"Tha  **you**
giving up

She shrugged, trying to play it off as if it was no big deal. "Like I told you the other day, I had the time off, so it's all good."

He nodded, and she tried not to take offense at the relief washing through his features. "Good, because I don't want you to get the wrong idea. I just need you to pretend to be my girlfriend when the others are around."

"Especially Mrs. Dankirk."

"Exactly. ..." He paused, his gaze transferring to something out the window behind her.

Was it bad to wish it was the woman?

A second later, she wondered if the colonel's wife was outside because when Ben's attention returned to her again, his gaze was hot and interested and...consuming.

Her heart tried to burst from her chest. Then he shifted closer, sexy smile on his face trapping the breath in her lungs. She couldn't blink. Forgot how to breathe. Just sat there watching the sexiest man alive lift a hand to cup her face.

Breathe, idiot! The last thing she needed was to faint. Not when she was about to get the kiss she'd dreamt about since puberty.

God, she hoped she was about to get the kiss she'd dreamt about since puberty...

What they're saying...

About Her Uniform Cowboy:

"Ms. Michaels pens a tale with pure heart and true grit! This story will hit so many readers close to home there is not one part of the plot that will feel foreign. No super models here, just true, down to earth servicemen and woman getting back to their place in the world. The characters and plot have a wonderful arc and the laughter, tears and emotional ride readers get to take on this journey will not disappoint."
—InD'tale Magazine, Crowned Heart of Excellence 4.5 Stars
--Voted BEST COWBOY in a Book/Reader's Choice-LRC

About Her Forever Cowboy:

"Ms. Michaels has done it again! Book four in this series is another great success. The author knows how to lure her readers in by telling them a wonderful story that's wrapped around characters we get to know and love as if they're real people. This book was no exception. I highly recommend this book and this author!"
—Night Owl Reviews, *Reviewer Top Pick*

About Her Fated Cowboy:

"As always, this author perfectly blended an amazing storyline, which contained characters you just can't help but fall in love with and she worked her magic in creating a masterpiece of the heart. I even enjoyed her sense of humor sprinkled throughout, which was placed in all the right places. This is one story I highly recommend and one author I just can't read enough from. Since this is the first book in the Harland County series, I'm eagerly looking forward to the next book."
—Night Owl Reviews, *Reviewer Top Pick*

Dear Reader,

Thank you for purchasing Wyne and Dine. This is the first book in my new Citizen Soldier Series, a Harland County Series spinoff. *Guarding the hearts of the Pocono Valley.*

This series showcases the National Guard brothers of the heroine from the third Harland County book-Her Uniform Cowboy. The Harland County clan will make an appearance for Brandi and Kade's wedding to be held up in the Poconos.

This first book is about Brandi's brother Ben, whom we met in her story. Ben is fulltime National Guard and set in his ways with a sour outlook on love. All the women in his past have left him to make it big in the Big Apple. It takes a woman who understands him, knows him, loves him completely to supply the Bn. S4 with another option.

Lea Gablonski is that woman. She's Brandi's best friend who has known Ben practically her whole life, and has had a thing for him from way before he and her older sister started to date. She has an MA in History, her sights set on a job in one of New York City's museums and Benjamin Wyne.

When he asks Lea to pretend to be his girlfriend at a weekend retreat, they discover they have chemistry. Of course, Ben fights it tooth and nail, until he realizes he's about to lose the woman who has always been there for him.

This hot, heartfelt, sexy read, is the first in this series and will include several characters from Harland County, as well as introduce you to a few future National Guard heroes.

Thanks for reading,

~Donna
www.donnamichaelsauthor.com

Also by Donna Michaels

~Novels~
Captive Hero (Time-shift Heroes Series-Book One)
The Spy Who Fanged Me
Her Fated Cowboy (Harland County Series-Book One)
Her Unbridled Cowboy (Harland County Series-Book Two)
Her Uniform Cowboy (Harland County Series-Book Three)
Her Forever Cowboy (Harland County Series-Book Four)
She Does Know Jack
~Novellas~
Cowboy-Sexy
Thanks for Giving
Ten Things I'd Do for a Cowboy
Vampire Kristmas
~Short Stories~
The Hunted
Negative Image
The Truth About Daydreams
Holiday Spirit
~Do-Over Series~
Valentine's Day Do-Over
Valentine's Day Do-Over Part II: The Siblings

UPCOMING RELEASES:
Cowboy Payback (Cowboy-Sexy Sequel)
~Time-shift Heroes Series~
Future Hero—Book Two
~Harland County Series~
Harland County Christmas (Novella/Brock and Jen)
Her Healing Cowboy (Book 5/Jace)
~Citizen Soldier Novels~
Wyne and Chocolate (Book 2/Mason)

Wyne and Dine

A Citizen Soldier Novel
Book 1: Ben

By
Donna Michaels

Thanks for reading!

Donna Michaels
RT 2017

WYNE AND DINE

A Citizen Soldier Novel//Book 1: Ben

ISBN-13: 978-1502549174
ISBN-10: 1502549174

Print edition September 2014
Book 1 in Citizen Soldier Series

<u>Dedication</u>

To Donna Michaels' Minions-my wonderful Street Team, thank you for your continued support! To Harland County fans, I hope you enjoy this spinoff series and the story of Brandi's brother Ben, the set in his ways military man with trust issues.

To my husband Michael and the PA National Guard for inspiring me to write this series. I'm honored to create a series around all of you.

To my family, my cp JT Schultz, and the HOODS. And finally, to my editor, Stacy, and to Emily for their help in the final stages. ♥

Chapter One

"Sit on my brother Ben and make the bugger call me," Brandi Wyne, soon-to-be Brandi Dalton, ordered from the other end of the phone.

Lea Gablonski choked on the bite of cinnamon raisin toast she'd just sat down to eat with her morning coffee. Her bright idea to take advantage of the lull in the breakfast rush at her family's diner—The Pocono Eatery—just hit the dimmer switch at her best friend's blurted request.

She blushed.

Dammit.

Still, it was a miracle she didn't self-combust given the amount of heat rushing through her body at the thought of settling her backside on the lap of the virile, prime beef that was Sgt. Benjamin Wyne. The sexiest man alive.

So sexy, so potent, he could set a lake on fire.

And did.

The National Guardsman had actually achieved the feat, along with her brother Ryder, back when she had been eleven, and they were seniors in high school. Something to do with an inner tube and a birthday celebration gone wrong. Lea couldn't help but feel her sister had been involved, too.

Her perfect, blonde-haired, blue-eyed, older sister, Gwen.

The now famous New York model, Gwen.

She had always suspected Gwen, a year younger than the boys, had caused the mishap, and Ben, being the

1

knight-in-shining-armor that he was, and dating her sister only a few weeks at the time, had taken the blame.

"Even with today's technology we've been playing phone tag for the past two days," Brandi continued, bringing Lea's mind back to the present. "I can't even reach him on Skype."

Living in Harland County, Texas and planning a wedding in the Pocono Valley of Pennsylvania had to be hard. Lea was doing whatever she could to help.

Ever since befriending the new girl in fifth grade, she and Brandi had become best friends. How could they not? They were so much alike. Clumsy introverts with a love of classical as well as country music…and Belgium chocolate. A bond that had strengthened when they both lost their mothers in middle school. Where Brandi had turned to practicing the violin, Lea had shoved her nose into books. Many, many books, and her love for history was born.

As well as her appreciation of the male physique, thanks to hanging out at the Wyne household, or as she silently dubbed, *The Hot Spot*. Each of Brandi's four step-brothers had set the bar high for boyfriend standards. The combination of responsibility, compassion and humor, coupled with their good looks and ripped bodies, made Lea's search for a viable mate near impossible. She'd started to doubt one existed beyond the Wyne household, until last year when she had met Brandi's fiancé. Kade Dalton was a little bit of all right. Okay, he was a *lot-a-bit* of all right. He was flippin' gorgeous and steadfast, and so respectful of Brandi that Lea had hoped she might actually discover one for herself outside of *Wyneville*.

Her friend had assured her Harland County had an overabundance of good-looking, charming, respectful cowboys and had been badgering Lea to head to Texas.

But since her siblings had thriving careers, the job of keeping the restaurant afloat while her father recovered from back surgery fell onto her shoulders. She wasn't going to go anywhere but crazy.

On a fast train.

With no brakes.

"I'm pretty sure he had drill down the Gap this weekend and was probably too busy to get on the computer," she replied before taking another bite of her toast.

With the restaurant located right across from the National Guard armory, there were soldiers in and out of the Pocono Eatery all day long. The scuttlebutt of drill dates, activations and deployments always found her ears. Besides, her brother had mentioned it. Even though Ryder owned his own construction company, he was still a part-time soldier in the National Guard.

"Oh. That explains it." A sigh filled her ear. "Cell phone reception is spotty down there."

"True," she agreed, nibbling more toast.

"But since it's the Monday after drill," Brandi continued, confidence strengthening her tone, "and my brother is nothing if not predictable, he'll be into work early to get a jump on the paperwork, and that means he'll also be in to see you this morning."

Lea's heart dropped to her ribs where it raced the sudden fluttering in her stomach. God, she *wished* Sgt. Hotty was coming in to see *her*. But, it wasn't her he stopped by to sample every morning. She should be so lucky. Just the thought of that firm jaw scraping her skin as those full lips kissed a path to parts south had her sighing in her coffee—the very thing that drew the man into her restaurant. Not her sigh. Her coffee.

3

Sure, he was friendly. He'd always been friendly to her. In fact, Ben treated her special, like one of the family.

Too bad so sad for her; she wanted to be treated like a lover, not family. To know him intimately. But, family was all she was ever going to be to the man, and she'd learned long ago not to wish for more. Wishes didn't come true. At least, not for Lea Gablonski.

If that was the case, she'd be putting her Masters Degree in History to good use, working in one of New York City's many museums…and sleeping in Ben's bed at night.

She glanced at the train-shaped clock on the wall. The one she'd purchased from the local train and anthracite museum where she worked one Sunday a month. The old, black locomotive wasn't going anywhere, and neither was she. Her responsibility rested with her family. She loved them, and they loved her, and she'd do what was expected, helping her dad out at home and at the restaurant since her siblings were busy with their successful careers. Though she'd given up her position at a museum in Philadelphia to come home until her father was well, she also made a promise to herself. She vowed to reach for her dream by applying for a job in the Big Apple. It was time she put herself first.

After she made sure her dad was back on his feet, of course.

"Yeah, it's nearly nine am," she said, bringing her mind back to the conversation. "Your brother should be here soon. He usually comes in this late after drill weekend."

Twisting around in the booth, she strained her neck to see if the hotty had snuck in while her back had been turned. Nope. Only Mary, her server, and a few locals dotted the restaurant. A young couple held hands as they

4

sat on the same side of a booth; a happy family of four enjoyed breakfast before heading out on one last summer adventure; old man Tierney argued about the Mets at the counter with old man Simpson who, in turn, argued about the Yankees.

Yep, business as usual.

"Well, until he does, I want to thank you for all your help, Lea."

"Hey, that's what maid-of-honors are for, right?"

She was so happy her friend had found someone who appreciated her friend, unlike *jerkman*, Brandi's former boyfriend who had been using the talented woman as a status symbol. Not an issue now. A fact that had been more than evident when Lea had met Kade last Thanksgiving. The gorgeous Texan was a man of few words, but his expression had said all she wanted to know. He adored his fiancée.

"You go above and beyond," Brandi stated. "So, why don't you tell me more about your date with Clark last night?"

Lea silently cursed her friend's sudden change of subject, no doubt due to the slipup she'd made at the beginning of the call, telling her about running into an old schoolmate. She should've known her astute confidant wasn't going to let it go. She straightened back around in her booth—the one she and Brandi had shared so often over the years her dad had dubbed it the B/L booth—and she shrugged as if her friend were seated across from her. "It wasn't a date. We met by accident at the Confection Connection and decided to share the Special of the Day since it was so dang huge."

"Huge? What the heck did Jill come up with this time?" Brandi asked.

Jill Bailey, a New Yorker who knew her way around all things chocolate and decadent, wasn't afraid to combine ingredients to create new desserts. Much to everyone's delight—and their waistline's dismay.

"A double-decker banana split. It was to die for." Just thinking about it made her mouth water.

"And Clark didn't mind sharing?"

"No" she replied, then lowered her voice when she heard customers settle into the booth behind her. "He was very generous."

"Wow, Clark generous. That's new. He was always so bossy."

She laughed. "True, but not last night. He let me go first."

"I'm shocked."

"I know, right? He's usually demanding, but this time I got to eat my fill, and let me tell you, I did."

She could always count on Jill to take care of her chocolate fix. If only the woman had a recipe to satisfy her unreasonable craving for the unattainable Benjamin Wyne.

Full-time National Guardsman, Sgt. Benjamin Wyne slid into his usual booth across from his brothers, Keiffer and Mason, ready to order his usual breakfast and recharge his batteries from three days of training before he jumped back into the after-drill workload. He hated when people didn't do their jobs and was tasked with picking up their slack, but sometimes it was as unavoidable as his after-drill headache.

He'd kill for coffee.

One thing he'd learned from eating at Gabe's, the name he, his father and three brothers had come to call the Pocono Eatery, was he could always count on the delicious, homemade food to pull double duty in decimating his appetite and the pounding in his head.

Until today.

Until he heard his sister Brandi's sweet, good-natured best friend Lea Gablonski talking about giving a blow job. What the hell was she doing talking about oral sex on the phone in her family's restaurant? She knew better. She was reliable, responsible and...

And, why the hell was it turning him on?

That was sick. Lea was an honorary sister in the Wyne household. For over a decade and a half, ever since his father had married Brandi's mother, and Ben had gained a step-sister. Brandi and Lea had been fast friends, and the little girl had practically become a fixture in their house. She'd been great for Brandi. Still was, just not so little anymore.

Or innocent, apparently.

He blinked, glancing past his smirking brothers and no longer seeing the little girl with long brown pigtails. The one who used to follow him and Ryder around, the sweet girl with big blue eyes. The one he used to help with homework, bait hooks and taught how to ride a horse.

No, the girl with her back to them, unaware of their presence, sighing seductively into her phone was definitely no longer a girl.

When the hell had Lea grown up? And how could he find a way to go back to thinking of her as a child?

"I explained to Clark that I don't normally like them that big," she continued, voice dropping an octave. "And believe me, this thing was huge. The girth was unbelievable. I never knew you could grow them that size, but darnit, it wasn't just drizzled in chocolate. It was covered. And you know how I can't resist chocolate."

The image her words created should've induced bile; instead, the vision of her enchanting mouth working a certain kind of magic was testing not only his integrity, but the integrity of the zipper in his ACUs—his Army Combat Uniform.

"I kind of went a little crazy. Licked it clean. So clean it sparkled."

She let out a throaty sigh that wiped the smiles off his brothers' faces and sent heat skittering down his spine.

"I latched onto that sucker and didn't come up for air until every last, delectable inch was gone."

She had all three of them squirming. He wanted to alert the woman of their presence, clear his throat, cough, anything to give her a clue, but that would require control of his faculties...of which he had none. Somewhere between *delectable* and *inch* he'd lost the ability to breath. Now, his head was no longer the only part of his anatomy pounding in tandem.

"Man, you should've seen the look on Clark's face when I lifted my head. It was priceless. And his eyes about bugged out when I licked my lips and told him I wanted seconds."

God bless Keiffer.

And youth.

Or whatever the hell it was that gave his youngest brother the ability to snicker, because the woman stiffened and stopped talking.

Alleluia.

Her mouth finally shut, and there were two things he no longer had to face. His honorary sister talking about *lollipopping* some dude, and the fact he wished it were him.

Both should be disturbing. They weren't.

Now *that* was disturbing.

Lea twisted around, dark hair swinging from the motion, phone poised by her ear, blue eyes round and unblinking, while her mouth parted to form a perfect O.

X-rated thoughts of licking scenarios rushed through his head. Ah, hell. The heat in his veins scorched.

She smiled and stood. "Hey, Ben. Just the man I wanted to see."

His mind blanked, and because he never suffered a blank mind before, he blinked. "F-f-for?" Damn. His voice cracked like a pubescent teen. He cleared his throat, refusing to glance at his snickering brothers. "For what?"

She nodded. "Yeah, Brandi, he's here, along with Keiffer and Mason. Buggers all snuck up on me," she said, holding their gazes, not in the least bit embarrassed at having been caught talking blow jobs with his sister.

His sister.

Bile finally made an appearance in his throat. He cleared it again.

With a grin that shouldn't seem so damn sexy, the woman stepped over to his side of the booth in a dress looking tighter and shorter than normal. "Do you still want me to sit on Ben so you can talk?"

Hell... "No," he said, a little louder than intended. This garnered more snickering from his *deadmeat* brothers. "Just give me the phone." He thrust his hand up, hoping—praying—she'd relinquish the device without question, and without expecting him to make eye-contact, because that was not going to happen anytime soon.

Not until he got his body back under control.

Thank God she handed him the phone. He was acting like a high schooler with raging hormones. *Christ.* Back in high school, his hormones had raged for Lea's older sister. This was all too weird for his psyche to handle. So he didn't.

9

"Hi, Ben."

He cleared his mind of everything surrounding him and concentrated on his sister's voice.

"You're a tough guy to get a hold of," Brandi stated, smile in her tone.

"Sorry, it was drill weekend. I didn't get your messages until last night, but it was too late to call. So, what's up?" He trained his gaze on the table, vaguely aware of *Ms. Licktober* dropping off a coffee pot and cups before disappearing into the kitchen, mumbling about getting the usual.

He was never going to associate that word with Lea ever again.

Damn it.

"I just wanted to ask you to double-check Dad's schedule to make sure he's around next month for the wedding, and not off at some meeting or exercise. He promised me he was all clear, but he does tend to book and forget."

A smile tugged his lips. "True. But I'm on it. Don't worry. He'll be here," he reassured, pouring coffee into his cup. The hearty aroma hit his nose and lessened the pounding in his head.

"Thanks. I don't know what I'd do without you and Lea."

Since he was doing his best to stay off the Lea subject, he decided to change it. "How's Kade?"

"Wonderful," she gushed. "Now that he's no longer sheriff, he's concentrating on his horse sanctuary. It's been great working with him. He seems so much at peace."

Ben blew out a breath and smiled. "I'm glad. He's a good guy, Brandi. And he makes you happy. I can hear it in your voice."

Both Mason and Keiffer murmured in agreement as they drank their coffees. Their sister had blossomed into a confident, content woman since moving to Harland County, Texas a year and a half ago. It had been tough on his family, but she'd been determined to leave, and adamant she needed to go alone. Now that it was all said and done, Ben was damn glad she'd gone and rediscovered herself. Brandi was no longer the sullen, self-depreciator she'd been when she'd left.

"That's because I am happy." She sniffed.

Ah, hell. Tears. He hated tears. He didn't mean to make her cry.

"I just wish you and Mason and Keiffer and Ethan could be this happy." Another sniff hit his ear. "And Lea. She's always doing for others. It's time she thought of herself and took care of her own needs."

All the control Ben had managed to muster the past two minutes slipped out the door. The mere mention of Lea and *her needs* conjured up images that had his groin tightening again.

"I tried to get her to come down for a visit this past spring. There are a few nice cowboys here who would love to meet her," his sister informed.

The news tightened his gut for some strange reason.

"But she said Ryder and Gwen were really busy with work. Between you and me, Ben, I don't think she even asked if they'd cover for her and help their dad out at the restaurant. She never wants to impose."

True. Nothing new there. Lea was always eager to please. Always put others first. Hell, she'd quit her job in Philly and came rushing back to the Poconos so her siblings could continue with their lives. He wasn't sure if that was responsible or irresponsible. That was no way to build a career.

11

"It's time she found someone who appreciated her," Brandi continued. "That's where you come in."

"What? How?" His constricted gut quaked with an invisible blow.

"Relax, Romeo. I'm not asking you to court her—even though she's had a crush on you since you and her brother were on the same little league team—I just want you to help me talk her into flying back to Harland County with me after the wedding."

Ben's mind was still filtering in the crush news for something he should've known, but didn't. He was having a tough time with all the eye-openers this morning. It was like a switch had been flipped the moment he'd sat down in the booth, and he wished to God he could flip it back.

Life had been perfectly fine when he'd thought of Lea as his sister's safe, reliable, sweet best friend. Not the sexy seductress, smelling all flowery with mouthwatering cleavage winking at him as she leaned across the table to hand out their food.

What the hell? Now she had mouthwatering cleavage? What was next? A delectable ass?

A clanking sound had her straightening upright as she glanced over him and shook her head. "Oh, hang on, Mr. Tierney. Let me get your cane."

Don't turn.

Do not turn around.

Shit. He turned in time to see the woman bend down to retrieve a cane from the floor.

Damn. She did have a delectable ass.

Swallowing a curse, Ben twisted around to find his younger brother grinning across the table at him.

"See something you like, bro?"

"What's Keiffer laughing at?" his sister asked, reminding him he still had the phone pressed to his ear…in a killer death grip.

"Nothing," he replied, loosening his hold before the cell cracked in half. "The goof still thinks he's actually funny."

"Well, give chucklehead and Mason my love. And tell Lea I'll call her later. I can't wait to see her with Kevin. Wait 'til you see how great those two are going to look standing up together with their dark hair and blue eyes. Those pictures are going to rock. Love ya. Bye, Ben."

And just like that, the line went dead.

But he had questions. *Damn.* Like, who the hell was this Kevin dude? Some Casanova cowboy ready to put the moves on sweet, innocent girls? The clanking of the phone echoed when he set it on the table a little harder than necessary.

"What the hell did Brandi say to make you look like you bit into a lemon?"

He ignored his gawking brothers and stabbed at his eggs, scrambled just like he liked them. Lea always did know what to serve him without asking. The woman deserved better than a Casanova.

By the time half his plate was gone, his missing common-sense returned. Brandi would never set her friend up with someone unworthy. And, as he'd just recently realized, Lea wasn't an innocent girl, she was a twenty-six-year old woman capable of doing who and what she wanted.

His stomach knotted on that one, but he refused to examine the reason.

Somewhere in the recesses of his fogged mind, he had data on a cowboy named Kevin, and he aimed to find it. A few more forkfuls of delicious bacon did the trick. Bacon always cured what ailed him. The smokey goodness was his go-to fix. Ben began to relax and the fog continued to lift. Kevin was Kade's cousin and his best man. And most importantly, *engaged* to be married in October.

Funny how the food suddenly didn't taste like cardboard anymore.

"You know, Mason, I think our brother's look had something to do with Lea talking about giving a—"

"Enough," he barked at Keiffer just in time to stop the words his newly under control body couldn't handle. "Don't the two of you have clients to take hiking today?"

Not only were he and his brothers in the National Guard together, they also owned a resort that catered to the outdoorsman year round. Since it was still summer, the place was booked for hiking, fishing, boating, and white water rafting, of which his three brothers happily obliged. Ben was more of a silent partner, working full time in supply in the guard. Keiffer, Mason, and Ethan were part time guardsman while they ran the place their sister had redesigned and renovated three years ago.

Lea appeared to replace their empty pot of coffee with another. "Can I get you guys anything else?"

"Chocolate," his idiot younger brother replied with a grin.

The guy was a dead man.

She smiled and leaned her hip against the booth near Mason. "I love chocolate."

"We know," Keiffer said, scratching the bridge of his nose with his thumb, still smiling that stupid smile.

Ben was ready to scratch his brother's nose with his fist. Why the hell was the idiot bringing that up?

"I'll put it on just about anything, but even I won't put it on eggs. Pancakes, sure, but not eggs."

Keiffer cocked his head. "So…eggs—no, men—yes."

"Men?" She straightened with a frown, color tinting her cheeks. "What do you mean?"

Mason cleared his throat and spoke for the first time. "We kind of overheard your conversation with Brandi."

"Okay." The groves in her forehead deepened as her gaze bounced to each of them. "So?"

His brothers transferred their gazes to him.

Ah, hell no. Not gonna happen. He sat back in his seat, folded his arms across his chest and stared them down. No way in hell was he going to further the conversation.

"I'm confused. I wasn't talking to Brandi about a guy. I was talking about a banana split."

Right. Ben snickered. "Since when did you start naming your dessert, Clark?" *Damn.* So much for staying out of the conversation.

"Clark?" She blinked. "I…oh my God." She laughed, then laughed some more. So much so she sank down in the booth next to him, her warmth vibrating, stirring parts of his anatomy that shouldn't be stirred as she silently shook. When the woman finally sobered, she took one look at their faces and start laughing again.

Ben exchanged glances with his brothers, hoping they had a clue as to the cause of Lea's laughing fit. He wasn't sure his aroused body could take much more of the sweet torture. But given their shaking heads and shrugging shoulders, he guessed they were just as clueless as him.

"I'm sorry," she said a minute later, wiping her eyes. "That was just too funny."

"What was?" he asked.

"The three of you thinking my conversation had to do with licking chocolate off of Clark's…*banana.*"

"It wasn't?"

"No."

Thank God.

"Then what was it?"

"I told you. I was talking about eating one of Jill's banana splits."

Mason grunted into his coffee while Keiffer nodded. "Oh, Jill. That explains it," his younger brother exclaimed, grin consuming his face. "That woman sure knows her way around chocolate."

Now, Lea was nodding while she tossed her hands up. "Amen."

"So, let me get this straight." He turned to the great smelling woman smiling next to him and nearly forgot what he'd wanted to stay. "You were talking about a banana, not a…" Ah hell, he couldn't do it. Couldn't utter the name of the very thing throbbing for her touch. A new ache he'd never experienced before, at least, not with Lea.

She glanced around the now vacant restaurant, then settled her amused gaze back on him. "It's okay to say penis, Ben. I know what one is. I've seen one. Heck, I've even *touched* one." She sucked in a breath and slapped a hand over her mouth, faking a shocked expression.

"Very funny." He did not like where this conversation was heading.

Her smile turned positively sinful. "Trust me, there wasn't anything funny about it."

Shit.

"Enough," he ground out again. "We're not having this conversation."

Neither one of his heads could take it.

She shrugged, not in the least put out by his tone. A tone that had many supply sergeants quaking in their boots.

"You all started it, although, I wish I had known you mistook my conversation with Brandi."

"Why?" Keiffer grinned. "So you could've played it up?"

"Hell yeah." The exasperating woman's head dipped in quick affirmation. "I would've mentioned my sticky—"

That's it. "Let me out." Shoving the laughing woman from the booth, he swallowed a curse as he shot to his feet. "Since my brothers seem to be in a jolly mood, they can pay the bill. I have work to do."

With one last, stern glare at the three of them, he pivoted around then strode from the restaurant. What the hell had gotten into her?

Once outside, he jammed his hat on his head and crossed the street. The woman in there smiling and spouting the word 'penis' was a far cry from the sweet, innocent blue-eyed girl who used to follow him around.

Two days later, as Ben was leaving work, he realized he had been mistaken about Lea.

She *still* followed him around.

He couldn't get the damn woman off his mind. Just when he thought he had a handle on things, he'd hear her voice in his head, talking about chocolate and his favorite body part, or see her mouth curve into a seductive smile.

It was damned annoying.

She was his best friend's baby sister, and his baby sister's best friend. He had no business thinking of her in that context. And she sure as hell had no right to invade his dreams, with her lush lips and generous cleavage, turning them into fantasies that even made him blush.

He took the stairs inside the armory at a hurried pace; the muffled sound of his boots clapping off the steps followed him to the ground floor. So did his irritation.

He was a military man. From a military family. Order, control and discipline were not only a code of conduct, they were a way of life. He thrived on them. They were ingrained. A part of him. These recent, foolish, unwanted flashes of lust were for schoolboys. He'd had his shot at allowing his heart to rule his mind at the end of his senior year with Gwen Gablonski, and failed. Miserably.

A month after he graduated, the long-legged, blonde-haired, blue-eyed beauty had signed with a New York modeling agency and became supermodel Gwen Gabel at seventeen. Ben had been so proud that his girlfriend had been a model. He'd left for boot camp, foolishly believing they'd make a long-distance thing work. That he could have the girl and a future in the military. Five weeks later, he received the Dear John letter. She left him for a French photographer while he still had eleven weeks of training to go.

That's when he woke up. Got a clue. Set his sights on a military career. Reliable. Tangible. Doable. He focused on things he could control. And others' feelings weren't one of them. Relationships fell last on his list.

Besides, in his experience, he'd seen too many fail, unable to withstand a military schedule. It had happened to his own parents. His mother had left his dad after fourteen years of marriage. Fourteen years. Rachel Wyne claimed she was tired of supporting his career while hers took a back seat. They shared joint custody and got on well; she even attended his father's second wedding to Brandi's mother, saying they made much better friends than man and wife. That was fifteen years ago, but Ben still took that lesson to heart. It had shown him, early on, the military and relationships didn't last.

That was why he was selective with his lovers. They knew a relationship was out of the question. He didn't want one. Just a warm body and great sex when needed. Nothing serious. Just physical.

Charisse, his current go-to girl, was out of the country representing her company at some trade show. She didn't expect a ring, or exclusiveness. They called each other up when they felt the need to work off some steam. Perfect set up.

Great sex.

Zero commitment.

Life was good.

Pushing through the front door, he exhaled a breath and noted his shoulders felt a lot lighter than when he'd exited his office a minute earlier.

"Sgt. Wyne. Just the man I wanted to see."

Ben stopped and silently uttered a curse, tightness returning to stiffen his body once again. He knew without turning around who stood on the sidewalk behind him. He recognized the voice of his superior officer's superior.

Colonel Dankirk.

The man with the authority to stop promotions, like the one Ben was eligible for at the end of the year.

The man with a wife half his age who continually hit on Ben whenever her husband's back was turned.

His father's friend and old war buddy who'd left two messages inviting Ben to his house for the weekend for a small get together with a few officers…and his promiscuous wife.

There was no way to duck the invitation now. Nor could he afford to refuse. Damned if he did, and damned if he didn't. He knew when his career allowed him to do his own thing, and when he needed to jump through hoops. This was a jump-through hoops kind of weekend.

Pasting a smile on his face, Ben turned around and held out his hand. "Colonel Dankirk, how are you, sir?"

The man shook his hand and cocked his head, gaze direct and sharp as usual. "Fine, Ben, but I'd be better if you'd tell me you're coming to the house this weekend. It'll be a mixture of work and play. Mira has her heart set on it. You've made quite an impression with my wife. She loves that wit of yours, son. I hate to disappoint her."

And he hated to be fired. Blackballed. Manhandled. Or caught in a compromising position not of his choosing.

He was screwed.

He couldn't go.

Couldn't not go.

And he couldn't just tell the Colonel the reason. No man liked to hear shit about his girl, even if it was the truth.

Yeah, he was screwed.

"Hey, Ben. Colonel Dankirk. Sorry to butt in." Lea's voice carried across the street and he could've cheerfully kissed his sister's best friend for the interruption.

"No worries, my dear." The colonel transferred his direct gaze to the woman rushing toward them, her blue checkered apron blowing in the wind. "How's your dad?"

"Misinformed," she replied, slight quirk to her top lip. Over the years, she'd waited on the two of them plenty of times at Gabe's, so he wasn't surprised by her greeting or the colonel's inquiry. "He thinks if he rushes through therapy, he'll get back to work sooner."

His superior chuckled. "Not on your watch."

"Exactly, sir." She smiled, then turned her blue gaze on him as she waved at the restaurant. "I saw you from the window and wanted to catch you to let you know I just got off the phone with Jill. We have an appointment at six o'clock tonight to sample wedding cakes."

Colonel Dankirk reeled back slightly, brows raised, small smile tugging the corner of his mouth. "Congratulations, Ben. Your father didn't tell me you and Lea were seeing each other."

"Oh…uh…" Her pretty face turned the exact shade of pink as the Hello Kitty pencil shoved behind her ear. "It's n-not for us," she stammered.

Never one to look a gift horse in the mouth, Ben quickly slipped an arm around Lea's shoulders and drew her close, a little surprised at how soft she felt. "Yeah, it's for my sister's wedding next month. Lea and I aren't rushing things. We're taking it slow, sir."

She stiffened against him, and for a moment, his heart stopped. *Damn.* The last thing he needed was for her to push away. But she must've heard his silent message, or noted the pleading in his gaze, because she suddenly relaxed and melted against him.

The colonel nodded. "Smart man."

A moment later, Lea really got into character. She slid a hand around his waist and snuggled closer, reminding him once again she was no longer a little girl. The plump softness of her breast pressing into his side alerted him of that fact. *Shit*, he did not need to know she felt that good. Or that she was that stacked. And, *oh hell yeah*, she was stacked if he could feel her breast through the thickness of his ACU jacket.

"That he is," she said, resting her head against his shoulder while she patted his chest. "But he still has a few things to prove to me first, don't you, *snookums*?"

He swallowed a curse. She did not just call him that in front of his superior.

Colonel Dankirk laughed. "Good for you, Lea. Make him squirm."

Oh, he was squirming all right.

"Hey, Ben." The colonel turned to him, wide smile on his face. "Why don't you bring Lea with you this weekend? The others are bringing their ladies. I know Mira would love to meet your girlfriend, too."

"Thank you, sir," he replied, relishing the fact he'd found his buffer, and that his *girlfriend* had stiffened again as he glanced down at her. "We'd love to."

Blue eyes stared up at him, and he grinned, doing his damndest to keep from laughing. He didn't think he'd ever seen her look so shocked. Not even when she'd walked in on him and Gwen making out in the Gablonski's basement the night before he left for basic training.

She lifted her chin, a devilish gleam entering her gaze before she turned her attention to the colonel, and left him shaking in his combat boots not knowing what the hell was about to come out of her pretty mouth...

Chapter Two

"Yes, sir. We'd love to," Lea replied, adrenaline, confusion and a few other 'uns' running through her body, taking turns increasing and decreasing her temperature. "Benny promised to row me around his lake, but so far he hasn't found the time. I know there's a small one next to your property. Maybe he can finally take care of me this weekend."

"Absolutely, young lady." Colonel Dankirk nodded, casting a stern glance at Ben who blinked down at her.

She clenched her teeth to keep from laughing. Poor guy hadn't looked that shocked since she'd walked in on him and her sister going at it hot and heavy in her basement the night before he left for basic training.

The confusion clouding his green eyes suddenly cleared and her heart leapt in her chest when his gaze gleamed a deep emerald. "Perfect, because you deserve to be taken care of, *sweetheart*."

One octave. That was it. A single octave lower was the difference between innocent and trouble. And *holy crow*, his voice had dropped an octave with that phrase.

Her stomach fluttered, and neglected good parts tingled. *Damn.*

She was in trouble.

"Wonderful. I'll expect you both at eighteen hundred Friday night." Their future host pivoted around and strode toward the parking lot on the side of the building before either of them had a chance to reply.

They must've stood that way a good four minutes until the colonel's car disappeared down the street. During those four minutes, Lea soaked it all in. The hard muscles under her palm. The solid strength in the arm surrounding her. The promise of heat in the hand caressing her hip. She inhaled two, three—five times, enjoying the pure male scent that was Benjamin Wyne. The sexiest man alive. The man holding her close.

In the middle of the sidewalk.

In broad daylight.

Across from her father's restaurant.

The one with customers pressing their faces to the window, smiling at them, hoping to see who knows what.

Ben must've noticed, too, because he stiffened, released her and stepped back so quick and rigid she half-expected him to go straight into an about-face and march away.

But the sexy sergeant stood there and gave her a firm nod. "Thanks, Lea." The palm with the heat she could still feel on her hip skimmed across his head after he momentarily removed his cap. "Sorry to drag you into this."

She cleared her throat, doing her best to sound nonchalant. "Exactly what is *this*, Ben?"

"*This* is me asking you to pretend to be my girlfriend, just for the weekend," he replied, jamming the hat back on his head. "I hope you didn't have work at the museum this Sunday."

"No," she replied. "I would've said something to the colonel if I had." She only worked one weekend a month at the anthracite museum, and she'd already put her hours in this month.

He nodded, relief easing the stiffness from his shoulders. "I need, you, Lea. Your help, I mean."

She heard it. Really, she did. She heard his added clarification, but latched on to the *I need you, Lea* part and *oh Lordy*, her body basked in the rush of heat his words created. Words she'd longed to hear practically half her life. "S-sure, no problem. But I have to admit, I find it hard to believe you need a pretend girlfriend."

He laughed, and dammit, the sound warmed her from the inside out. "Thanks. Colonel Dankirk was pressing me to stay at his place this weekend."

"Which is horrible. I know, what with his estate being so big and all." She made a tsking sound with her tongue as she shrugged.

This won her a smirk. "Smart ass. I needed a buffer from his wife and wouldn't have asked you, but Charisse is out of the country, so I needed a substitute and fast."

Oh, swell. She was a substitute. A stand in for his goodtime girlfriend.

Still, Lea couldn't bring herself to feel bad. For two whole nights and three days she was going to be Sgt. Benjamin Wyne's girlfriend. Which meant she had to touch him and cuddle with him, and show signs of affection in public.

Yeah, sucked to be her.

Four and a half hours later, Lea was in the middle of a Skype call with Brandi and her bridesmaids, Jordan, Kerri and Shayla, discussing the cakes she'd just sampled with Ben, when the truth in that earlier statement hit her for the first time.

It *did* suck to be her.

"Okay, I know that look," Brandi stated, her pretty face moving closer to the screen. "What did Ben do now?"

Darn woman really was too astute. "Nothing. Not really."

"Explain."

"Gosh, you're so bossy," she said with a laugh.

"I'm a Wyne. We can't help it," Brandi stated. "Now, stop changing the subject and spill it. What is going on with you and my brother?"

"Ooh, are you seeing the sexy Benjamin Wyne? Do tell." Jordan moved closer, brown gaze alight with mischief.

"No. I wish." *Pretty please with sugar on top.* Now was probably not the best time to entertain thoughts of licking sugar off the man's ripped torso. Twice.

"But…? Come on, tell us," her friend urged.

"Yeah, we want the scoop," Kerri said, gathering close, along with a nodding Shayla.

Darn. She knew when she was busted. "It's nothing really." She sat back in her chair and petted Marlow, her dad's black cat currently curled up on her lap. "I'm just pretending to be his girlfriend while we're at Colonel Dankirks this weekend."

A dawning lit Brandi's eyes, turning them the same shade as her namesake. "To keep Mrs. Dankirk at bay."

"Exactly."

"Do you have to share a room?" Shayla smiled.

"I-I don't know. Maybe." She hadn't even thought to ask. Something fluttered in her belly, but Lea wasn't sure if it was excitement or dread. It would suck to be so close to the man and not be able to be *close* to the man.

"Probably," Brandi answered. "I went there once with Ed, and each of the couples had their own room."

The fluttering increased to double time in her stomach, robbing her of breath. She would be sharing a bedroom with Ben the whole weekend. What should be considered a dream come true left her worried.

"I'm not gonna make it." She palmed her face.

"What do you mean?" Kerri asked.

She dropped her hands and shook her head. "I don't think I can be cooped up with the man that long without, you know, touching him."

Jordan shrugged. "Then don't."

This turned Lea's nervousness into laughter. "Don't share a room? I don't think I can request another."

"No, I mean don't resist touching him," the brown-eyed, long brown-haired beauty clarified.

"Easy for you to say. You're competent and gorgeous. Did I mention gorgeous? I'm just…" She paused to wave at her average body. "…boring me."

Brandi narrowed her gaze and shook a finger at the screen. "You are far from boring, Lea Gablonski. And you're practically the fantasy of every soldier in that armory."

Now she was laughing outright. "You are so full of shit, Brandi."

"I'm serious. You forget I've been around those soldiers. They were always talking about you with your silky, dark hair, light blue eyes and killer body." Her friend was laying it on thick. "Half of them think *you* should be modeling next to Gwen."

That sobered Lea up real fast. "What?" She blinked, but her friend's smug face didn't change. "They did not."

"Yes, they did. *Including* my brothers."

"Why wouldn't they?" Kerri frowned. "You're so beautiful. It's time you believed it. Because, trust me, once you believe in yourself, the world changes for the better."

"Amen." Shayla nodded, brilliant smile lighting her happy face.

"So, you're saying Ben thinks I should be a model?"

"Something like that. I doubt he'd want you to be, though. He just agreed you're beautiful enough to model."

Ben thought she was beautiful…

A rush of warmth settled over Lea, leaving her feeling all kinds of tingly. Then reality set in. "Too bad he thinks of me as his little sister."

"Then this weekend is the perfect time to change his outlook."

"Change? How?"

"I have one word for you," Jordan cut in, that mischievous grin consuming her gaze. "Negligee."

"Negligee?" Her heart dropped to her ribs and rolled around. "I-I don't own any."

"Buy some," Brandi stated with the bridesmaids all nodding in agreement.

"I can't do that. It feels dishonest. Like entrapment or something." Besides, she didn't have the guts. What if he turned her down? She'd die. Simply die. No, she couldn't do it.

Could she?

As she silently argued with herself, the girls discussed what style and color would work best for her. It was all too surreal. Time to change the subject.

"So, back to the cakes," she said, regaining her best friend's attention. "They were all excellent, but…"

"The chocolate one, right?" Brandi eyed her closely.

Lea slapped a hand on her chest and moaned. "It was orgasmic. Jill mixed in Belgium chocolate. Pure bliss." Just thinking about it had Lea closing her eyes and sighing. "It was so good I finished my slice, and then Ben's."

Right from his fork. He just blinked at her, mouth dropping open as he watched her lick her lips. Poor guy. A flash of fear skittered through his mossy green eyes.

"It takes a smart man to know better than to get between a woman and her chocolate," Kerri stated.

She opened her eyes and nodded.

"Unless the man is *covered* in chocolate." Jordan winked.

"Yeah."

"Amen."

"Yeehaw."

The women snickered. Lea balked. They were killing her. In stereo.

She hadn't been with a man in, well, almost a year. She'd dated a few guys while in college, and last year, she'd even had a fling while penthouse sitting for her sister. Gwen had asked Lea to watch the place while she was in Cairo for a shoot. The freedom, the energy of the city had been great, but she'd been most at home at the library. It was huge and inviting, and the big, stone building itself had been so full of history she felt right at home. That's where she'd met a handsome professor, and soon their daily lunches and friendly discussions had turned to nightly rendezvous…until she'd discovered the jerk was married.

Even now, her stomach soured just thinking about it. She shivered as a wave of distaste rolled through without mercy. Since then, she'd learned to be more selective. Though, no need. There hadn't been anyone else.

Her sex life was dead in the water.

Sure, guys glanced her way and smiled, a few of the customers even flirted, but for some reason, they never asked her out. And she got to wondering if maybe they'd been smiling at her for other reasons. Like maybe she had jelly on her butt or some other form of food. It'd been known to happen. She was always brushing up against the stack of dirty dishes while rushing around the kitchen.

"Okay, so we're going with the chocolate cake," Brandi said, making notes on a legal pad.

"Like there was ever any doubt." She snickered.

"Hush, you." Her friend pointed at her. "Now, let's get back to discussing your upcoming weekend with my brother."

"Yeah, the enigmatic Ben." Kerri smiled. "You should make him his favorite food."

"Bacon?" She laughed. "I'm not sure I'd be able to sneak that in."

The girls chuckled.

"Probably not," Kerri agreed.

"All you need is that negligee," Jordan insisted. "Trust me. It worked for Brandi."

"It did?" She leaned closer, and this time shook her finger at the monitor. "You've been keeping things from me. Good things. It's your turn to spill, woman."

Color swept into her friend's face, turning it practically crimson, but the satisfied smile curving Brandi's lips cancelled out the blush. "It was a pink bra and thong set. When I dropped my robe, Kade dropped his resolve, and well, he…"

"He what?" Lea's face was literally inches from the screen now. "Don't leave me hanging."

Her friend's color deepened, along with her smile. "He took me against the door."

Shit.

"Amen."

"Heard that."

"Done that."

The bridesmaids all giggled, while Lea sat there in an un-*serviced* pile of need. She'd never been taken anywhere but on her back, unless she wanted top. Yeah, she was boring. And apparently uninspiring. "I want to be taken against a door."

"Then buy the negligee." Jordan smirked. "The guys can't resist."

"Yeah, but…what if Ben did?" She shivered again.

"Then at least you'd know," Brandi spoke up. "Look, Lea, you've been carrying this torch for my brother ever since you first met him. It's time to call him out. See what happens."

"Nothing will happen." She sighed, already knowing the outcome. "He sees me like he sees you, or worse, as his childhood sweetheart's little sister." She dropped her head into her hands and groaned. *Thank you, Gwen.* "I'm doomed."

"No, you're just uninformed."

She glanced up to see Brandi fold her arms across her chest and nod.

"And it's time you learned the truth," her friend continued. "It's better to know than to go on always wondering, right?"

"Hell ya," Jordan replied, face devoid of her usual mirth. "Trust me. I've been down that road. It eats at you."

She nodded. "Yes, it digs and digs." God, she was so tired of the digging.

"Then it's settled," her friend said. "This weekend, you're going to proposition Ben and see how he really feels."

Friday evening, Lea paced in her room, phone to her ear while Brandi tried to talk her out of a panic attack. Ben was due to arrive any minute to pick her up for their pretend weekend.

She didn't want to pretend.

But Ben didn't do the boyfriend thing. The confirmed bachelor avoided relationships like men avoided the tampon aisle at the grocery store. Made a wide birth. The guy was married to the military. Fine with Lea. She didn't want a ring. Just some fun. She wanted to taste the man…all of him. Get him out of her system before she embarked on her own career. But she wasn't sure she wanted things to change between them either. Because no matter how the weekend turned out, they would never be the same.

"I'm not sure I want to risk his friendship," she said for the third time in ten minutes.

"Is his friendship enough for you?"

"No." *Dammit.* "It's not."

"Then you have to risk it, hun," Brandi told her in a tone meant to sooth, but Lea was still anxious. "It's time to put my stubborn brother to the test."

"What if he fails?" There, she said it. She voiced her biggest fear. What if he avoided her after this? She couldn't bear it.

"Are you wearing the negligee Jordan sent?"

The gorgeous silk teddy had arrived that morning, via express mail from the incorrigible woman. Her gaze shot to the small suitcase opened on her bed. The sexy, sky blue outfit with black lace stared up at her. She walked over, unable to resist fingering the silky material.

"No. But I did pack it." Lea still wasn't sure she could be that daring, no matter how beautiful the negligee made her feel.

"Good enough," her friend said. "Now shut the suitcase and zip it closed before you change your mind."

She did what she was told, grumbling the whole time. "You're so bossy. Just like Ben."

"Yeah, well, it came from growing up with those guys. And you love every bit of it."

"True." She laughed. "And I love you, too. Thanks for putting up with me, Brandi. Especially when I'm supposed to be helping you with your wedding."

"My wedding plans are going just fine, thanks to you and Ben. Now, you both deserve some fun, and I want to make sure you take advantage of all this weekend has to offer. You've been waiting forever for this chance, Lea."

She still couldn't believe she was spending two nights with the sexiest man alive. And with the task of pretending to be his girlfriend. The opportunity really was a gift.

Lea zipped her suitcase and stood tall. "I'm ready to see where this leads."

"Good for you."

Movement outside the window caught her eye. She drew closer and watched through an opening in the blue-flowered curtains as Ben parked his truck in front of her father's house.

"He's here," she said on an indrawn breath.

Dressed in civilian clothes, he unfolded from behind the wheel and walked to the sidewalk, gaze a bit uncertain as he stared at her front door. Goodness, he was mouthwatering. The gorgeous man filled out his clothes, testing the seams in jeans and the gray, button-down shirt that showcased powerful arms beneath his rolled-up sleeves. Her pulse tripped, and for a moment, she forgot to be nervous.

Lea usually saw the man in her restaurant or on the street outside the armory, and habitually in his ACUs. The National Guardsman was potent and just a little bit intimidating in his uniform, but without it? He was more…human. Accessible. He was just as gorgeous. Just as hot. But now he appeared more approachable. And the way he hesitated on the sidewalk, muscles rippling in his forearms as he flexed his fists, caused something inside her to catch. She didn't often see the vulnerable side of Sgt. Benjamin Wyne. In fact, Lea didn't think it existed any more. Not since he'd come back from basic training.

"Well, then you don't need to be talking to me. Grab your stuff and go get him."

Lea jerked her head at Brandi's voice in her ear, having forgotten she was still on the phone.

Chimes from the doorbell echoed loudly through the older, two-story house. The butterflies swarming in her stomach increased their frenzy. But it was going to be okay. Ben was anxious, too. No doubt nervous about jeopardizing their friendship.

He needn't worry. It was like she'd told the sullen teen with the fresh crew cut all those years ago when she'd sat down beside him on the dock at the lake. She'd always be there for him. Always be his friend.

After promising to fill Brandi in on Monday, Lea hung up the phone, then grabbed her purse and suitcase and headed downstairs where she could hear her dad opening the door. Henry 'Gabe' Gablonski hated to be treated like a baby, so she'd deliberately waited until he'd welcomed their guest. The doctor had said a little exercise was good for him. It was tough at times, but Lea had to force herself to stop playing mother hen and allow the man to do more. Answering the door fell on her list of acceptable chores.

Now, she had to accept hers.

The weekend was happening whether she was ready or not. No sense in delaying the inevitable.

Rushing down the stairs before she could change her mind, she heard her father talking to her *date* in the front room.

As usual, Ben's deep baritone did funny things to her pulse. Willing herself to remain calm, she stepped onto the foyer and set her suitcase down. The rush of nerves hiccupping through her veins was as unavoidable as breathing. With her shoulders back, she headed to the front room where her dad enjoyed sitting in his recliner watching reruns of *Kojak* and *The Rockford Files* on TV.

The swoosh of her periwinkle sundress brushing just above her knees proceeded her into the room. Lea had no idea of the dress code for the weekend, so she went with the suggestions from Brandi and the bridesmaids to keep things casual chic. Comfortable white lace flats, minimal make up and jewelry, hair pulled up and secured with a clip at the top of her head. If she was dressed totally wrong, it was too late to change now.

"Hi, Ben," she said, smiling when the man rose to his feet. A gentleman with great manners. All the Wyne brothers had them. Judging by the approval in eyes, she had dressed appropriately.

"Hi, Lea. You look nice."

Her dad sat in his chair, gaze bouncing between them, big smile on his face.

Ah great, here it comes.

"'Bout time you two got together." He pointed a finger at Ben. "I always said you were dating the wrong daughter."

Her sharp intake of breath echoed loud enough to rival the car chase on TV. "Dad! I was eleven when he dated Gwen."

"I know. He just had to wait for you to grow up, that's all." He chuckled as he jabbed a thumb in her direction. "There she is, Ben. All grown up."

More like all red in the face. *God*, she was so ready for the proverbial floor to swallow her whole. Now. Right *now* would be really good.

"I know."

Her gaze snapped to the guardsman. What did that mean? And did he have to look so darn unhappy while saying it?

Deciding to ignore the sourpuss, she walked to her father, set her hands on her hips and frowned down at him. "I told you the truth about this weekend. You know it's just f— "

"Yeah, yeah. I know what you told me. You're there to keep Mrs. *Velcro* off Ben." He waved a hand at them. "But mark my words...it's more than that." Carefully folding his arms across his chest, he cocked his head and dared her to argue.

Since the weekend *was* more than that to her, she had no argument, so she bent to kiss his cheek instead. "You're incorrigible. Love you. Call if you need me. Ben will call out the National Guard."

"True," Ben said, genuine smile finally lighting his face. "Just say the word. I have them on speed dial."

Her father laughed. "Of that I have no doubt. You hang onto him, Lea. He's a good man."

"Will do," she said, knowing it was easier to get out of the house if she played it safe. "I labeled the food in the freezer and—"

Again her dad waved her off. "I know. I'm not an invalid. I'll manage. I've been cooking since I was a toddler. You just go and have a good time." He grabbed her hand. "You deserve it. You work too hard. And you shouldn't even be here. You should be in the Big Apple talking about historic buildings and such, not waiting on people at the eatery, or talking about coal on weekends."

"But I enjoy both. And I'm right where I want to be." Mostly. She couldn't stop her gaze from shooting to Ben.

His green eyes were intent, studying her, reawakening her pulse that had finally slowed to normal.

"Well, I just feel bad that you're saddled with me," her dad continued, drawing her attention away from her date.

"I'm not saddled. I love you, and if it makes you feel any better, I sent out a few resumes this week."

"You did?" Joy beamed from her father, erasing the sudden haggardness from his face, making her feel less guilty at the little white lie she'd just told.

The resumes *were* written and sitting on her hard drive; she just hadn't hit Send yet. She needed to know her dad was going to be all right first.

Lea straightened her shoulders and lifted her chin. "Yes. So, who knows? Maybe I'll be in the Big Apple this year after all."

Before the holidays would be great. It was so pretty there that time of the year. She still had time. If she sent them out in the next few weeks, and they went through channels and up against boards and committees, she might have a job by Christmas.

"I'm so glad, sweetheart. I hate that I'm holding you back."

"Nonsense. You know I love it here, too. And everyone at the restaurant. The regulars and the soldiers from the armory." She nodded to Ben whose face wore a neutral expression. "I'd ideally like to commute."

On weekends. But, she'd definitely commute daily if the guardsman asked.

He continued to stare at her, emotionless.

Her dad patted her hand, regaining her attention. "Well, as long as you do what's right for you. I don't want you commuting because of me."

A shaft of guilt pierced her heart. Her father hadn't been the original inspiration behind the mention of commuting. Still, she'd certainly be willing. She bent to look him in the eyes. "I promise, commuting is what I want."

The smile returned to soften his features. "Okay. So, now you need to concentrate on having fun this weekend and getting to know your future husband better."

"Dad!" She straightened up. How was she going to be able to face Ben now?

"It's okay. The two of you will come to terms with it at your own pace," he insisted, then nodded toward the door. "But you'd better get going before traffic gets too thick."

"Yes, sir," Ben said, already standing in the doorway, holding her suitcase.

Poor guy. He was more than ready to get the hell out of Dodge. She didn't blame him.

And had no idea what to say to him ten minutes later, in his truck, heading for the colonel's estate. But she had to say something. Her father had just pushed her on him in no uncertain terms.

Lea chanced a glance at the silent man. The strong hands gripping the steering wheel weren't white-knuckled. That was good. Her gaze wandered up his muscular arms. An image of those forearms flexing while they had up-against-the-wall sex flashed through her mind. *Damn*. She shifted in her seat. Where the heck had that come from? Her *wishful-thinking well*, that's where. It was bottomless and full of similar images from years of crushing on the guy. Besides, her Skype conversation with Brandi and the girls had planted that baby in her head two days ago.

"You okay?"

She stifled a giggle. "Yeah." And if he hadn't been wearing mirrored aviator sunglasses, looking all stoic and sexy-as-hell, she would've been able to tell if he was, too. But his gorgeous green eyes were now covered, and their secrets hidden from her view for the moment. "I'm sorry about my dad back there."

His firm mouth twitched into a lop-sided grin. "Don't be. He just wants you to be happy."

She sighed, twisting around to face the front. "I'll be happy when he's back at the restaurant, doing what he loves."

"What about you?"

She turned to blink at him. "Me?"

"Yeah, did you really send out resumes?" Something in her gaze must've given her away because he shook his head and smiled. "You didn't send squat."

"No," she admitted. "But I will."

"Sure."

His tone was less than believable, so she punched him, no doubt hurting her hand more than his rock hard bicep.

"I will. You'll see," she insisted, rubbing her fingers. "Once he's back at the restaurant."

"Right. Then you'll need to stick around to help Ryder, or fill in for Mary or—"

"They're legitimate reasons," she defended, turning back to face the front, folding her arms across her chest.

"More like legitimate excuses."

"Look, I'm not going to argue with you about this."

"Again."

"Yes, again. I know you've been harping on me for years."

"Then do something about it, Lea. Use your degree. You deserve to do what you want. Not what others need. You had a good job in Philly. It bothers me that you gave it up."

It did? Why? Was he that uncomfortable around her?

She cleared her throat. "I know. And I will."

"When?"

"I told you. After my dad is back to work."

"That could take months."

She lifted her chin. "So be it."

"You're afraid."

Her gaze snapped to his face. She wished she could see what was going on behind those damn glasses. "I'm not afraid of anything."

Other than something happening to her family and friends. She'd experienced enough loss, and the community had seen enough during the past decade. With each deployment, the pictures increased on the wall above the Fallen Soldier's Table her father had set up in the corner of the restaurant to salute those who never made it home.

"Except what?" he prodded. "Come on. I can see it your eyes. You thought of something."

She nodded and considered lying to shelter him from the pain she knew her answer would cause. But Ben despised liars, and she'd already fibbed to her dad today. Besides, he'd know if she made something up. Damn man was the best lie detector she knew. He should've been a cop like their friend Jeremy.

"Well? Spill it. You know I'll get it out of you."

She stared at her reflection in his glasses. "Except adding another photo to the wall at the diner."

He stiffened, and after a second, gave her a curt nod, and the rest of the trip was made in silence. Not exactly a good start to the weekend, but this weekend was about truths, and they were not going to be selective truths.

A half-hour later, Ben pulled through the opened wrought iron gates to the colonel's estate, and Lea admired the vast, manicured lawn, trees and shrubs that surrounded a circular drive with a working fountain in the middle.

"That's…um…interesting," she said, as he parked behind another truck. Lea was unsure whether to laugh or gawk at the bronze statue of a very well-endowed, naked man with water spewing from a plate he held in his hand.

"I know." Ben grimaced. "Mrs. Dankirk had it commissioned and flown in from Italy."

Total waste of money. "It could be worse," she felt compelled to say.

He shut off the ignition, removed his glasses and turned to stare at her, brows knit together, gorgeous green eyes narrowed to mere slits. "Worse? How?"

Her lips quivered. "What if he had no plate? I'd hate to think of where the water would come from then…"

It took all of two seconds before Ben tossed his glasses on the dash, threw his head back and laughed. The warm sound reverberated through the cab to her very core, and Lea's good parts quivered in response. She twisted to lean her back against her door for support as she faced him. Goodness, the man was potent in close quarters.

When he finally sobered, the warmth remained in his gaze as he smiled at her. "What am I going to do with you?"

Several scorching and decadent suggestions flashed through her head at the same time, but none made it to her lips. "Put up with me, I guess," she said instead. "You're the one who invited me."

"True."

His gaze sobered and lost some of the warmth, and she suddenly felt cold.

"Thanks for helping me, Lea. I appreciate you giving up your weekend for me."

She shrugged, trying to play it off as if it was no big deal. "Like I told you the other day, I had the time off, so it's all good."

He nodded, and she tried not to take offense at the relief washing through his features. "Good, because I don't want you to get the wrong idea. I just need you to pretend to be my girlfriend when the others are around."

"Especially Mrs. Dankirk."

"Exactly. …" He paused, his gaze transferring to something out the window behind her.

Was it bad to wish it was the woman?

A second later, she wondered if the colonel's wife was outside because when Ben's attention returned to her again, his gaze was hot and interested and…consuming.

Her heart tried to burst from her chest. Then he shifted closer, sexy smile on his face trapping the breath in her lungs. She couldn't blink. Forgot how to breathe. Just sat there watching the sexiest man alive lift a hand to cup her face.

Breathe, idiot! The last thing she needed was to faint. Not when she was about to get the kiss she'd dreamt about since puberty.

God, she hoped she was about to get the kiss she'd dreamt about since puberty…

Chapter Three

"I hope you have some acting skills, Lea, because we have an audience," he informed through that delicious smile still lingering on his approaching lips. "Don't freak out, but I'm going to kiss you."

Freak out?

She was going to freak out if he *didn't* kiss her. *Bring it on, Bucko, I'm ready* seemed a little too anxious. "Okay," she whispered instead, hands clenched in a ball on her lap to keep from grabbing his collar and yanking him close.

That would appear too desperate, and she wasn't going for desperate. She wanted demure, mysterious...and the rest of her thought process went to hell in a designer bag when his lips finally brushed hers.

A fission of some sort skittered down her shoulders and spine. He must've felt it too because he drew back to blink at her. She inhaled, lost in his incredible manly scent mixed with fresh soap and something cedar. But Lea had waited a long time for the kiss and was having none of that air between them. She reached up to cup his face and pulled that sexy jaw and sensual mouth back where they belonged. On her.

To her joy, Ben needed no coaxing. Tentative and light at first, his lips resumed their private tasting; then, as if a switch had been flipped, he increased the pressure, deepening the kiss, driving her out of her rapidly fogging mind.

He did not disappoint. His quiet strength and raw passion she sensed hidden just under the surface felt even better than she had imagined.

Hotter. Stronger. Just…more.

It was all too much. She closed her eyes and melted into him, clutching at the collar she tried so hard not to clutch. Again and again, he tasted her lips, and she willed his tongue to slip on over for a visit while she fought to keep her tongue to herself, to refrain from exploring his domain. Wanting, willing him to make that first move.

This was their first kiss. They'd have more this weekend. She'd have plenty of opportunity to sample all of Benjamin Wyne.

Of course, if he wanted to sample more, she was happy to oblige. Right there. In his truck. In the middle of the colonel's driveway…

She stiffened a half a second before him, each apparently realizing where they were at the same time.

"Damn, Lea," he said, drawing back, lop-sided grin tugging the warm mouth she already missed. "You are a great actress."

Actress?

He friggin' thought she had been acting?

The deep, consuming need to touch and taste had nothing to do with acting and everything to do with feeling. It was real. They had a connection. And she would've told him, but he was already slipping out of the truck.

Acting my ass.

She sucked in a few breaths and cleared the fog from her brain. By the time he reached her door, doubt had set in.

Maybe his need and passion had been faked. Maybe *he* had been acting. That made sense. Why else would he have been kissing her like his life had depended on it?

Because it had. Sort of. His *promotion* life.

Idiot.

44

Here she'd thought it was her. That she was the reason he couldn't seem to get enough. That he finally awakened to the realization she was no longer a child.

Darn man zapped her common sense along with her brain cells.

"Watch your step, sweetheart," he said, taking her hand to help her out of the truck.

Catching sight of Colonel Dankirk and his wife approaching with another couple behind Ben, Lea conjured her best smile and slid slowly to the ground, using his body as a buffer.

A rock, solid, hard buffer.

"Thank you, Benny." She lifted up on tiptoe to kiss his cheek. Only she could see the shock widening his gaze. Maybe he wasn't as indifferent to her after all.

Satisfaction was a warm blanket to the soul.

"There you two are," the colonel said, hand extended to Ben. "How was traffic?"

They drew apart so the two men could shake.

"Not bad, sir," her date replied.

Mrs. Dankirk stepped forward. "Good to see you again, Ben."

Lea half-expected the woman to look like an aging porn star, not the attractive, polished blonde in designer clothes and posture as perfect as her plastic surgery. If Brandi hadn't informed her the Velcro vixen was in her forties, Lea would've guessed early thirties. Whoever did her face and boobs was one heck of a doctor.

Her hostess with the mostess pulled Ben into a hug that started out innocent enough, until she skimmed a hand over his ass.

Nice. And right in front of her husband's nose, too. Lea was doing her best to keep the distaste from showing on her face when the woman turned a cool gaze on her.

"And you brought a friend."

Her date immediately stepped close and dropped an arm around her shoulders. "This is my girlfriend, Lea Gablonski."

"Gablonski? Funny." The woman didn't laugh. "You don't look polish."

As much as she wanted to counter the remark, she curbed her inner snark for Ben's sake. "I know. I think most of it went to my older sister."

The woman stared at her like she didn't know what to do with her, which made sense to Lea because she didn't know what to do with herself either.

Ben introduced the other three couples who had gathered near, and she wasn't surprised to find each of them were customers from the diner. Thanks to her upbringing in the restaurant, Lea suspected she knew everyone in the county.

"Come on inside and Malloy will show you to your room," Colonel Dankirk said, leading the way.

Room.

Her heart leapt. So they *were* sharing a room. Maybe the negligee would see the light of day—or moonlight— after all. Of course, she had to get up the nerve to wear it in front of her *boyfriend*.

Stepping into the two story house, she found the foyer open and airy with high ceilings and gorgeous crown molding. At every turn was an antique, a piece of history Lea longed to explore, but the dowdy housekeeper was already heading upstairs expecting them to follow, so she had to drool on the run.

When they were finally alone in their room, she brushed past Ben and took advantage of the opportunity to openly covet the furniture.

"I can't believe this, Ben. Look." She pointed to an ornate vanity dresser. "They have a Chippendale. A *Chippendale*. I think I've died and gone to heaven," she said, gently running her hand over the mahogany wood. "Who would've guessed the house would be full of such treasures? Especially after seeing that fountain."

He shrugged. "It's just furniture."

Her intake of breath filled the room when she punched his arm. Hard.

"Ouch."

"Exactly," she said, frowning at him. "These aren't just pieces of furniture. They're history. Someone's history."

Again he shrugged, unzipping his duffle bag to remove a modern day shaving kit. "If you say so."

"I do." She nodded, moving on to examine a settee in the corner.

It was a Victorian walnut settee from the 1800s, and in excellent shape. Excitement rushed through her veins. This wasn't a museum piece; she was allowed to touch. Drawing in a shaky breath, she gingerly sat down, then stretched out and smiled.

"I left room in the—" Ben reentered from the adjoining bathroom, stopped mid-sentence and stood staring at her as if he'd walked into a pole.

"What?"

He blinked and gave his head a slight shake. "What?"

Lea turned on her side, propped her head in her hand and smiled. "I asked you first."

Ben blanked.

Again.

Why the hell did that keep happening? He couldn't seem to filter in Lea's words or form a thought, other than she was so damn beautiful and sexy lying on the old couch, come-hither stare fastened on him through eyes the same unique shade as her outfit.

Damn.

The urge to strip her naked and join her was so sudden and strong he nearly doubled over.

What the hell?

The same unexpected need had hit him when he'd kissed her in the truck. That wasn't supposed to happen. The simple staged kiss in front of the colonel's wife to show he was off limits had turned into anything but simple. It should've been like kissing his sister. Unfeeling and unpleasant.

But it wasn't.

Hell no. The instant his lips had brushed hers, a wave of heat had shot down his body and stirred his groin. He should've stopped and pulled back, but Mrs. Dankirk had been watching from a distance, and he'd wanted to make sure she got the message.

Bullshit, his mind balked. It had been all Lea. He couldn't get enough of the blue-eyed beauty. He'd wanted more, needed more, and it was all he could do not to thrust his tongue into her mouth and sample her essence. Luckily, common sense had kicked in. She wasn't offering—she was acting.

At his request.

So, what was she doing now? There was no audience. Just them.

He needed to cool it and get his thinking back on track. Use his other head. He cleared his throat and nodded toward the bathroom. "There's room for your stuff in there."

"Thanks," she said, then scooted back and patted the cushion in front of her. "Come here and try this out, Ben. It's more comfortable than I thought."

He swallowed a snort. "No, I might break it." And by *it,* he meant his resolve not to touch the woman while they were alone. He could tell by just that one kiss things could get out of hand fast. At least, on his end. He glanced at the clock on the nightstand. "We'd better get downstairs. It's just about time for dinner."

A flash of reluctance crossed her face. He could relate. He was not looking forward to mysteriously ending up next to Mrs. Dankirk again. At the last party, he had to endure her grab-hand tactics under the table.

"Okay." Lea scooted to the edge of the chair, flashing a good portion of supple leg and thigh before standing. "Let's go see your girlfriend."

"Very funny." He wasn't amused.

A few graceful steps brought her to him at the door, where she hooked her arm through his then glanced up and smiled. "I know."

Despite himself, his lips twitched into an answering grin as he opened the door and ushered her into the hall. No matter what life threw at the woman, she was always upbeat and positive, ready with a smile. A Godsend for Brandi and the whole Wyne family. And it was never more apparent as they entered the dining room a minute later.

"There you are, Ben," Mrs. Dankirk smiled and patted the chair on her left. "Just in time."

Damn. He didn't think he could take another dinner with the hostess feeling his crotch.

Lea stepped forward. "Oh, would you mind if I sat there, Mrs. Dankirk? Benny is left handed, and we'll do nothing but bump elbows all night if he sits there."

The woman hesitated, and he held his breath until she forced a smile and nodded. "But of course."

God he could've kissed Lea. She actually got him out of the hotseat. And with the truth. He *was* left handed.

"Thank you," Lea said when he held the chair out for her.

He bent down to whisper in her ear as he pushed her in. "I owe you."

She turned to him as he took his seat, mischievous grin curving her lips. "Yes, you do."

He should've been afraid, but he wasn't. Not this time. He was still enjoying the high from not having to sit next to their hostess. Then a twinge of guilt shifted through him. This meant she was going to endure Mrs. Dankirk's wrath for getting in the way.

"So, tell me, Lea," the woman began as she shook out her napkin and settled it on her lap. "What exactly do you do?"

"Right now I'm working at my dad's diner," Lea replied, smoothing her own napkin over her thighs, shoulders relaxed, not in the least put out by their hostess' condescending tone.

He was noticing this pattern with her lately. She wasn't easily put out. Maybe her time alone in a big city had matured her. And maybe he shouldn't find that trait so attractive. That was asking for trouble.

Colonel Dankirk leaned forward and cocked his head. "She's being modest, my dear. Lea also has a Masters in History."

The colonel's wife jerked her head. "Really? Why in the world are you waitressing? Seems like a waste of time."

Lea shrugged, expression still amicable. "My dad is recovering from surgery, so I'm just filling in until he's back behind the counter."

"And she works at the train museum," one of the other women at the table spoke up.

Distaste broke through and soured the corner of Mrs. Dankirk's mouth. "I see," she said, reaching for her wine.

"Oh my," Lea exclaimed, gaze trained on the woman's hand. "What an exquisite Fede Gimmel ring. It's Victorian, right?"

And just like that, the distaste in Mrs. Dankirk's eyes disappeared to be replaced by delight. "Yes, it is. Do you know jewelry?"

His date smiled. "No, but as they say, I do know history." She fingered the ring still on their hostess' finger. "It's actually three rings that fit tightly together to form one. This piece is incredible."

"Yes, it is," their host repeated, removing the ring and spreading it to reveal three parts.

The women around the table all murmured their delight at the thin gold ring with a hand on one, half a hand on another and twin hearts on the middle. When fit together, it appeared to be two hands clasping the double hearts. Ben never would've guessed it was a set, or expensive.

"Then you'll probably love our dinner plates. And here they are now."

The staff set out their first course and Lea sucked in a breath. "My God. These can't be real."

"I can assure you, they are," the colonel said with a shake of his head. "They cost a pretty penny."

Lea started to shake. "I can't believe I'm eating off of sixteenth century china."

"Believe it," Mrs. Dankirk said, big smile lighting her face. "What do you think of the candle sticks?"

Ben spent the next half-hour eating in silence, enjoying Lea's expressions from shocked to delighted to awestruck, as well as her explanation for each piece their host mentioned. His date practically vibrated in her seat.

Before he knew it, dinner was through, and he survived without being groped once.

A novel experience for him in that house.

"Well, my dear, why don't you show Lea our art collection while the guys and I shoot some pool?" the colonel suggested, pushing back in his chair.

Lea stilled. "Art collection?"

"Yes, we have an extensive one in the other room," Mrs. Dankirk replied, rising to her feet to hook elbows with his *girlfriend* and lead her from the room without once subjecting him to an inappropriate stare.

Yeah, he owed Lea big time. All evening, she held everyone's attention and worked the table like a pro, without even trying. She was just being Lea. Her usual *well* of knowledge. This allowed him to actually enjoy a meal at the colonel's house, for once.

Best damn idea he'd ever had was bringing her along.

He stepped into the study, ready to talk shop, curious to know if the colonel had heard about gaining another company, but as soon as the door closed behind him, he received backslaps and handshakes from the snickering guys.

"Wow, Serge. You're a sly dog."

"And a lucky one."

"Now the truth is out. All these years of warnings, biting everyone's head off and threatening to spit it down our throats if we even so much as looked at Brandi or Lea the wrong way had nothing to do with Lea being like a sister to you."

Yeah, it did.

"Truth is out, Serge. That was bullshit."

"You just wanted her for yourself."

Damn. He'd forgotten about that. Once the girls had turned fifteen, he and his brothers had taken it upon themselves to warn off any of the soldiers who showed interest. It had worked for the most part. But the guys were right, he was still doing it. Just last week, he caught a new transfer eying up Lea's legs when she'd leaned across a table. He'd ripped the kid a new one. She deserved better. Someone without possible deployment and uncertainty in their future.

Brandi is happy with Kade, his mind interjected. He ignored it.

"Na, he's just smart," Colonel Dankirk said, shoving a drink in his hand. "That woman's a keeper, and he knows a good thing when he sees it."

"Yes, sir."

But he didn't. Not really.

Ben had no idea what a good thing was because he avoided it like the plague. Lea was definitely white-picket, and he was camouflage. Hell, until a few days ago, she was like his little sister.

Not after that kiss today.

He'd never consider her that way again. *Damn*. He lifted his glass in a salute, then drank the scotch and contemplated his dilemma as the liquid burned a path to the knot in his stomach. It felt as if he was in a sinking rowboat in the middle of a lake with no paddle.

"So, Colonel, is it true we're acquiring another SIGNAL company?" one of the lieutenants asked.

Ben welcomed the change of subject, even if he'd already heard the news unofficially last weekend when he'd drilled down Fort Indiantown Gap. More communications equipment to inventory and add to the books.

"Yes, as of fifteen May twenty-fifteen, the armory at Myersville will be under our command." His superior hit him with a frank stare. "That means, Ben, we'll need to make provisions for their equipment and so on."

He nodded. "Yes, sir." He knew the drill. The amount of companies they'd gained and dropped in the past two years kept him hopping.

Another scotch and two games of pool later, Ben emerged from the house in search of his *girlfriend* who was supposedly outside watching the sunset. He'd had about all the shop talk he could take, and as much as he wanted to avoid the new temptation, he couldn't, in good conscience, let her alone, or worse, at the mercy of Mrs. Dankirk.

"Ah, so you've emerged outside without peril," Lea said when he rounded a tall hedge in the garden.

"Yep," he replied, having truthfully forgotten *Mrs. Velcro* was on the loose. "How was your art tour?"

A laugh escaped her throat and echoed around them. "Swell, got any valium?"

Ben's smile disappeared when he stopped next to her, noting the head-to-toe tremors wracking her body. He grasped her shoulders and twisted her to face him. "What's wrong? Are you okay?"

Weird, he hadn't sensed anything, and he usually did when family and friends were in some kind of trouble. A type of sixth sense he'd inherited from his mother's side of the family.

"Swell, got any valium?"

"Lea, I'm serious."

"So am I."

Cursing under his breath, he dragged her to a nearby bench and forced her to sit down, then sat next to her, rubbing her arms. "What is going on?"

"Oh, nothing. I just ate boxed macaroni and cheese off a rare Victorian plate worth more than I make in a month."

He let out a breath, and swallowed a few curses. "Is that all?" Jesus, she scared him.

"Is that all? Is that *all*?" she wailed, punching his shoulder.

She certainly seemed to enjoy punching him today.

"Didn't you hear me? It's priceless. Rare…as in antique. It should be in a museum, not soaking up grease and cheese and placed in a microwave." She sucked in a breath and squeezed his arm. "Oh my God. You don't think they put it in the microwave, do you?"

Ben had no idea, but for the sake of his arm and blood supply to his fingers he shook his head. "No."

She exhaled and released her hold, but she still shook. "I won't even tell you where they're hanging their Rembrandt." She swallowed visibly. "On a wall, in direct sunlight."

He didn't know much about the arts, but even he knew that was a big mistake.

She stood, then began to pace. "I'm not sure I can do this, Ben. I want to help you. I really do, but they have such incredible treasures with no regard to their preservation."

He shot to his feet and stepped in front of the distressed woman. "Hey, it's okay," he said, grabbing her hands and placing them on his chest. "It's okay."

"How?" she asked, shaking beginning to subside. "Didn't you hear me? They're washing King George I's dishes in the *dishwasher*. How is that okay?"

He bent at the knee and smiled down at her. "Because he doesn't need them anymore."

Big blue eyes blinked twice before her gaze cleared and she slapped her palm off his chest. "You're a goof, you know that?"

"So I've been told."

She laughed, then wrapped her arms around his neck and hugged him close. "Thanks."

He tried not to notice the generous breasts crushed against him, but without the jacket of his uniform as a barrier, he felt every delectable curve. "For what?" he drew back enough to stare down into her pretty face. "I owe *you* the thanks. You saved more than my ass tonight at dinner."

The left-side of her mouth tugged upward into a grin. "What? She didn't get to play hide the sausage?"

This time he laughed, then groaned at the thought. "No, and it would be *grab* the sausage."

"Not if I were playing." Her hand flew to her mouth as her face turned beet red. "Tell me I didn't say that out loud."

God, she was adorable.

"Okay," he answered, unable to stop the smile from spreading across his face. "But you did, and I'd really like to know what you meant by that."

As her color deepened, so did his attraction. *Damn it*. He was playing with fire. He needed to release her. Get as far away from the temptress as possible. Once his hands and feet complied, he'd hightail it up to their room for a cold shower.

"Uh oh." She glanced at something behind him. "I think I saw someone."

Ah, hell. Just what he needed. Now, he had to continue to hold her close, which made his body yell, *Hell yeah*. Then she really kicked up his pulse when her hands inched back up around his neck, and she tugged his face toward her.

"Don't freakout," she whispered a mimic of his earlier words. "But I'm going to kiss you now."

For a beat, they shared a breath before her sweet lips took his, tasting and nibbling. And heaven help him, her tongue lightly brushed his lower lip, shooting a spike of heat to his rapidly tightening groin. That was it. He didn't give a shit about who was or wasn't watching them. Even King George I himself. All Ben knew was he wanted to taste more of the amazing woman.

A lot more.

Cupping the back of her head with one hand and her supple ass with the other, he crushed her close, thrusting his tongue inside her warm, wet mouth, exploring her hot taste fully for the first time. She was exquisite. Her soft, sexy moan wreaked havoc with his pulse, and when their tongues touched, his erection throbbed.

Jesus, he'd never been this aroused this fast by just one kiss. Damn woman had him so off kilter he lost sight of the horizon. He couldn't get enough. She was addicting. Even when they broke for air, he needed to taste her, had to keep his mouth on her delicious body. With her hair piled on top of her head, he had full access to her throat and began to kiss a path down her neck. Her second moan, and the way she clutched at his back, stiffened his groin until the zipper bit into his flesh.

So he bit into hers. Behind her ear.

The hitch in her breath fueled his hunger, and if it hadn't been for the sound of laughter and approaching footsteps on the garden pavers, he might've taken the embrace a lot further.

Which pissed him off.

He was acting like a horny teenager again. The lack of control was disturbing. Especially since his good friend was the cause. He'd watched her grow up. They'd shared triumphs and sorrows, and a lot of pizzas in between, but through it all, they'd remained friends.

Where the hell had this attraction come from? Better yet, where the hell had it been?

No, that was not a good question. Not a safe one, anyway. He had to keep his wits about him. Today was almost over. He just had to make it through one more day.

"There you two are," Mrs. Dankirk said, rounding the corner with one of the officers and his wife. "I was just showing the Bartons the garden, but it's getting dark."

"Yes," Lea said, voice still a little throaty and way too sexy. "But it's still lovely."

Their hostess smiled. "Thank you. We're getting ready to turn in. It's been a long day."

"Us, too."

Lea shifted closer, and his heart dropped to his ribs. He was in no condition to be alone with the woman.

"Wonderful. Before you go up, Ben, my husband said he wanted to see you in the study."

Thank God. "Okay."

With a nod, their hostess and the Bartons headed back the way they came. Leaving him alone with Lea.

He released her and stepped back. "I'd better see what the colonel needs."

They walked back in silence, mostly because he had no damn clue what to say. Hopefully, she'd believe his kisses had been for show. Because, regardless of his arousal, he had no intention of acting on their unexpected attraction.

Leaving her at the bottom of the steps, he waited until she cleared the second landing before he pivoted around and marched toward the study, thankful for the reprieve.

Twenty-four hours to go. How hard could that be?

He walked into the darkened study and stopped dead. Where was the colonel?

"I was beginning to think you weren't going to show," Mrs. Dankirk said, pushing him against the door that shut behind him, while sneaking a hand beneath his shirt as she kissed his neck.

Son-of-a-bitch!

He grasped the woman by the shoulders and shoved her none-too-gently away. "Enough." He flipped on the light. "We've been through this before. I'm not interested. Your husband's a good man. Show him some respect."

"I know he is," she replied, straightening her dress. "He's just not...enough."

"Well, look elsewhere. I'm not interested." Without waiting for a reply, he whipped open the door and strode out.

The unfaithful woman just solidified what he already knew: Relationships and the military did not mix. He'd tried and failed. Mason had tried and failed with his bride walking away the day of the wedding. His dad had tried and failed, once; the second to Brandi's mother didn't count since Catherine's life was cut so short. Then there was his older brother Ethan. His wife had died in a skiing accident while he'd been deployed, but Ben had suspected the woman had been cheating. Not something his older brother needed to know. But it had certainly added to his own disillusionment.

And what the colonel's wife just pulled cemented his views on women and relationships.

They weren't worth it.

With a new resolve strengthening his control, Ben entered his room and shut the door, relief easing the tension from his shoulders. At least he'd be safe from their hostess for the night. He turned around...and stopped dead.

Holy hell...

Stopped breathing.

Didn't blink.

Mind blanked.

Again.

The most beautiful, erotic vision emerged from the bathroom, gorgeous breasts spilling out of the light blue silk and black lace corset thing causing a stranglehold on his breathing and tight grip on his groin.

Lea smiled, then twisted completely around, giving him a glimpse of her perfect, spankable cheeks, nearly sending him into cardiac arrest. He rubbed his chest, fighting the heat and fog overtaking his body. God, she was stunning.

The urge to press her against the wall and sink into her lush, hourglass curves shook through him. And because he wanted to, with every hard, throbbing muscle in his over-heated body, Ben did the only honorable thing he could.

He turned around and walked out.

Chapter Four

He left.

Lea stumbled to the bed on shaky legs and sank onto the mattress. He walked out. Why? Had she misread his kisses? Did he really only see her as a kid sister? Her jumbled mind tried to latch onto an explanation, but none were forthcoming.

Oh God, what have I done?

Before mortification set in, she got up and changed into a T-shirt and shorts, resisting the urge to trash the nightie. She fingered the silky material. It had been a sweet gesture from Jordan and the girls, and didn't belong at the bottom of the dump. The floor maybe, after great sex, but not the dump. She shoved it back in her suitcase, then turned out the light and crawled into bed.

So much for up-against-the-wall-sex.

Why did she have to get the broken negligee?

Turning her face, she laughed into her pillow because it beat crying. *Idiot.* She swallowed past her swollen throat. Leave it to her to scare the guy silly. Geez, he couldn't get away fast enough. Hot tears filled her eyes and slid down her cheek without her permission. *Dammit.* She didn't want to cry.

It wasn't as if he hadn't found her attractive because, although Ben hadn't said a word, a fierce hunger had blazed in his green eyes, turning them a delicious emerald. Her good parts were still tingling over that. Thank goodness he hadn't been repulsed.

Otherwise, yeah, she'd really be mortified.

Right now, Lea lingered somewhere between embarrassed and humiliated. She hiccupped a laugh. The

61

nightie wasn't exactly broken. He found her attractive, just not enough to overlook their past.

She rolled over and buried her head under the pillow. Now, if she could just pretend to be his girlfriend without seeing him for the next twenty-four hours…that would be great.

How in the world was she going to face him now?

The sound of the door opening and closing made it to her ears despite the pillow. Crap. She wasn't ready. Not yet. The shuffle of boots on the hardwood floor signaled he'd drawn near. She could feel him watching her. The urge to burrow deep was strong, but she didn't move. Not one muscle.

"Lea, are you awake? We need to talk."

Yeah, she'd get right on that.

"Come on."

The click of the lamp echoed in the silent room while light cast away the shadows she could see from the edges of her sanctuary.

"I know you're not sleeping."

"Yes, I am. Go away."

He didn't, but the pillow did as he lifted it up and set it aside. "Can't." He knelt beside the bed to stare into her heated face. Compassion and remorse mixed to cloud his gaze and soften his tone. "I'm really sorry, Lea."

"For what?" She snorted. "Not wanting to have sex with me? It's fine. Really. I just have to get through the mortification process. I'll see you in about ten years." She made to roll away, but a large, firm hand pressed into her shoulder and held her in place.

"That's not what happened."

"Really, Ben? Because it sure seemed like it from where I was standing—in a damn sexy negligee, I might add. With practically everything on display." She fought hard to resist the urge to pull the sheet up over her head. "But you walked out uninterested."

"That's not what happened," he repeated, then released her, troubled gaze boring deep. "I walked out because I *was* interested, Lea. So damn interested I couldn't see straight. Still can't."

Her heart rocked hard in her chest, dislodging a startled gasp. "Really?"

"Yes." He straightened from the floor and sat on the edge of the bed. "You're beautiful, Lea, and damn sexy. Don't think for one minute it was easy to walk away from you, because I wanted nothing more than to take you up against that damn wall."

She smacked his nearest shoulder. "Dammit, Ben. I *wanted* up-against-the-wall sex."

"Jesus." He vaulted to his feet as if the mattress had caught fire, then stumbled toward the wall. "You can't just say things like that. What are you trying to do, kill me?"

"No, I'm trying to make sense of this." She sat up and waved a hand between them. "If you're attracted to me, and I'm attracted to you, what's the problem?"

"I watched you grow up," he replied in a solemn tone. "You're Brandi's best friend."

"Who do you think sent the negligee?"

His head snapped back. "What?"

"Well, her and Jordan and the other bridesmaids."

"Thanks. Now I know whose necks to ring when I see them," he stated, while leaning his long frame against the Victorian dresser.

Her inner historian screamed in protest, but she refrained from warning him to be careful. At the moment, discussing her sex-appeal was a damn sight more important than the antique.

She lifted her chin. "So...you really were turned on?"

63

"Yes."

"But not enough to stay."

Expelling a breath, he walked back to sit on the bed and reached for her hand. "As great as the sex promises to be, you're a good friend, Lea, and I don't want to ruin that friendship with great sex. Would you?"

Yes, please. Take me now! But because that sounded wanton in her mind, she swallowed the words and shook her head. "No." He was right. She wouldn't want any awkwardness between them.

He dipped his head, a ghost of a smile tugging his lips. "So…we're good?"

No. She wanted him to want her as much as she wanted him. And because that barely made sense in her fogged up brain, she lied. "Yes."

As long as he only saw her as a friend, they'd never be okay.

"Let's get some sleep. Tomorrow's going to be a long day," he said, rising from the bed. "Breakfast is at O-eight hundred, followed by a full day of outdoor activities, including the lake. Thanks for that, by the way. Seems I'm supposed to row you around."

She smiled big. "Don't mention it." Bugger was going to row her twice around. He owed her at least that for walking out earlier.

"Yeah, I thought you'd be pleased."

She watched him grab a pillow from the bed and toss it onto the floor. "What are you doing?"

"Going to bed."

"On the floor?"

"Yep." He pulled a camouflage liner from his duffle bag and threw it next to the pillow before sitting on the chaise to remove his boots.

"This is a queen size bed, Ben. There's plenty of room for us both."

He grunted. "I'm barely hanging on by a thread here, Lea. I don't think I'll ever get the image of you in that damn corset thing out of my head. No way in hell are we sharing anything."

Funny how his discomfort made her feel better. Even though she knew it wouldn't take much persuasion to get him to break his resolve tonight, she stayed put. His body may want her, but his heart and mind did not, and they were actually more important. Their lack of participation would dampen her pleasure.

Until Ben came to terms with his wants and needs—*if* Ben came to terms with them—she would not be making any more advances. Sure, she'd continue to play the dutiful girlfriend thing tomorrow, and enjoy every damn second, but if he wanted in her bed, he was going to have to make the next move.

Ben had never taken a cold shower before. Ever. Not even during his adolescent years. But last night, after images of Lea battered his mind in that damn sexy blue getup with a sultry, inviting expression on her beautiful face, he'd lost the battle and used the cold water as a deterrent to crawling into her bed to seek relief to the heat and need throbbing his body. The bed had been closer than the bathroom, and a hell of a lot more appealing, but he couldn't get past the fact it was Brandi's friend in that bed. His friend. The little girl from down the street. Those were the thoughts that helped him turn on his heel and march into the bathroom.

But those thoughts were eventually going to fade. Heaven help him then. And *now*. He entered the dining room, holding Lea's hand for appearance sake, and did his best to ignore how right it felt. Time to get his mind back on work, and socializing with his peers. That was the reason he was here this weekend.

"Good morning, Colonel. Mrs. Dankirk." He nodded to their hosts already seated. With any luck, by the time they filled their plates from the buffet style breakfast set up along the far wall, they'd be able to sit on the other side of the table. "Smells almost as good as your cooking," he said to Lea.

"Then we'd better hurry," she said, tugging him to the food. "We don't need them running out of bacon. I don't want to have to put up with Mr. Crankypuss all morning."

He stopped, and when she turned to face him, he frowned at her. "I don't get cranky in the morning."

She laughed.

The lieutenant and his wife ahead of them looked up from the buffet. "Sure you do, Serge, but you always come back in a better mood after eating at Gabe's. I thought it was the food, but now I know better."

Lea blushed. "Nah. He's addicted to my coffee."

"True." He smiled and received a smack from her on the arm.

"That's because I know what you like." Her gaze was open and friendly with just a hint of mischief darkening her baby blues to steal his breath. "You like bacon with your bacon with maybe a side of eggs."

The other couple laughed as they continued down the buffet.

"True," he told Lea again, handing her a plate before falling in behind her.

He had to admit, the view was great. His gaze traveled down her white tank top with blue anchors, exposing a neckline that haunted his dreams, and his body tightened at the way her navy pants hugged those sweet cheeks he'd glimpsed…and walked away from.

Idiot.

He was beginning to regret his decision last night.

"You can get your revenge on him today, Lea," the colonel stated from across the room. "Because, after horseback riding this morning, we're all heading to the lake for a picnic, and he can finally own up to that rowing."

"Perfect," she said, then loaded scrambled eggs and some delicious smelling bacon onto the plate in his hand. "You need to keep up your strength, Benny. I'm going to give you a workout."

The others laughed, even Mrs. Dankirk, so he forced his lips to curve upward. But he wondered if she was serious or just acting her part. It shouldn't matter.

So, why did it?

An hour later, Ben was still contemplating the answer as they all walked to the stables. Breakfast had been smooth and uneventful, and once again, he was blown away at how well Lea handled the wide range of topics from politics to fashion to celebrities. The pretty woman at his side was eloquent and intelligent, and he was ashamed to admit he hadn't realized just how intelligent. Made him wonder what else he'd taken for granted about his sister's friend.

Like conversation. Today, he noticed she wasn't initiating dialogue with him, only speaking when spoken to. Which should make things easier. Keep them off personal subjects. So, why did he feel as if something was missing?

"As you can see, we don't have enough horses for everyone, so a few of you will have to double up," the colonel announced when they reached the stable where the horses were already saddled and ready to go. "I'm sure Ben and the lieutenant won't mind sharing their mounts with their women."

"Of course, sir." The way the weekend was going, Ben wasn't surprised by the turn of event, but he was surprised by the look of reluctance that flashed fleetingly through Lea's gaze. Why wouldn't she want to ride with him?

Normally, he enjoyed a ride through the country side. The area was spectacular with pine, oak, maple and birch trees standing tall and majestic, with only an occasional creaking branch breaking the silence in the wind. And the slight rocking of the horse and soft thud of hoof beats on the forest floor usually soothed away his troubles.

Not today. Negative. Today, he experienced a different side to riding. A very enjoyable side. With a woman sitting behind him, but not just any woman—Lea, with her soft, supple body pressed against his back, hitched breaths hitting his neck when the horse rocked them together. Damn, he could feel her nipples and her heat, and heaven help him, he loved every minute. Even guided the horse into a trot just to feel those beauties poking, raking, testing his control, and down a few hills so she'd cling tighter and longer. By the time their ride ended back at the stables, he wasn't sure he could walk, but his extra ministrations had been worth it.

Anticipation upped his pulse when he slid off the horse and turned to help Lea dismount. It wouldn't be inappropriate to steal a kiss from his girlfriend, and he was more than ready to feel those delectable curves brushing the front of him this time.

Those thoughts were wrong, and the fact he knew it and didn't care was a testament to the amount of fog in his brain.

But when he helped her down, she placed her hands on his shoulders, then slid them to pat his chest while she lifted on tip-toe to kiss his check. "Thanks, Benny," she said, then walked over to the other women and was soon laughing at something one had said.

What the hell just happened?

No kiss? No curves? No Lea melting into him?

Yeah, her display of affection was still girlfriend-ish, so he couldn't very well remind her he needed her help. But at the moment, he wanted…

Ah hell, he didn't know what he wanted.

Two hours later, he was more than a little frustrated and confused as hell. A walking contradiction of need. On one hand, he needed to keep her at arm's length; on the other hand, he wanted his hands on her. He was all mixed up, but one thing was clear, he couldn't do both.

The colonel drove them to the lake where they hiked, then a few of the women played a bit of Frisbee while the men talked more shop, but after watching Lea jump a few times, Ben realized it wasn't such a good idea. He couldn't take the bounces. They rippled through him with a power punch to his libido.

"Time for the rowing I owe you," he said, needing her to stay still so he could calm his mind and regroup.

After helping her into a wooden dingy, he stepped in and carefully pushed them from the dock. The urge to distance himself from something had taken over. Problem was, he had no idea what he was distancing from, but he already felt better. As he rowed them toward the middle of the lake, he concentrated on the horizon, using controlled, even strokes, and not paying any attention to the woman lounging in front of him, with her head tipped back, eyes closed and a look of pure rapture on her face.

No. He wasn't paying any attention to that, just rowing and rowing, and waiting. Jesus, was she really not going to talk to him unless he started the conversation?

He pulled the oars out of the water and set them inside the boat. She still didn't open her eyes. Ben crossed his arms and waited. Finally, after another minute of silence, she opened them and lifted her head…and a brow, but said nothing.

Damn, stubborn woman. "Spill it. What gives? What's wrong?"

"You stopped."

He dropped his arms and expelled a breath. "That's not what I meant, and you know it."

Her shoulder lifted. Was she trying to get a rise out of him?

It was working, damn it.

"Is this about last night?"

Color rose up her neck and settled in her cheeks, enhancing the blue of her eyes.

"No. Not really, Ben. I'm just trying to keep things on an even keel, pretending to be your girlfriend like you asked, but not hanging all over you." She stilled, then narrowed her gaze. "Why, did you want me to hang all over you?"

Yes. He did. *Damn.* "No."

"Then what's the problem?"

That *was* the problem. "I just wanted to make sure things were okay between us," he said, realizing it was the truth. A truth he didn't want to delve too deeply into, but knew for some reason it was important.

"They're good." Her gaze dropped to the hands curled tightly in her lap.

She was lying. But he chose not to pursue the issue. Mostly because she was right. Things had changed between them. Not better, not worse, just different.

"But if you want to make up for last night, then you better get rowing," she said, smile tugging her lips upward. "I'm not getting any younger."

He laughed, adopting her friendly attitude. "Yes, ma'am." They were going to be all right. "Let's put all of that aside for now and just have fun today, okay?"

"Okay," she replied with a nod. "I'd like that."

Ben picked up the oars and started to row, shoulders feeling a little lighter after having cleared the air, even if it was only in a small way.

Things were good until Lea reached for the buckle on her pants, then the zipper. The sound ripping straight through him as he sat there, unable to move, or think, or row.

She frowned at him. "What's wrong?"

"You're stripping. Why are you stripping?"

"Because I want to take advantage of the sun." She pointed to the cloudless sky above, then turned an almost wounded gaze on him. "Don't worry, I'm not making a move on you. I've learned my lesson. Trust me, that will never happen again." She yanked off her tank top and pointed to her bikini. "See? I'm wearing a bathing suit. It's all good. You're virtue is safe."

To hell with his virtue. He was worried about his sanity. Any shred he'd managed to hold onto landed in a heap on the bottom of the boat—with her pants.

Damn.

It had been close to a decade since he'd seen Lea in a bathing suit. She and Brandi had been swimming in the pool in their back yard, talking about college, excited about life. He'd been sitting there with her brother and his, and remembered thinking she was going to be a knockout someday.

As the oars sliced through the water, and he pumped the paddles back and forth until his shoulders burned, he realized with a start that someday was now. Her trim curves had filled in…and out…and she wasn't the only one bursting at the seam.

With a content sigh rippling through her, she stretched out her sunscreen coated legs to set her feet alongside him on the seat, and leaned back, resting her elbows on the sides of the boat. Closing her eyes, she let out another sigh. "This is the life."

More like the death…of him.

He spent the next hour rowing her around, talking about their fathers, Brandi's upcoming wedding, his job, her supposed job pursuit in the Big Apple, everything but the noticeable current flowing between them whenever they accidentally brushed.

The connection was not welcomed. He didn't want, nor need it in his life, especially with his sister's friend. She had plans and dreams, and he did not fit into them, just as she didn't fit into his agenda. He was a companion only type guy, and Lea deserved a relationship type guy. The two of them simply did not mesh.

Damn her, and her talk about banana splits last week, because that was when everything changed. Something had happened. She'd woken up his body, and he'd been trying to get the damn thing to go back to sleep ever since.

By the time they returned to the dock, Ben was more than ready to jump into the lake fully clothed. Luckily, he'd had the foresight to bring his board shorts, and after a quick change in the public restroom, he sought solace in the cool water.

Then she joined him.

As did the others, all except the colonel and his wife, who headed back to their estate to pick up the lunch their staff prepared.

If the morning was a test of his control, he hoped he passed, because after lunch, they got dressed and joined a few locals in a game of baseball. Despite the attraction flowing between them and the danger of such a lure, he was having a hard time not enjoying himself in Lea's company. He always did like her company, but this time, it was…different.

Despite calling herself a book nerd, the beauty was very athletic. A natural. And her competitive side, he discovered, was a turn on. Big time.

With their team down by two, he was on third when she came up to bat. "Come on, baby," he called to her. "Hit me home."

She blew him a kiss, then pointed to left field before settling into her stance. A stance he'd taught her when she was eleven. Feet shoulder-width apart, she held the bat, elbows out and wiggled her butt.

Catcalls and whistles filled the air and an unexpected heat spread across his shoulders and tightened his chest. The feeling was unpleasant, reminding him of when he'd hear one of the guardsmen talking about sampling her *cooking*. The more the local guys vocally admired her, the more irritated Ben became, to the point where he almost missed her swing. But the crack of the bat regained his attention, and as the ball sailed far into right field, he took off for home plate.

Thata girl, he thought to himself, pleased she'd retained what he'd taught her well over a decade ago, the stance *and* faking where she'd intended to hit the ball. After he scored, Ben turned around and watched Lea running to third base while the centerfielder finally reached the ball.

"Come on," he cheered, alongside the rest of the crew. Even Mrs. Dankirk was on her feet yelling. She was the tying run.

Positioning himself in line with home plate, but keeping far enough away so as not to interfere with the play, he opened his arms and cheered again, "Come on, baby! Come home."

And she did, right into his arms. She was safe, but he wasn't. Deep down, Ben knew he was in trouble, but at the moment, he didn't care. Using her momentum, he twisted the laughing woman around, and when he set her feet on the ground, he grabbed her face and kissed her square on the lips.

"Great job," he told her when he pulled back, chest tight with some emotion he knew better than to analyze. Today was about fun, and that was all he would concentrate on. He told her that earlier, and he never gave an order he didn't follow himself.

Color entered her face as pride and satisfaction deepened the blue of her eyes. "I had a great teacher."

For the next half-hour, Ben rode the high her words and gaze created, and after they won the game, he found himself sitting with her on a blanket, sharing some incredible homemade sangria. The combination of strawberries, lemon and wine were surprisingly refreshing.

"Where did you learn to make this? And when did you have time?"

She laughed. "Kerri McCall sent me the recipe last year."

"Kerri who?" The name was familiar, but his mind was a bit too fogged by the woman in front of him to place the face.

"McCall. From Harland County."

"Oh." The light bulb went off in his brain. "Jordan's sister. The chef."

"Yes."

He hadn't realized Lea knew anyone else from Texas. "How long have you all been friends?"

"Since Brandi introduced them last Christmas on Skype. I Skype with all the bridesmaids now."

He lifted his glass. "Well, I'm glad, because this is delicious."

"I'll be sure to tell Kerri." She nodded, sipping her drink.

"I know you didn't bring this with you yesterday, so when did you make it?"

She smoothed out the blanket and glanced at her hand. "Last night. I snuck down to the kitchen and made a batch."

"Last night?" He reeled back. "When? I didn't hear you leave."

"You were in the shower."

"Oh." He had hoped she hadn't heard him.

She glanced down at her glass. "I…ah, found myself in your boots, so to speak."

"You did?"

"Yeah, either leave or do something I might regret."

He dipped his head to catch her gaze. "What in the world would you have regretted?"

"Me? Nothing," she replied, blush creeping into her face. "But I'm not sure how you would've felt about me climbing in the shower with you."

His heart dropped to his feet. The shower? *Shit.* He swallowed to relieve his suddenly dried throat. The thought of soaping up that incredible body he'd drooled over while rowing made his jeans painfully tight. He shifted to relieve the ache.

She bit her lower lip and stared at him, waiting for him to respond.

He needed to stay the course. But he didn't know which course to stay. The one where they *stayed* friends and ignored their needs, or the one where they maybe *stayed* friends and relieved each others' needs.

"Um, Ben." She glanced over his shoulder. "Mrs. Dankirk is watching. Do we need to do anything, or is it enough that we're sitting close on the blanket?"

Relief washed through his body in a warm, welcomed wave. A legitimate reason to kiss her. Had all his brain cells been firing, Ben would've realized his libido had compromised his logic. Too bad he wasn't thinking with his northern head.

He cupped her face and brushed his thumb over her trembling, lower lip. "I'm going to do what I've been wanting to do. All. Damn. Day."

She nodded, and stopped his heart when her tongue snaked out to touch his thumb. With a groan rumbling in his throat, he captured her lips in a kiss that was too long overdue to be tender. His hunger for Lea was fierce. There was no taking it slow. Not even close. He jumped right to intense, demanding, taking as he plundered all she had to give. Kid gloves were off. No playing around. No pretending. No thinking of her as his younger sister's friend.

She was a woman. A very desirable woman who matched his hunger, meeting his tongue's demands, taking what she wanted right alongside him.

He told himself his need was born from not being with a woman for the past few weeks. No Charisse. No casual hookups as of late. It was as if he was getting bored. But there was no denying his increasing hunger for the woman in his arms.

Pressing her into the blanket, he ran a hand down her side, brushing her breast, sweet curve of her waist, down to her thigh, then slowly back up, slipping under her shirt to stroke her skin just under her bra.

So damn soft...

He rocked against her in a show of need and half-expected her to put a halt to his advances, but she had a hand clamped to the back of his head, holding him in place while the other snuck under his shirt to trail heat up and down his back from her roaming fingers.

If his brain hadn't registered the giggling from some nearby teenagers, Ben had no idea how far he would've gone.

The thought scared the hell out of him.

He stilled. He'd never lost control like that. Ever. Slowly drawing back, Ben recognized the same confusion he felt flashing through Lea's eyes as breath rasped in and out of her lungs. Rolling to the side, he removed his hands from her soft, warm flesh and inhaled long and deep in a show of solidarity. She wasn't the only one knocked on her ass.

"I should apologize for letting things get out of hand," he said, voice a little hoarse because he was still a lot hard.

She sat up and stared straight at him, gaze clear and open and unpolluted. The woman was too damn sweet for someone like him.

"Don't you dare apologize."

Surprised by her reply, he was now faced with the challenge. The question. The unspoken invitation in her words and direct gaze.

He was too damn jaded and set in his ways for someone so fresh and open and giving. She could do so much better. She shouldn't waste her time on the likes of him.

The light dimmed in her eyes. "I see. That was for show again." She made to get up, but he caught her arm and waited for her to meet his gaze.

"Lea." His heart hammered an unrecognized cadence in his chest. She was killing him. "I wasn't acting."

She studied him, caution clouding her baby-blues.

"That was raw need," he added.

With his admission, her smile returned, and warmth rolled through his bewildered heart with the force of a Humvee.

"Me, too." She rose to her feet and glanced down at him. "They're starting another baseball game. Perfect for channeling this pent up energy."

Without waiting for a reply, she turned on her heels and headed toward the others, not once asking him for any kind of declaration.

Ah hell, he was so out of his league.

As Lea got ready for bed that night, she contemplated what had changed that day. Because something most definitely had.

Last night, she not only made a batch of comfort sangria, she'd made a vow. Today she would act her usual self around Ben. She'd play it cool. Socialize with the others. Not hang all over him. She was proud of herself for following through. She didn't mislead him or make the first move. All the warnings Lea had given him about being watched had been truthful.

And fruitful.

Damn the man was hot.

The kiss they'd shared nearly caught the blanket on fire. He'd initiated it. Devoured her. Curled her toes inside her sneaks. He was the one who kept staring at her all day, and if he didn't have a quizzical expression on his handsome face, a frown creased his brow. It was as if he was seeing her in a new light, but didn't exactly know what to do.

She had a few yummy suggestions, but knew the man had to come to them all on his own if she were ever to have any shot with him. Now, if she could just find the strength to wait and not make another fool of herself, she may just survive the weekend.

With that thought in her head, she came out of the bathroom in her T-shirt just as *Sgt. Hotty* entered the room. All the nerve-endings on her body stood at attention. His gaze was dark and delicious, and when he closed the door behind him and started to walk to her, nervousness set in.

"H-how was your meeting?" When the women had headed upstairs for the night, the men had gone to the study to shoot pool and talk shop.

"Too long."

A giggle escaped without permission. "But you've only been down there ten minutes."

He stopped in front of her, gaze deliciously dark with a determined heat that stoked her to a slow burn.

"Ten minutes I could've had up here with you."

She couldn't breathe. Couldn't think. His presence was all consuming. Finally. *Finally,* the man was saying things she'd longed to hear for forever, and here she was, a trembling puddle of need, leaning against the wall for support. If only one brain cell would fire up and give her something witty to say.

She had nothing.

Chapter Five

Lea attempted to suck in some air, but it clogged her throat the second Ben palmed the wall by her head and lifted a finger to trace a path from her ear to her jaw.

"I was trying to keep from crossing that friendship line, but you and I both know it is now so damn blurred it's a permanent smudge."

With her voice still on hiatus, she nodded.

"No matter how I calculate it, this leaves us with a problem, Lea," he said, voice deliciously low and oh so sexy she shook.

"I-it does?" she squeaked.

He nodded, finger now skimming her lower lip, sending jolts of heat straight to all her good parts.

"Yes. I can't get your taste out of my head."

"Good."

Oh, his eyes darkened on that one and jaw clenched tight. "No, it's not good, because I really want to take you against this wall. Right here. Right now."

"Do it."

His other hand hit the wall as he muttered a curse, closed his eyes and sucked in a breath. "You're going to be the death of me."

What the heck did he think he was doing to her? Proclaiming he wanted to take her against the wall, then doing nothing. *He* was killing her.

Opening his eyes, Ben stared down at her, gaze dark with need, yet clouded with restraint. "I'm not long-term, Lea."

"I know." Finally regaining control of her limbs, she lifted a hand to palm his solid chest while her other gripped his hip. "You're married to the military."

He nodded, still making no move to touch her. "And you still think this is a good idea?"

She smiled. The very fact he'd asked that question signaled he was coming around to her way of thinking. "Yes. I do." And to prove it, she snuck both hands under his shirt and skimmed his hot flesh all the way to his pecs, and was rewarded with a hiss of breath when she grazed over his nipple. "You know I'm hoping to leave in a few weeks to work in the city."

He nodded. "I don't want to hurt you."

"I know. And you won't. Unless you leave this room again." Her heart pounded out of control, taking her breath, leaving her throat dry. He blinked as if trying to comprehend her words. Her meaning. So she clarified, "Why can't we have fun this weekend?"

A glorious palm touched her shoulder, then skimmed down the front of her, brushing lightly over her breast. "This weekend, huh?"

Heat rushed between her legs, and heaven help her, she arched into his touch. "Yeah…" Her voice was soft and breathy, but hell, at least she still had one considering his thumb lingered on her peak, brushing it back and forth, exploding brain cell after brain cell.

"Okay, I had to be sure." He pressed her against the wall with his rock hard body before he shoved his hands in her hair and kissed her without restraint.

A real honest-to-goodness Benjamin Wyne kiss.

Long and deep. Thorough and complete.

Holy smokes, the man could kiss.

Her mind was fogged and body throbbed with need. Gone was his self-discipline. She sent up a silent *Allelluia* to the proof he no longer saw her as a little sister. He kissed away her sanity. She couldn't even pick out a Picasso from a caricature at the moment.

On and on, he devoured her strength, his tongue stroking hers, his hands skimming down her torso in a blaze of heat. When they came up for air, she stared at him, trying to grasp onto a coherent thought, but they dissipated in the steam need created in her head.

Dragging in air, he cracked a sexy smile she caught with her heart. Damn, he looked scrumptious. Shirt undone and hanging open to reveal the dusting of hair her fingers were still stroking. The sight of the ridges in his abs did funny things to her breathing, which wasn't steady to begin with, and the fact she'd somehow managed to unbutton his shirt and unbuckle the top of his jeans without realizing proved she'd lost her equilibrium.

Off kilter and out of her league, she was loving every damn minute of it. He pushed her boundaries, took her out of herself, just as she'd always known he would. With luck, she was doing the same to him.

She set her forehead against his collarbone. "Wow. I've been missing out."

He slipped a hand under her shirt to stroke her back and the other into her panties to cup her ass. "So have I. But no more."

His hand dipped lower, and fingers brushed the part that ached the most for his touch.

"*Ben*." His name ripped from her throat in a voice full of hunger and need as she spread her legs in a welcomed gesture.

He needed no instruction. "Wet and sweet." He caught her mouth in a hot, hungry kiss as he stroked her again.

Lea saw stars and every damn planet in the universe. Possibly another galaxy. But she really needed to have him naked. And in her. She pushed his shirt all the way off, then stood there trembling as he bunched hers up to her ribs and stopped to gaze at her purple zebra printed panties. Thank God she'd had the foresight to only pack the bikinis that made her feel sexy.

The raw need deepening his gaze to moss green made her sweat in secret places.

Ben lifted her shirt higher, and she watched mesmerized as his gaze darkened further at the sight of her bared breasts.

He let out a rough groan. "Killing me."

That was good. She hoped. Because she was dying.

"I need—Oh…that." She moaned when he drew her nipple into his mouth and teased with his tongue. "Yeah, that works—" He transferred his delicious attention to her other breast, and she gripped his arms, closed her eyes and sucked in a breath. "That—works really—well."

Whether it was her hitched breathes or rushed words or both, something spurred him on because he had her shirt up and over her head and panties off before she opened her eyes.

"Beautiful." He stared at her nakedness with the same hunger scorching her veins.

His turn. She unzipped him, then tugged until his clothes fell to his ankles where they caught on his boots. But his fundamentals were free. And, *oh Lordy*, she was going to have *fun* with his *damentals*. Inches more than she'd ever had, he was big and hard and thick, and she needed to touch him pronto.

But he dropped to his knees and gently spread her legs. Before she could blink, he leaned in and put his mouth on her, stroking her with his tongue.

She sucked in a breath that sounded strangled and needy to her ears, but she didn't care. He was magic and on a mission because he added a finger, sliding it inside her as he flicked his tongue over her aching center.

Her gasped turned into a moan, and both echoed around them. This seemed to spurn him on. He upped his pace and zapped her strength. With legs reduced to liquid, she dug her fingers into his head and used him as an anchor as he continued to take her out of this hemisphere. Unable to control her hips, they rocked against him in slow, erotic circles. She was on the edge, teetering.

"Ben," she said, half-questioning.

He glanced up, gaze delectably dark with a fierce hunger and determination that was nearly her undoing. He responded by sucking her gently into his mouth.

That was it. She was done. All those years of wanting, wishing, waiting to be with him came to fruition at that very moment. Lea burst, and Ben used his expertise to prolong her pleasure as he held her hips and kept her from falling to the floor.

When the ringing subsided in her ears and her vision returned, she rediscovered her legs. She let out a sigh and smiled down at him. With eyes blazing pure male satisfaction, he released her to dig a condom from the pocket of the jeans bunched around his ankles. His body vibrated with a tension she felt clear to her core. Needing to have him inside her, she reached out and helped roll the condom over the length of him.

He uttered a curse, breathing heavy, a sheen of sweat breaking out across his brow. "Killing me."

Feeling inspired, she smiled and leaned in to flick her tongue over his nipple. He cursed, lifted her up and, thunking her against the wall, entered her in one, delectable thrust.

The man filled her so completely she was nearly brought to tears. *This* was what she'd wanted for so long.

But since she knew tears were a no-no when it came to sex, she blinked them away.

"You okay?" He stared, concern replacing some of the heat.

"Yes. Absolutely. Please, don't stop." And to prove she meant it, she wrapped her legs around his back and locked her ankles.

This drew him in farther, and their sounds of approval mingled in the air.

"Damn, you feel so good."

He began to move, and she moaned again, clutching at his shoulders. Over and over, he withdrew and returned, holding her against the wall for his slow, exquisite thrusts.

There was no doubt now, he was killing *her*. He had control. His grip on her hips prevented her from upping the pace. He was in command, and heaven help her, she loved it.

As if his vigilant, purposeful thrusts weren't enough to drive her out of her ever loving mind, he bent forward to capture a nipple in his mouth. She cried out, her eyes rolling in the back of her head as he made his way to the other. The incredible, mindless pleasure took her right up to that blissful edge, again.

"*Ben*." She clutched his shoulders.

"I know," he said, voice rough as he kissed her neck and continued to stroke her with those fierce thrusts. "Me, too."

Knowing he was just as lost in the mindless pleasure was all it took to send her off the cliff into her second foray with the man who'd so often ruled her dreams. But dreaming of him and being with him were two entirely different things Lea discovered as she clung to his heated body while their shared release shook them to their knees.

Nothing could compare to the real deal.

The weekend had been a success.

As Ben drove them home from the colonel's on Sunday afternoon, he breathed a sigh of relief. He'd dodged the bullet that was Mrs. Dankirk. He'd also been privy to information from the higher ups on upcoming moves. It was always good to have advance warning rather than have work sprung on him and told to make it happen.

Yeah, the weekend had definitely been a success.

Then there was Lea.

He glanced sideways at the silent woman who sat staring out the passenger window in a pretty, frilly, purple sundress. Silky hair fell past her shoulders to settle on the ample chest he'd had the pleasure to taste hours before. She'd been an unexpected surprise. He'd only wanted her to pretend to be his girlfriend to deflect the colonel's wife. But he'd gotten a whole hell of a lot more.

More than he should have…more than he deserved.

His gut tightened.

Last night, he'd woken up, exhaustion still weighing down his limbs, thanks to the woman curled into him like a pretzel. Her head had rested in the crook of his arm while she tossed a leg across both of his and placed a hand on his chest. When he realized his hand covered hers, and the other covered the sweet curve of her ass, his body had gone hot…then cold.

The urge to leave, to carefully untangle himself from the sleeping beauty and retreat to his spot on the floor had been strong. He never went to sleep with women. Sure, he went to bed with them, just never fell asleep. That was asking for trouble, showing the slightest bit of commitment, which he never did. Not even with Charisse. They never slept together. Ever. Just had sex, then depending on where they were, one of them left.

No strings. It was all good.

With his chest tight and breathing a chore, he'd needed to leave the bed, put things into perspective. Interject a distance so she didn't get attached. But then the beauty had moved, and opened her eyes, and smiled a sleepy smile.

"Hi," she'd said, hugging him closer. "Mmm…If I could feel my legs, I'd so do you right now."

His heart had cracked opened, just a little, just enough for him to kiss her nose, tighten his hold on her succulent ass and tell her he'd take her up on it, but his legs seemed to have waltzed out with hers.

She'd laughed, yawned then fell back to sleep.

And he couldn't do it. He couldn't hurt her by leaving her bed to sleep on the floor. No. Because she was a friend—a good friend—there was no way he would've hurt her like that. The impersonal act would've been a slap in the face to the woman he'd known most of his life. If he'd ever found out a guy had done that to her, he would've kicked the sorry-sonofabitch's ass. Since it was his ass that would've needed kicking, he stayed right there in her arms.

Besides, he really couldn't feel his legs. Ben had never been so relaxed, so spent, so completely satisfied in his whole life. She had been incredible. All three times. *Jesus,* he couldn't believe they'd had sex three times in three hours.

The woman *was* trying to kill him.

Not really. He knew she'd acted on impulse like he had, which led to an incredible night. The first time, the sex against the wall hadn't been just for her. Sure, he'd wanted to fulfill her request from the previous night, but it had also been for him. No way in hell could he have waited to carry her to the bed. After having his mouth on her, and she gave herself over to him so completely and without question, he couldn't get enough of her taste, couldn't back off. He had to lap up every bit of her. She was exquisite. She'd also had him wound so tight he'd been ready to burst if she even looked at him the right way. Yeah, the bed was never a contender that first time.

Or the second.

They'd made it to the shower and put the built-in seat to good use. Excellent use. A smile tugged his lips and body heated at the thought. The image of her all wet and slick, head thrown back, gorgeous breasts bouncing as she straddle him would be forever imprinted on his brain.

God, she'd been great. Too great. The last time nearly *did* kill him. He'd asked her to put on the blue corset thing so he could show her properly how much he loved it. Try to make up for being such an ass the night before. Just remembering how damn sexy Lea had looked in the silky thing with all her mouth-watering curves spilling out sent heat skittering down his body to stiffen his groin. A true vision. A vision he'd wanted on the bed, sprawled out where he could devour every delectable inch. And he had. But he hadn't expected the same treatment. The woman was full of surprises. She'd flipped him onto his back and licked and touched and tasted every damn inch of him. Without mercy.

It had been incredible.

Too bad it had to end.

But it did.

The weekend was just about over.

"What are you smiling about?" she asked. "Me, I hope."

He held back a snort. Yeah, her and that damn corset. Not something she needed to know. Especially since their time was up.

"Yes. I wanted to thank you for all your help with Mrs. Dankirk. Other than one time, she hadn't bothered me all weekend."

Some of the sparkle left Lea's gaze. Ben's gut tightened, but he ignored it. It had to be done. It was for her own good. They had no future.

"Good, I'm glad I could help."

"You did." He tried to formulate the words that would be the least hurtful. *Ah hell,* this was why he didn't want to give into his need. "Look, about what happened—"

"Hey, don't worry about it," she rushed to say, soft hand on his arm as she tipped her head and winked. "It's all good. I *Wyne'd.* I dined. But the weekend is over, and so is our foray."

He pulled up outside her father's house and parked, shock stunning him silent. Yeah, she was full of surprises. Here he was trying to come up with a way to let the woman down gently when she did the letting down.

"Don't look so shocked. We agreed to one weekend, and we had our weekend." Still smiling, she patted his arm. "And don't worry. I'll still respect you."

He laughed at that one. She was something else. "Thank goodness for that. I was concerned."

"I thought so." She grinned and made to remove her hand.

He grabbed it and squeezed. "Seriously, Lea. Thank you, and not just for Mrs. Dankirk, but for one hell of a memorable weekend."

If what Brandi had told him was true, then Lea had wanted to sleep with him for a while now. He just hoped he hadn't disappointed. Sometimes living up to one's expectations were impossible. No one knew that better than him.

He also didn't know if he'd lived up. And apparently, she wasn't going to give him any clues, either.

"Right back at you, Ben."

Okay. Maybe a crumb.

Her blue gaze was frank and friendly. God, he could get lost in them. Thoughts like that sent a red flag to his brain. Same went for the urge that rushed through him to lean in and kiss her lush lips.

He gave himself a mental shake and lifted her hand to kiss her fingers instead. "Thanks again."

"Right back at you, Ben," she repeated, then tugged free to reach for her overnight bag on the floor.

"Wait, I'll get it for you," he said, making to take the small bag from her, but she brushed his hand aside and smiled.

"Don't be silly. I've got it."

And before he could argue further, or walk her to her door as he'd intended, the damn woman exited the truck and was halfway to her porch in a matter of seconds.

He knew he'd hit pay dirt. He really did know. Relief was the customary emotion a guy experienced who had just been let off the hook from what could've been a very messy situation.

As he drove away from the woman who had rocked his world the whole weekend, the woman who didn't even look back as she entered her house, Ben refused to label the tightness in his chest and the rippling in his gut as anything other than relief.

Even though he knew it was far from it.

Lea's Monday went by like every other Monday. Busy, fast and boring. Although, this one had another verb.

Avoided.

Ben never showed up for breakfast as usual that' morning. His brothers, Mason and Keiffer, were right on time, but no Ben.

Dammit.

She was to blame. She knew it.

The very thing she'd tried so hard to avoid was happening. The man of her dreams had slept with her, and now he was avoiding her. To say it didn't hurt would be a lie. A big. Fat. Lie

By the time she was getting ready to go home after the supper rush, and he still hadn't made an appearance, Lea kept her gaze fixed on the armory across the street. Maybe he hadn't gone to work that day. Or maybe he was visiting another armory, or down Ft. Indiantown Gap. That could explain his absence. But when that unmistakable smile, broad shoulders and familiar swagger came into view as he walked with another soldier to the parking lot, her hurt had turned to disappointment, then anger.

What the hell was his problem? She'd made it clear she had no hold on him. Wanted nothing from him other than for them to carry on as normal. And normal did not include avoidance. *Dammit.*

Her worst nightmare.

She was still fuming when Brandi sent her a text later that night as she was getting ready for bed. An invitation to Skype.

Shoot. She'd forgotten she'd promised to talk to her friend tonight about her weekend.

Until today, Lea had been prepared to discuss the wonderful night in Ben's bed. Now, she was too ticked off. Still, it was no reason to act like him. Nope. She wasn't going to *ignore* his sister because of his actions.

So, she booted up the laptop, settled in her seat, pasted what she hoped was a passable smile on her face, then opened the conversation.

"Tell us what happened," Brandi demanded, while three eager faces nodded in the background.

Kerri moved closer. "Did the negligee work?"

"Of course it did." Jordan smirked.

Shayla smiled. "Come on, spill."

Ah, hell. She should've ignored the text.

"Uh oh. What did my brother do?"

"Or not do?"

Four faces leaned closer to the monitor, gazes alert and out for blood.

"My brother is an idiot," Brandi scoffed, along with a few colorful words Lea hadn't known her friend even knew. "Do I need to get Ethan or Mason or Keiffer on him?"

"No." She laughed, a true laugh. "It's not like that."

"Oh." A collective sigh of relief hit her ears.

Except for Jordan. She still sat straight up, gaze intent. "Then what's it like?"

Now she understood why her friend called the woman a watch dog. She must be one hell of a sheriff.

"Did you at least get a kiss out of him?" the pretty chef asked with a grin, brushing back her straight bangs a few shades darker than her eyes.

Lea smiled. "Oh yeah. Several." A delicious warmth rushed through her body, and she sighed. "Damn, Brandi. Your brother can kiss. My brain cells were in danger every time our lips met."

"I still have that trouble with Connor." Kerri's face turned a pretty shade of pink.

"Cole." Jordan nodded, mouth curving upward.

Brandi nodded, too. "Kade knocks me for a loop every dang time."

"Yeah." Shayla frowned. "I swear Kevin patented some kind of invisible device, because mine go missing whenever we kiss. Damn man has enough brain cells, he doesn't need mine, too."

"Glad to hear I'm not the only one who gets wonky." Somehow, hearing them confess made her feel a little better about her weakness.

"So, what about the negligee?" Jordan prompted.

"Well, I waited until Friday night to put it on—which was absolutely gorgeous by the way—and he'd given me enough signs and unnecessary caresses for me to assume he was interested in taking it further."

"Oh, wow." Shayla's gaze narrowed. "Are you saying he wasn't?"

Lea snorted. "I'm saying he took one look at me, then turned around and left the room."

"Oh. He. Didn't," Kerri hissed between the fingers she'd slapped on her face.

"I'm gonna kill my brother," Brandi growled, eyes dark with concern as she moved closer to the screen. "Are you okay? I'm sorry, hun. He is so stubborn sometimes. Believe me, he was interested. That's why he left."

"I know."

"You do?"

"Yeah, he told me a little while later when he apologized."

"Oh, so is that when he got you naked?"

Lea laughed. "No. We didn't do anything that night."

Jordan sat back, big grin once again on her face. "So then, how did Saturday night go?"

"Much better," Lea replied. "I'd decided to play it cool all day, only pretended to be his girlfriend when Mrs.

Dankirk was around, otherwise, I slipped back into friend mode."

"Oh my God. You're good," Kerri stated.

Shayla nodded, her red hair rippling with the movement.

"I bet that drove him nuts." Brandi slapped the table and laughed.

Jordan nodded, too. "Very smart."

"Whether it was or not, something worked, because that night, I was coming out of the bathroom as he walked into the room…and headed straight for me. Before I knew it, he had me against the wall and completely turned on."

Kerri fanned herself while all four women wore matching grins.

"I hope my brother gave you your against-the-wall sex."

"Yes," she replied. "And then some."

Whistles and claps echoed through her room, and she was thankful her dad was downstairs. This was not a conversation she'd want to explain to her father. In fact, she couldn't believe she was having it. She wasn't usually the kiss-'n'-tell kind of gal.

"Please elaborate, without getting into too much detail, because although I love you and am so happy you've finally scratched an itch you've wanted scratched for years, it was with my brother, and I'd prefer not to get too personal."

"Then go into the kitchen so we can get the goods," one of the girls said.

Lea chuckled. "There's not much else to tell, other than it was fantastic. But it's over and time to move on."

"Whoa. Wait. Over?"

"Why is it over?"

"Yeah, if it was that good and you've wanted it for that long, why walk away?"

She shrugged. "Because Ben doesn't do relationships."

Her four friends blinked at her a second before they burst into laughter. She had no idea what was so funny. Lea glanced behind her to see if something hilarious was going on in the room. Nope. Just her spilling her guts. "I wish someone would let me in on the joke, because it isn't funny where I'm sitting."

"That's because you're as clueless as him," Brandi said. "But don't worry. You'll catch on."

She set her elbow on the desk and chin in her hand. "Then a little help would be much appreciated right now girls, because I've got nothing."

"Let me guess," Jordan spoke up. "You haven't heard from him today."

Lea straightened. "No, I haven't. Not that I expected a call or anything, but he's gone off his routine."

"He didn't show up at the restaurant for breakfast?" Brandi asked, and when Lea nodded, her friend frowned. "That idiot. He'll learn he can't outrun his heart."

"Whoa, wait, when did his heart get involved?" She blinked at them. "I didn't do anything to compromise the guy in that way. It was just sex. Okay, incredible, hot sex, but I never expected promises or picket fences and told him as much. Just the weekend."

"But you wanted more," Kerri said.

"Well, yeah, of course," she replied, but didn't tell them it was also the reason she accidentally-on-purpose shoved her negligee into his duffle bag. No way was she going to let him forget their night that quick.

"You'll get more," the beautiful, smart and—God she hoped—insightful sheriff told her, gaze once again serious and direct. "The very fact he couldn't face you today shows his heart is more involved than he'd like."

"True." The redhead nodded. "After our first time, well, our time in Houston, Kevin tried to avoid me, but within that first week, he showed up at my door and did that pressing against the wall thing you'd mentioned."

Lea's heart leapt at that admission. "Really?"

Shayla nodded again.

"And Connor couldn't stay away, even though we'd both agreed to be friends with benefits, it turned into something more real fast."

"Yeah, even Kade tried to stay away, but somehow he knew I needed him, and he came anyway. The man always knows when I need him."

Her friend smiled such a satisfied smile it took Lea's breath away.

"I'm glad for you all. Really I am, but Ben and I agreed to just the weekend. We don't want to jeopardize our friendship."

"It's already in jeopardy, isn't it?" Jordan asked quietly.

Damn, the woman was good. "Yes," she replied with a sigh. "So, what do you all suggest I do?"

Chapter Six

"Nothing." The sheriff shook her head. "He'll come to you."

"Yes, he knows right where you'll be, so mark my words, hun," Brandi said. "My idiot brother will show up at the diner sometime this week. He won't be able to stop himself."

"Amen." Shayla smiled. "Sometimes the southern head has more pull than the one on their shoulders."

"True," Kerri agreed, a blush infusing her pretty face again. "And maybe you should consider suggesting the friends-with-benefits thing."

"I don't know." She shook her head and sighed again. "He kind of has a woman named Charisse he sees when the need arises." Her stomach knotted just thinking of the man with another woman. The sexy, talented man who'd given her multiple orgasms.

Shayla's red hair bobbed closer to the screen as the woman leaned in. "Do you want more nights like last night?"

Magic? Hell… "Yeah." She nodded.

"Then make the suggestion. Trust me. After last night, Charisse is in his past."

"Really?"

"Oh yes," Kerri spoke up. "Considering the way he's already acting. You're under his skin."

"Okay, but I'm going to be going back to New York City in a few weeks, and he hates the city."

"Look, you're both smart. If anyone can figure things out, you two can," Brandi said. "Just don't worry about that right now. Enjoy yourself. You deserve it."

"Thanks, Brandi."

The idea of *enjoying* Ben a few more weeks until she left the Poconos for NYC made her smile. Of course, if the man kept avoiding her, that was going to be a real problem.

"And don't worry about seeing him," the all-knowing sheriff said.

Apparently the woman could also read minds. Must drive the bad guys nuts.

"It's like they said, he'll show up soon."

Shayla shook a finger at her. "And when he does, don't let him off the hook too easily."

"Yeah." Kerri folded her arms across her chest. "Make him beg."

"I couldn't do that. He already…" She closed her mouth, having revealed more than she'd meant.

"Ooh, no you don't. Clarify, woman." Jordan leaned closer to the screen and gave her the death glare. "He already, what? Begged?"

"You have to tell us now, Lea," Brandi stated, gaze alight with joy. "When did Ben beg? He's never done that, ever. So you have to tell me what happened to cause my brother to lose control."

Lose control? Is that what had happened to make him ask—practically plead—with her to don the negligee Saturday night?

She hadn't wanted to, was perfectly happy being naked and ready for round three, but the heated look in his eyes told her it would be worth the effort, so she had. And damn…it *had* been worth it. Her good parts tingled just remembering the special attention he'd paid them.

"Oh, wow." Brandi blinked. "More up against the wall sex?"

"No." A grin tugged her lips hard. "This involved him persuading me to put the negligee on so he could make up for walking out the night before."

"Yeehaw!"

"Sweet!"

"Then he definitely made up for it if that satisfied expression is anything to go by."

Her grin widened into a smile. "Oh, he did. Several times."

More cheers and laughter reverberated around her room, and Lea had to admit, she felt so much better than she had an hour ago. Leave it to her friends to put things into perspective. Between them, the women had been through enough to clue her in. Make her see that Ben's avoidance wasn't going to last.

Good, because she wouldn't either. They'd been friends for far too long to let sex—great sex—get in the way. Now, she just had to make him see they could enjoy both for a few weeks before she left for NYC.

By ten fifteen Thursday morning, Ben finally gave into his need to go to Gabe's. He'd skipped breakfast there on Monday, and every morning since, to keep things in perspective with Lea. Surely, a few days of breaking his routine was enough to show his friend he could do without her company if he had to. That they were just friends and required nothing more from one another, as she'd so easily told him in not so many words when she'd walked herself to her damn door Sunday evening.

She could do without him, and he could do without her.

Piece of cake.

Gabe's had the best breakfast in town. There was no need to flex the proverbial *control* muscle any longer. He was hungry. No reason to avoid the place any longer. Besides, his friend Ryder and Keiffer were already there waiting for him. He couldn't very well tell his friend he couldn't accept his invitation for a free breakfast because he'd slept with the guy's baby sister and didn't want her to cling.

Shit.

He'd slept with his best friend's sister. The man was going to kick his ass.

The man *should* kick his ass. He deserved a kicked ass. He never should've given into his need and had sex with Lea. Although, try as he might, Ben couldn't bring himself to regret the night.

No. He'd take the ass-whooping he deserved, and hopefully, they'd move on.

He certainly would've kicked Ryder's ass if he'd ever slept with Brandi.

Ben's footsteps slowed as he walked across the street, shoving a hand in a stop motion at an oncoming car. He didn't care. He was pissed. Jesus, had those two ever slept together? Brandi had always been comfortable around Ryder, and his friend had been unusually comfortable around her. *Sonofabitch.* Maybe they *had* slept together.

He was going to kill Ryder.

Stepping onto the sidewalk, he grabbed the handle, then yanked open the door. The bell above him jangled loud enough to wake the dead. Again, Ben didn't care. He had some dead memories to pluck from his friend's brain.

"Way to make an entrance, Serge." His buddy snickered along with his brother.

Good. They were alone. Almost. Ben glared at a man sipping coffee at the counter, folded newspaper in his hand as he turned toward him. And he continued glaring while the customer set his cup down, coffee sloshing over the side, threw money on the counter and quickly scurried out the door Ben held open for him.

"Wow, someone's having a bad morning."

"No, but they're going to," he said, striding over to the booth to glare down at Ryder.

"Okay, I'll bite. Did I do something wrong?"

Trying his best to keep a lid on his temper, Ben dropped into the booth next to Keiffer without losing eye contact with Ryder. Better to have a table between them to keep him from throttling his best friend.

"Depends."

"On what?"

"On whether or not you've slept with Brandi."

Coffee spewed from Keiffer's mouth and covered half the table, Ryder's jaw hit his chest, and the sound of dishes breaking in the kitchen echoed to their table.

"*What?*" Disbelief shot his friend's tone up a few octaves as the man stared slack-jawed at him. "Of course not, man. She's your sister."

Ah...hell.

Studying the guy's steady gaze and relaxed body, Ben had to conclude his friend was telling the truth. *Jesus*, this business with Lea had him nuts. He was off his game. Out of his mind. So far out he'd lost sight of it. Had been all week. He was beginning to think he and his sanity would never be reunited.

Discovering that sexy blue corset mixed with his clothes had held him prisoner all damn week. He couldn't walk past it without remembering her taste.

"What the hell is this about?"

Keiffer choked on more coffee. He slid him a sideways glance, but his youngest brother had grown immune to Ben's glares. The asshole just sat back in the booth and smiled, motioning with his hand to proceed.

Bastard knew. His brother's dark eyes were brimming with realization, and a whole hell of a lot of mirth.

He turned back to face his friend and tried to figure out how to come clean.

"Ben slept with your sister." Keiffer apparently decided to help.

Ryder shrugged. "Gwen? That's old news, pal."

This time Ben twisted in his seat and stared directly at his *deadmeat* brother. "Can it."

His glare must be broken because his brother just smiled and returned his attention to their friend.

"No, your *other* sister."

The crashing of more dishes sounded from the kitchen.

"Shit." His friend straightened in the booth and narrowed his gaze.

Ben held up his hand and nodded. "I think we should take this outside so you can kick my ass like I deserve."

Whatever the man had been about to say remained a secret as the kitchen pass-through door flung open and a fuming Lea stomped close.

"I'm so glad to see the three of you think so little of me you have to discuss my sex life in the middle of the damn restaurant."

Keiffer held up his hands and stared up at the furious female. "If it means anything, Ben made sure to clear everyone else out first."

"Well, thank you for small favors." She twisted on her heel and marched back into the kitchen, her ponytail swishing in her haste.

Ben's chest had never felt so tight. He had trouble breathing. Another first. He glanced from Keiffer to Ryder then jumped to his feet. "Excuse me," he said, then rushed after the seething woman.

If he'd stopped to think, he probably would've realized his actions gave away a clue he totally missed. All he knew was he never wanted to see the pure hurt and disappointment clouding Lea's beautiful blue eyes ever again. The fact he was the reason it was there in the first place twisted the knot in his stomach and made him pick up his pace.

He entered the kitchen to find it empty except for a cowering cook and pieces of broken dishes strewn across the floor. The cook pointed to the open door leading to the parking lot out back. Ben rushed outside and found her leaning against a tree, watching ducks swim in the nearby creek.

"Lea. I'm sorry."

She turned around and watched him approach through narrowed eyes. "Who are you and what have you done to Ben? He doesn't know those words."

The invisible vice squeezing his chest increased its hold. She was right. He'd never uttered those words. Didn't believe in those words.

Gwen. His mother. Mason's fiancée. They'd all used them. Even Brandi's mother had apologized to his dad on her death bed for not sticking around longer.

Sorry?

No, he didn't believe in the damn word.

Until now.

Because he *was* sorry he hurt her. Remorse soured his stomach and cancelled his appetite. "You're right. I don't know a lot of things, like how to mesh what we've done with our normal lives. It's got me acting out of character. I'm sorry."

She turned to face him, and waited until he stopped to palm the tree and stare down at her.

103

"What we've done, Ben, was give into a basic need. People do it every day. It's been going on since the dawn of time. There was no reason to act—" She paused to wave a hand at him and then the building. "—Neanderthal or whatever the hell it was you did in there."

"You're right," he repeated quietly. "I should never have—"

She slapped a palm onto his chest and cocked her head. "Don't you dare tell me you regret what we did, because it was the best darn night of my life."

He blinked as satisfaction and male ego increased his height by two inches. "It was?"

"Yes." She slapped him again. "You know it. So don't you dare say you regret it. Lie to me, I don't care. Just don't say you regret it."

He clamped a hand over her thudding palm and held it to his chest. "I would never lie to you, Lea. And I wasn't going to say I regretted it. I was going to say I should never have accused your brother like that. Let alone out in public. My only excuse is lack of sleep has clouded my judgment."

"You're not sleeping?"

No. She'd been invading his dreams, making him hot and hard all damn week.

"Why?" She removed her hand to palm his head then forehead. "Are you sick?"

Yes, he was. He had a fever, for her, and only just now realized it. *Shit.* What the hell did he do now? There was no way he was going to act on this newfound information. She deserved better than someone who waltzed around in public announcing they've been having sex.

Okay, technically it hadn't been him, but his actions had caused the knowledge to come out. So he was just as guilty.

Actually, he was the *only* one who was guilty.

"No, I'm not sick. But I have been stupid. I'm sorry. It won't happen again, Lea." He removed her hand from his face to kiss her knuckles.

"We've both been blindsided by our reactions to one another," she said, expression softening. "I certainly didn't expect our connection to knock me for a loop."

It had knocked him on his ass, and he was still trying to right himself.

"So don't try to figure this one out, Ben. I think it might be better to just agree it is what it is."

The huskiness of her voice upped his pulse without his authorization. "Which is?" Damn. He hadn't given his voice consent to reply, either.

"Which is—great chemistry—pure and simple."

There wasn't anything pure or simple about the way he felt when it came to Lea Gablonski, especially when she tapped his face before spinning around to walk back into the restaurant.

She hadn't asked for anything more.

Hadn't demanded anything more.

Hell, he didn't even know if she wanted anything more.

God, he was so damn confused.

As he watched her wiggle and the sexy sway of her hips, that great chemistry heated him from the inside out and left him hard. And hanging.

Was this going to be the new normal for him?

He needed to get laid. Thank God Charisse had texted him on his way in to work that morning to say she was returning tomorrow night.

If ever he needed a mindless coupling, it was now. His gaze continued to fixate on one hell of a beautiful ass as Lea stepped over the threshold into her restaurant and away from his view.

Yes, a few hours with Charisse should put his sex life back into perspective. And get his head out of...Lea's pants.

Friday night, Lea left work and headed to the Confection Connection on the next block to talk to Jill about placing an order for specially shaped chocolates for Brandi's bachelorette party next weekend.

Joy swelled in her chest.

She could hardly believe her friend was going to be here soon, and getting married. Excitement picked up her pace and sent her right into Ben. He'd rounded the corner when she'd collided with him.

Two strong hands clamped around her shoulders and steadied her. "You okay?"

"Yeah. Sorry," she stammered, instructing her pulse to settle down. It didn't listen. She glanced up into his concerned gaze and ordered her heart not to catch. It didn't listen either. *Dammit.*

They stared at each other a few beats. Heat began to spread throughout her body and her nipples hardened.

Great. She got perky for the guy. Right in front of...his date. Only now did she notice Charisse stood beside him. Lovely. Who does that?

Two people with great chemistry, apparently. Her gaze darted to the blonde at his side. The one whose gaze narrowed as she glanced from Lea to Ben then back again.

Yeah, this chemistry was definitely going to cause issues.

Ignoring her body and its unreasonable needs, she stepped out of his hold and straightened her shoulders. "My bad. I was on my way to—"

Clark waved from in front of her destination. "Hi, Lea."

She waved back, relief eating her tension as Ben and his date turned around to stare at her old school buddy. She suddenly didn't feel like such a loser. "Hi, Clark." Even though she'd had no idea the guy was going to be there tonight, she took advantage of the situation and stepped around the couple. "You ready to take advantage of tonight's special?"

"Something like that." He smiled as he stood in front of the store.

With a nod to Ben and Charisse, she said, "Have a good night," and could feel a gaze burning her back like a blow torch. She suspected it was Ben's, but didn't turn around to confirm as she crossed the street to meet her friend.

The man was on a date. No doubt moving on, and about to have sex with his groupie.

So much for suggesting a friends-with-benefits thing.

Shayla had been wrong. Charisse was not in Ben's past.

Lea was.

Ben needed a beer.

Two beers. Hell, a hole damn keg.

He'd just left Charisse's apartment...without doing the deed. Never in all his years had he had a performance problem. And although they hadn't gotten naked, yet, he knew there was an issue. No amount of kissing and heavy petting could start a spark in his jeans tonight.

What the hell?

He'd certainly enjoyed Charisse's body many, many times in the past.

Pulling up outside his brothers' resort, he blew out a breath and jammed his truck into park. It wasn't as if he was completely broken, because the spark had definitely been there when he'd run into Lea earlier in town. As soon as he'd grabbed her slight shoulders and inhaled her sweet perfume, a shaft of heat had shot down his body and his groin had twitched to life.

The longer he'd stood there holding her, the stronger the throb, until he was fully hard. In the middle of the sidewalk. In front of his date.

Who does that?

Apparently two people with great chemistry.

Muttering a curse, he made his way to The Knotty Pine, the bar on the main floor of the resort, relieved to see none of his brothers were around. He wasn't exactly in the mood for company. Just a drink. Or two.

Ben slid onto a stool at the far end and ordered a beer.

"Hey, Sergeant Wyne." Lieutenant Barton appeared out of nowhere and slapped him on the back before slipping onto a stool. "You here alone, too?"

He *was*. Damn.

"Yes."

"Same here." The man nodded. "Mason and I are going rock climbing tomorrow."

He wished he could climb his way out of whatever the hell kind of funk he was in.

"Why don't you join us?"

Ben immediately shook his head. "I promised my nephew I'd take him fishing." Besides, rock climbing required intense concentration. Something he lacked at the moment. He couldn't concentrate enough to walk a straight line.

"Well, maybe we'll run into each other tomorrow night. My wife's enjoying a spa day tomorrow with her sister and your girlfriend. I like Lea. She's a keeper."

Why did they keep telling him that? She wasn't his.

But what about the banana split guy? His gut twisted into a tight knot. The thought of her licking chocolate off the slick D's banana made him sick.

But it was none of his damn business. Last Sunday, he'd had every opportunity to ask to see her again.

His loss.

No. It had been smart. A safeguard. The two of them had no future, he reminded himself, sucking down his beer.

She was free to see whoever she wanted. City dude. Local dude. Guardsman. *Who-the-hell-ever.* He motioned to the bartender for another round.

It hadn't taken her long to hook back up with the city slicker.

Yeah, judging by the three-piece suit, Italian loafers and not a hair out of place, the guy worked in the city. Clark was of her people.

Ben was not. No way in hell would he ever be a city dweller. He loved the outdoors. Lakes. Pines. Open spaces. They could have New York City. He hated it. Ever since...

Swallowing unwanted thoughts of the past with a swig of beer, he concentrated on now. He'd take the Poconos any day.

He and Lea may have chemistry, but they had no future. No sense in going down that road.

Since the lieutenant had just given him advance notice about tomorrow, he'd make a wide berth on the way to the lake in order to avoid the spa area. Ben had thought he'd gotten past the avoidance thing, but until he regained control of his mind and body, distance was his new best friend.

Lea had passed on the body massage, but opted for the facial. Her body would get enough of a workout on Wednesday during her spa appointment with Brandi and the bridesmaids. She could hardly believe they were all arriving in a few short days. And that a week from today, her best friend was getting married. Even though she was immensely thrilled for her friend, Lea couldn't find her own *happy*.

Hopefully, today's exfoliation would peel away her blues, too.

It was silly. She knew it, but her mind wouldn't let go of the fact Ben had so easily moved on. It hadn't even been a week, and he was in another woman's bed.

Was I that unforgettable?

Her throat constricted, but she swallowed past the tightening and forced herself to relax. She doubted tears mixed well with whatever concoction was on her face. Time to suck it up. Ben had never promised her anything more. In fact, he'd told her straight out he wasn't long term.

Still, she couldn't stop her mind from rewinding to last weekend and how great it had been to spend time with him. To be the center of his attention for once. Warmth began to overtake the chill in her body. She sat there for a few minutes and basked in the memories while the technician peeled and buffed her face. When the woman finished, she smiled at Lea and gave her a thumbs up.

Guess she didn't look as bad as she felt.

"My sister and I are going to head for a pedicure, next. How about you, Lea?" The lieutenant's wife eyed her up expectantly.

"No thanks," she replied. Even though the accompanying foot massage was heavenly, she was too keyed up to sit. "You two go ahead. I'm done for the day. I think I'll go for a walk by the lake and enjoy what's left of the summer weather before fall hits us." ·

The women nodded and said goodbye before Lea made her way outside. She inhaled and closed her eyes. Fall was already in the air. But she didn't mind. She loved the fall, too. She could smell the change in the leaves and feel the slight chill in the air from lack of humidity.

It was one of her favorite times of the year. So colorful and picturesque. She couldn't wait to see the oranges, reds and yellows of the leaves reflected in the lake with a bright blue sky as a backdrop.

She took the trail leading to the lake, and let the silence of the woods seep in and calm her mind. How she missed this in the city. The Big Apple had many things, but this tranquility wasn't one of them. Sure, Central Park was nice, and the next best thing to the beauty of her hometown, but it couldn't compare on scope and scale. The Poconos were vast with mountains and lakes and trees and privacy.

As she came out of the clearing, she spotted several boats dotting the lake. The Wynes had designated the northern shore for water skiers so they didn't scare away the fish here at the southern shore. Here, people spent a lazy day fishing from boats or on several of the large docks. Some even fished from shore.

"Did you see that, Uncle Ben? That fish jumped right out of the water," a familiar young voice said a few yards to her right.

Lea glanced around a big oak at the six-year-old boy pointing to the lake, smiling at the man who had galvanized her thoughts all darn week. She had no luck. Or she had great luck. Depended on her outlook. Brandi's nephew Tyler was fishing with Ben near the exact spot she'd chosen to walk. An inner battle to stay or sneak back into the woods ended when the boy spotted her.

"Hi, Aunt Lea. Look what I caught!" Holding up a big fish, Ethan's little boy, the sweetheart her friend had helped raise after his mother died in a skiing accident, was growing so fast. His eager face, with warm brown eyes and a ready smile was always something Lea found hard to resist. "Dad's on an overnight hike, but Uncle Ben took a picture with his phone and sent it to him."

"Wow, Tyler. You did great. I bet your dad'll be proud." Smiling, she stepped closer to ruffle his hair.

"Yeah, he called and told me, and also said to catch a lot and kick Uncle Ben's butt." The boy giggled. "Can you stay and fish with us?"

She shifted her gaze to Ben, and her heart rocked in her chest. Damn, he looked great. Dressed in worn jeans and an old Army T-shirt stretched tight against his broad shoulders and chest, he took her breath. She cleared her throat. "I-I don't want to intrude, hun. I'm just out for a walk."

Ben's expression was neutral. He didn't appear upset at the intrusion. In fact, after a moment, he smiled a killer smile that curled her toes.

"It's not an *inclusion,* right Uncle Ben?"

"Right, Tyler," he replied, and the fact he didn't correct his nephew only added to his appeal. "I agree. Lea should join us."

Sensing a double meaning in that last sentence, she couldn't stop the heat from spreading to her core. Damn man was potent.

"Here. You can use my rod."

And bold.

He handed her his fishing pole, a wicked smile claiming his lips as he kept his back to his nephew.

Unable to respond in any suggestive way thanks to being in Tyler's direct view, she chose her words carefully. "Thank you. I think I remember how to *use* it."

Two hours, ten fish and a lot of laughs went by in the blink of an eye. Before Lea knew it, the sun was beginning its slow decent. On the way back to the resort, they talked about Tyler's first week of school and Brandi's upcoming visit and wedding.

"I can't wait to show Aunt Brandi the A I got on my first test. She's going to be happy," Tyler said, picking his way through the woods, his steps light and sporadic. "And Uncle Kade said if I did good this year, I can stay with them for a whole month next summer. So I'm going to do good, because I loved helping him and Cody out with the animals when Dad and I visited last month."

"I know you will." Lea had hoped to go to Harland County with them, but her dad had had a setback when he'd fallen from the bed. Maybe she'd visit next summer, too. "Did you have fun with Cody?"

"Yeah, and Amelia," the boy replied.

Brandi said it had been great to watch her nephew playing with Kade's nephew and soon-to-be niece. The three little ones had gotten on well.

"She was okay for a baby. And a girl."

"That's how it starts," Ben said under his breath, mischief glinting in his moss colored gaze he slid her way.

Gooseflesh raced down her arms, but she resisted the urge to rub them. That would give her away, and she was hoping he hadn't noticed.

"Cold?" A slight smirk twitched his lips.

He'd noticed. *Bugger*.

"A little." She leaned in to whisper close. "What are you gonna do about it?"

Without waiting for a reply, she caught up to Tyler as they cleared the woods. If Ben wanted to play with fire, she'd strike the match.

Chapter Seven

"Hey, Grandpa, look what I caught." Tyler proudly held up the string of fish he'd insisted on carrying as he rushed to the older man sitting on an Adirondack chair, drinking coffee on the large deck.

"Good job, Tyler. Looks like you came back with more than fish." Colonel Dennis Wyne, or as he'd always asked her to call him, Mr. Wyne, smiled at her and held up his mug. "Nice to see you again, Lea. So, who caught you? Tyler or Ben?"

She laughed. "Neither. I stumbled onto them on my walk. How are you, Mr. Wyne?"

"I'm good. How's your dad?"

"He's getting better, thanks. They're supposed to increase his therapy this week."

"Good to hear. I bet he's going stir crazy."

She nodded. Her father couldn't wait to get back to the restaurant. He complained about missing his people.

"I hope you're going to stay for supper and help us all eat the catch of the day," the older man asked, or rather ordered with a firm nod.

"Yes, Aunt Lea. Please stay.

"I'd love to"

"Okay, Tyler. Come with me and we'll get Cook right on them," Mr. Wyne said, rising to his feet. "This way Ben can take care of his catch. If he's smart."

Not one to blush often, she couldn't have stopped the heat that infused her face if her life had depended on it. Thankfully, the smiling man ushered the little boy through the back door of the resort without waiting for either of them to reply.

She could feel Ben stop behind her, his body heat blazing into her back, setting her nerve ends on fire. Twisting around, she stared up into his face, half-expecting annoyance to fill his gaze at having her thrust upon him.

Not an ounce appeared. There was a boatload of interest, though. And heat. Lots of heat.

"Seems I'm supposed to take care of you."

He was good at taking care of her.

A smug smile stole across his face.

Damn.

"Did I say that out loud?"

His smile widened.

Double damn.

He reached out and used a finger to push a piece of hair that had escaped from her pony tail behind her ear. "We should probably go in and wash up."

She expelled a breath she hadn't known she was holding and nodded. What she really needed was a cold shower.

He nodded for her to go ahead of him, and Lea was grateful to discover she still had use of her legs, even if they were a bit wobbly.

When she made to head to the public restroom in the lobby, a strong hand cupped her elbow and ushered her past reception to the residence wing of the resort, kept separate from the guest wings. Ethan, Mason and Keiffer lived at the resort, each with a separate entry to their own sections. During the redesign a few years ago, her friend had given her brothers their own built in residence, which connected to a common area if they wished to meet. Mr. Wyne stilled lived alone in their big house down the street from her dad's, and Ben had a private section here, too, but mostly stayed at his own cabin Brandi had redesign

116

years ago. The cabin was cozy. Lea had helped paint and decorate alongside her friend, secretly wishing the place was hers, too.

Silly thoughts from a young college girl.

Seemed she hadn't quite outgrown the silliness. Calling herself all sorts of ridiculous for the sudden shyness invading her, Lea walked silently with Ben, extremely aware of the hand he still had on her elbow. A strong, sure hand that had touched a heck of lot more than her elbow last weekend.

Unlocking the residence door, he led her into the cozy great room where a huge stone fireplace was centered on one wall, vaulted wood ceilings sported solid oak beams, and a back wall of floor-to-ceiling windows showcased the vista of trees and mountains owned by the Wynes. It never failed to take away her breath. Brandi had designed a beautiful space that blended in with the outdoors in muted greens, maroons and browns. A theme her friend had kept throughout the whole resort.

"You can use the bathroom down here," he said, stopping outside the door. "I'll be back down in a few minutes."

She watched him take the opened staircase two steps at a time, enjoying the play of muscles across his back, and the way his jeans hugged his firm butt.

"Aunt Lea?" Tyler appeared out of nowhere, staring up at her. "Want to see what I made in school this week?"

"Sure, hun. Let me wash up first."

"Okay, I'll be in the family room," he said, and ran down the hall.

Making quick use of her time, she washed up, splashed several handfuls of cold water on her face, then dried off and quickly called her dad on her way to join Tyler.

"I'm fine," he insisted. "Enjoy yourself. George came over with some pizza. We're watching college football."

"Okay, if you're sure."

"I'm sure. Have fun," her father said, then hung up.

She shoved the phone in her pocket then spent the next hour sharing a delicious meal with her friend's family. Just like old times. Except her friend wasn't there.

Yet.

Four more nights, then Brandi would arrive. It was going to be a great week. Even the dinner table conversation was alive with excitement of the upcoming nuptials and arrival of cowboys. At least, from her and Tyler's end.

Lea had gotten to know and became fast friends with all of Brandi's bridesmaids, so she couldn't wait to meet Jordan and Kerri's husbands, and Shayla's fiancé, the man she was standing up with. The handsome guy they all dubbed the Casanova cowboy. Sure, she'd seen pictures, but knew sometimes photos didn't do justice to the real thing. So she was in for a treat, because Kevin looked all sorts of fine in his photos. Movie star fine.

"Lea, are you going to take the girls into the city while they're here?" Keiffer asked as they ate their apple cobbler for dessert.

"Yes. Brandi said they wanted to visit the Big Apple. Especially, Kerri. She'd gone to culinary school there a few years ago. It should be fun."

"Well, if anyone knows that city, it's you," Mr. Wyne said with a nod. "I hear you're going to look for a job there soon."

Out of the corner of her eye, she saw Ben set his fork down.

"Yes, once I talk with the doctors this week to gauge my father's progress, I should be able to start applying, soon."

"Good for you." Mason smiled at her, a rare occasion, enhancing his breath-taking good looks, placing a sparkle in his brown eyes.

She smiled back.

"Yeah." Keiffer nodded, pointing to her with his spoon. "You're at home there."

"I like going to the city with you and Aunt Brandi," Tyler added, before shoving more ice cream into his mouth.

Ben fastened an unwavering gaze on her. "It's something she's wanted since she was small. Since her mother used to take her to the museums."

Her heart caught, not just from the memory, but from the fact *he'd* remembered. It was an admission she'd only shared once. When she'd been eleven years old, just before her mother's car accident. She'd just gotten back from a day trip to the city with her mom and sister. Ben and Ryder had rushed to help with the armful of bags. Gwen had been gushing about all the fashions and stores and all the clothes she'd bought, while Lea had carried a lone bag with a book on Teddy Roosevelt from the Museum of Natural History. When he'd asked if that was all she'd gotten, she'd told him it was enough because some day she'd work there or in another museum in the city.

Lea couldn't believe he'd remembered, especially when her sister had gone on to model all her outfits for him, looking stunning as usual.

She nodded, holding his gaze. "It's what I've wanted since I was little."

And for the life of her, she couldn't decipher if she meant working in the city, or him. The longer she stared, the louder the pulse pounded in her ears, and the more the room began to fade.

"Well, it won't be long now, I'm sure," Mr. Wyne said, breaking the spell as he pushed back from the table. "It's getting late. Time I headed home."

"Night, Dad." Mason rose to his feet. "Come on, Tyler. That dinosaur movie you wanted to watch comes on in less than a half-hour, and I promised your dad you'd take a bath tonight."

"Ah, do I have to, Uncle Mason?" At his uncle's firm nod, the boy relented. "Okay. Goodnight, everyone." A second later, he disappeared with Mason through the door leading to his uncle's place.

"Guess I'd better go before I get stuck doing the dishes," Keiffer said as he stood. "Have fun." And with a salute, he pivoted on his heels and strode down the hall out of sight.

Ben cracked a smile from across the table. "You can leave, too, if you want. I'm used to cleaning up everyone's messes."

"Nope." She shook her head as she rose to her feet, already stacking dishes. "Sorry, I think you know by now I'm not a deserter."

Her heart caught again, because the strange expression that flickered across his face told her he didn't know. Too many women had disappointed him by doing that very thing. Deserting him.

As they cleaned the table in silence, two things became clear to Lea. One, they made a good team, both having learned efficiency in their jobs, and two, they made a good team physically because every brush of the hand or arm or thigh as they worked side-by-side sent awareness through her body and set her temperature on simmer.

He wasn't immune, either. The more they brushed, the hotter his skin felt.

After Ben shut the dishwasher and hit the ON switch, he turned to face her, green eyes full of the heat rushing through her body.

"So, how was your banana split the other night?"

Completely thrown off by his question, it took Lea a moment to blink through the haze of desire and grab onto the memory of her time at the Confection Connection the night she'd bumped into him and the blonde.

"Good." She shrugged, then countered. "How was your date with Charisse?"

"Fine."

Uh oh. Guy code for not fine. She'd learned that early on in the Wyne household. But she kept her trap shut. *Not going there. Not going there.*

She wanted to go there.

Lea also wanted to go outside. She walked past him, opened the French door and stepped out onto the private deck, lured by the setting sun.

It had been years since she'd watched a sunset.

A warm glow hovered over the mountains, sending orange shafts of light through the trees, illuminating the shadows in a last ditch effort to remain. God, she could relate. Sinking onto one of the cushioned benches, she watched the rest of nature's spectacular display with Ben, who'd followed her outside and silently settled in beside her.

After it was over, and none of the sun's rays remained, only the glow from strategically placed solar lights, she wiped the wetness from her cheek. "Why haven't I done that sooner?"

"Done what? Cry?" he asked, using his thumb to wipe away a missed tear.

"I'm not crying."

A sexy smirk crinkled his face in a very good way. "Of course not. Your eyes leak all the time."

"Only when I'm moved." She reached up to touch the corner of his mouth with her thumb. "Are you ever moved, Ben?" Some of the playfulness disappeared from his gaze as he shrugged, and she'd be lying if she said that hadn't hurt just a little. "I don't move you?"

He stiffened and caught her wrist to remove her touch from his face. "Don't, Lea," he warned, setting her hand on her lap.

"Don't, what, Ben? Feel? Too late." She quickly grasped his arm to keep him from leaving. "It's what I do. It's ingrained in me. You know I'm a *feel* person."

"Don't feel for me."

His expression was as grim as his deprived heart, and she wanted to reach in and guard it close, hold it safe.

"You're wasting your time. Once people get to know me, I tend to tick them off or disappoint and..." His voice trailed off, leaving her to fill in the blanks.

She didn't like the blanks. "I'm not ticked off, and I know you really well, Ben." He just stared at her so she continued. "You make me smile. You make me happy. Sometimes you annoy the heck out of me, and other times you make me so hot I think I'm going to self combust." She bumped his shoulder and winked.

This got her a smile, but it never quite reached his eyes. Her heart snagged on that one because she realized he wasn't sure what to do with her. He wasn't used to a female staying in his life. First his mom. Then Gwen, then Brandi's mom. Even Brandi was now technically gone.

"Look, I just don't want to hurt you, Lea." His gaze was direct and bleak. "Please don't fall for me."

A smile tugged her lips despite the seriousness of their talk. "Conceited much?"

His soft chuckle filled the night air. "You know what I mean."

"Yeah." She nodded. "I do. And it's okay. I'm leaving in a few weeks, remember? We're good. I promise."

Now was a great time to mention the friends-with-benefits thing, but the heat that entered his gaze zapped the brain cells connected to her voice. And when he cupped her face and lowered his head, she was lucky she remembered her darn name.

"We're very good," he said a second before his mouth captured hers.

Yes, they were.

Lea slid her hands over his wonderful chest and touched her tongue to his, eliciting a rough groan from the man who was taking her right out of herself. He kissed her long and wet and deep. Her body trembled in anticipation. Still holding her face with one hand, he skimmed the other down her side to her hip, where he snuck under her shirt to stroke her flesh. She moaned, and that's when things got a little nuts.

He thrust a hand through her hair to cup the back of her head, pressed her against the cushions and brushed a thumb over her nipple straining the lace of her bra. Liquid heat pooled at her core.

Needing to touch all of him, she ran her hands up and down his hard, hot body, stroking his taut abs all the way down his happy trail.

How long they kissed and stroked, she had no idea. She was lost. Lost and drunk. Drunk on her desire for Benjamin Wyne. When they broke for air, she blinked at him.

"Every time," he muttered, lowering his mouth to her neck, kissing and licking a path to the curve of her shoulder. "Every damn time."

Did that mean he'd been lost, too? God, she hoped so. It was no fun being lost alone.

He sank his teeth in the soft spot behind her ear, and breath hitched in her throat as she clutched at his shoulders.

"Mmm…"

"I agree," he said, brushing his lips down her jaw to her mouth, where he proceeded to kiss away what was left of her strength.

A rubbery pile of mush. That's what she was. Warm mush. Warm, throbbing mush.

Skimming her hand down his torso again, she found him the opposite of mush. He was deliciously hard. And thick.

"Lea," he said, breaking the kiss, voice so rough and sexy she shook.

Or was that him?

His wicked hand slid up and down her belly, making it very hard for her to concentrate on even the simplest things like breathing. She glanced at his hovering lips, wondering, waiting, needing to taste him again.

With a strangled groan, he lowered his mouth, then stilled. A second later, he released her and shot to his feet.

"What is it? What's wrong?" she asked, fixing her shirt as she stood, glancing around to see if someone had joined them.

"I'm not sure," he answered distractedly as he fished the phone from his pocket and dialed a number. "Ethan? What's going on?"

Lea's heart rocked against her ribs as she watched his face. It was his gift. His sensing thing he'd inherited from his mother. She chewed her lower lip and continued to study his face for a clue to his older brother's well being. Tyler had said his dad was on an overnight hike. Maybe Ethan was okay. Maybe Ben's sixth sense was off.

Okay, it had never been off. Ever.

One summer, he'd been at her house, playing football in the backyard with Ryder and his brothers when he'd gone all still. And a little green. His gaze had crashed into hers. And she knew. She knew something bad had happened before the state police had shown up at the door with the news about her mom's accident.

This was not going to turn into that. They all had had enough tragedy. Especially little Tyler. Nope. She wasn't going to allow it. Thinking good thoughts, happy thoughts, willing away anything bad, she turned around and glanced over at the mountain, having no idea where the oldest Wyne brother was camped.

"I can barely hear you." Ben frowned, glancing at the mountain as his youngest brother came rushing out of the house.

"Is that Ethan?" Keiffer asked, holding up a phone. "We were talking when all of a sudden the line went dead. But not before I heard a gunshot."

Ben's whole body stiffened, and the urge to grab his hand and squeeze shook through Lea, but she stayed put, out of the way as the two brothers banded together.

"Ethan? Are you there? Did you fire your gun?" Ben frowned as he strained to hear on the phone. "Okay." He nodded, and her sigh of relief mingled with Keiffers. "Where are you? Give me the coordinates."

If she could feel her legs, she'd have rushed inside to grab a paper and pen, but she needn't have worried. He fished both from a pocket in his cargos and started to jot something down.

125

"Got it," he said. "You need Scott?"

Her heart hit her ribs again. Scott Holden was one of her brother's guard buddy, and a paramedic. If he was needed then...

"No? You're sure? Okay." Ben was nodding again, some of the tightness easing from his face and body. "All right. Keiffer and I will meet you at the bottom of the mountain in two hours." He hung up the phone and blew out a breath.

His younger brother cocked his head. "Let me guess, bear spooked someone?"

"Yep." He nodded, mouth tight. "And now they're insisting on coming in tonight, even though Ethan explained it's more dangerous to trek down the mountain in the dark than sleep with a bear on the prowl."

Keiffer plopped down on one of the chairs and shook his head. "There's always one or two every year."

"Yeah." Ben glanced at her and blinked as if forgetting she'd been there. He walked over, small smile tugging his lips as regret filled his eyes. "Sorry. We're going to have to break out the gear and go get them."

She nodded, answering his smile with one of her own. Sex was out of the question, but she was okay with that. Ethan needed help. "I'm just glad everyone is all right. My heart is still in my throat."

"How do you think I feel having heard that damn gunshot?" Keiffer asked, rising to his feet, face still a little pale.

The three of them shuddered.

And because the last thing Lea wanted to be was in the way, she said her good-byes and went home, but not before she got Ben to agree to come over to her dad's for dinner the next day.

Déjà vu rippled through Ben's mind Sunday afternoon as Lea's father led him into the Gablonski kitchen where the delicious aromas of homemade pot-roast beckoned like a long lost friend. A lifetime ago, he'd practically been a fixture at their house for supper. Not that the food hadn't been good at home while Brandi's mom had been healthy, it was after she'd become sick and the duty of cooking meals had fallen to the boys that he looked forward to invites at Ryder's. He loved his brothers, but unless it was Mason who had kitchen detail that week, Ben had taken to eating cold spaghetti out of a can. Much more appetizing than anything the rest of them could cook.

Truth be told, after a few visits, it hadn't just been the food that had drawn him there. Ryder's sister, Gwen, had been everything his teenage body had yearned for, a popular, beautiful, blonde cheerleader. Yeah, he'd been in heaven when she'd actually started to flirt with him. And he'd enjoyed Lea's company, too. The young girl had been a great friend to his new sister. And smart. Like Brandi, she hadn't been the type to play with dolls. And if she didn't have her nose in a book, she liked sports and the outdoors, and was a quick learner. There was nothing superfluous about the youngest Gablonski

Unlike Gwen.

Funny how he'd never realized that before.

He also never realized just how far from superficial the woman was either. Walking into the kitchen, they found her placing the roast on a hotplate on the table. She wore a jean skirt and a simple baby blue, scoop-necked shirt with her hair pulled back in another ponytail and no fancy necklace, or earrings or bracelets jangling from her limbs. The only piece of jewelry she wore was a pinky ring that used to belong to her mother. He knew this because Brandi wore one of her mother's rings the same

127

way. He remembered the two girls donning them around the same time.

"Something smells great in here, Lea," her dad said with a smile as he slowly sank into his chair.

"Of course it does. It's your recipe."

She smiled back, then transferred that gaze to him, and his heart rocked hard in his chest.

"Hi, Ben. You're just in time."

Felt more like he was years late. He'd been walking around with blinders on or something, because although he'd always found her beautiful, he just never really looked beyond skin deep. Peering past the surface was always a risk, and one he'd learned never to take lest he risk getting hurt. Or disappointed. Again.

But he couldn't help it now. Her blue eyes sparkled with warmth and acceptance. No judgments on his lack of dress clothes, which was good, because he wore a uniform all damn week so on weekends he relaxed in a T-shirt and jeans or cargos. She didn't seem to care in the slightest. In fact, her gaze had lingered on him, as if she wanted to add him to the menu.

His ribs took a jolt on that. The woman didn't pull any punches. And that was okay with him. Just like yesterday. He'd vowed to stay away from her, but the minute she'd stumbled upon him fishing with Tyler, he'd caved like a man starved for her attention. Because he was. Damn it.

"Thanks for the wine."

Wine…

Remembering the bottle held in a death grip, he thrust the red wine toward her and cleared his throat. "Hope it's the right compliment to your hard work."

A blush colored her cheeks, deepening the blue of her eyes. "I'm sure it will. Thank you."

Pure and real, her beauty fogged his mind and stole his breath. He rubbed at his chest in an attempt to relieve the tightness squeezing without mercy.

"Have a seat while I get some glasses."

Once she removed her debilitating gaze, he found his breathing returned and the tightness slowly dissipated.

"So, I heard Ethan had a bunch of pansies on the mountain yesterday," Mr. Gablonski said, and the dinner conversation centered on bears, mountain lions and rookie hikers.

A half-hour later, having just barely resisted the urge to lick his plate clean, Ben acknowledged he was one mouthful away from a food coma. The pot-roast had melted in his mouth the instant it hit his tongue, and the mashed potatoes...*ah hell*, the mashed potatoes were real. And hearty. And had just a hint of garlic enhanced by the rich, thick gravy she should patent and sell to every damn bachelor on the planet. The delicious meal was the stick-to-your-ribs kind of meal a guy longs to have after a hard day's work.

Then she'd placed a warm-from-the-oven peach pie— made from scratch—on the table.

Two mouthwatering slices later, that damn food coma had him by the shirt tails.

"Well, Ben, what do you say we go catch what's left of the four o'clock football game?" her dad suggested, rising to his feet and slapping his belly.

He glanced from the mound of dishes on the table to Lea. Who smiled and waved him toward the front room. "Go ahead. I've got this. It'll be nice for Dad to watch the game with someone other than me...you know, someone who actually *likes* the NFL."

She sat and watched games with her dad?

Lea Gablonski was the most warm-hearted, kind and giving person he'd ever met. That damn tightening in his chest returned. Nodding to her, he left the kitchen, rubbing his chest, again, and wondering how he could reverse the effects.

"How are the wedding plans coming along?"

It took Ben a full five seconds before he realized Lea's father had been asking about Brandi's plans and not his. *Jesus*, his heart had stopped for those full five seconds, too.

"Good, sir," he replied, settling into the other recliner facing the TV. "The resort has the rooms reserved for all the Harland County guests, and the banquet hall details are complete down to my sister's favorite color. The cook has the menu figured out. Lea took care of the flowers and cake arrangements. And my brothers and I will be standing by to pick everyone up at the local airport when we get the call on Wednesday."

The older man nodded, then smiled. "How is your dad through all this? Is he ready to give his little girl away?"

Normally, Ben would've responded with a yes, of course. But lately, he'd caught his stoic, no-nonsense father lingering over photos of Brandi hanging on the walls at home. "I believe, so, sir."

"Yeah, even your dad will feel the punch to the gut, I'm sure."

Ben nodded, suspecting the man was right.

"At least Brandi is marrying the right man."

"I agree."

"Sometimes you think you know what you want, and don't realize how wrong you are until you discover the right one was in front of you all the time."

Since he wasn't sitting across from the man, and could only gage him from the side, Ben had no idea if Lea's father was referring to him...or Brandi. Thankfully, Lea chose that moment to waltz into the room and save him from himself.

"Okay, you've had Ben for a half-hour, so now it's my turn to torture him," she stated with a smile sparkling in her gaze.

"Oh boy. That sounds like more wedding stuff, Ben." Her father grimaced. "Sorry. You're on your own, there."

"*Hey.*"

She jammed her hands on her hips, and he really tried not to notice how the movement thrust out her mouthwatering breasts. But he was a guy. And her breasts really were to die for.

"He'd promised Brandi he'd help. And it's not that bad. I need to show him the silk leis for the horses."

"Oh, that's right." Her dad's face lit up. "Kade was happy about that, I bet."

Ben nodded with a smile tugging his lips. "Very. They're all rescues the resort is proud to own. Brandi and Lea's idea to reach out to the local shelters up here was brilliant."

"Yes, it was."

"Thank you very much," she said, hooking her arm through his and tugging him forward. "It's time to go look at the leis and tell me if they are too girly or not."

He said a quick good-bye to her chuckling father and found himself descending back into that déjà vu territory again. The basement. The make-out den where he'd copped his first feel, ever, and with her sister Gwen, which now just made him feel a lot weird.

Weirded out.

But as he reached the bottom and glanced around, he realized the place had been completely overhauled and brought back no twinges of the past. It was still a rec room with a TV, a bar and couch, but they were new, and the room was set up differently.

"Ryder remodeled the place five years ago," she said, opening the door to show him a full bathroom that had once been a small half-bath. "The rest is similar, but he changed the layout to be more functional."

Placing his back to the couch, Ben worked on curbing errant thoughts of getting Lea naked on the cushions and sinking in to her warm, wet...

He cleared his throat. "It seems bigger, too." He motioned toward the table against the wall by the steps where the silk pieces for the horses rested.

"Yeah, I like it down here now."

This caused him to frown. "I don't remember you not liking it down here."

Pink settled in her cheeks. "Some memories weren't that great."

Even though she was clearly embarrassed, the woman held his gaze, unafraid if he read them. And he did. He knew exactly which memories she'd meant.

Him and Gwen making out on the couch.

They were quickly turning into some of his least favorites, too. If he'd been of his right mind, he would've realized that analogy was cause for a massive red flag and would've required him to hit the stairs running.

But, he was far from his right mind. In fact, he only had a one track mind. The one that wanted Lea on the couch. Naked. And screaming his name.

He had no idea where the last part came from, but it worked for him.

"Wait." She stepped back, apparently seeing his intent in his eyes. "You haven't said what you thought a-about the leis."

132

"They're one of my most favorite things." He moved toward her. "In fact, I'd love to get *lei-d* right now."

"Ben."

"Lea."

She choked on a laugh. "What's going on in that head of yours?"

"That it's time you had some new memories down here. Good memories," he said, stalking her, backing her up until the back of her knees hit the couch, and she fell onto the cushions.

Chapter Eight

"I—"

Ben followed her down, swallowing her words with his tongue, covering her body completely with his. God, she felt great, all warm and soft and trembling. Her hands were on the back of his head, holding him close, brushing her thumbs across his neck, sending goosebumps down his shoulders and spine.

Groaning, he ground into her, eliciting a sexy moan as her hands skimmed his back to grab his ass and press up into him. *Ah hell*, she had him on the fast track in under a minute. He broke the kiss and pulled back just enough to yank the shirt up and over her head. Breath hissed in his lungs at the sight of her white, lacy bra barely containing her breasts. He lowered his head to kiss her cleavage, and she grabbed him again, this time his head as he pulled the lace aside and sucked a beaded nipple into his mouth.

"Yes…" Her breathing came shallow and ragged.

Her body was hot, and he needed to touch all of her.

Slipping his hand under her skirt, he shifted his weight so he could push the denim up to her hips. He released her nipple and glanced down, nearly coming undone at the sight of her matching lace panties barely covering her mound.

"Don't stop," she begged, pulling his head back down to her chest.

Needing no further instruction, he kissed his way to her other nipple, pressing the pert peak to the roof of his mouth with his tongue. She moaned, arching into him while his fingers slid over her sexy lace panties… finding them damp.

A deep, hungry groan filled the room, and it took him a moment to realize the sound had come from him. He didn't care. He was too far gone, lost in the slick heat and soft curves of the responsive woman writhing beneath him.

"Ah, Ben? Lea?"

The interruption from the top of the stairs had him on his feet and pivoting around before his eyes could even focus. Thankfully, the wall prevented her father from seeing down into the room from the very top, and the back surgery prevented Mr. Gablonski from using stairs.

Jesus, what the hell had he been thinking? They weren't teenagers. But he sure acted like one, a horny one, whenever his mouth was on any part of the woman.

"Sorry to bother you, but the cat knocked the cable out of the wall again, and there's only two minutes left in the game," her father explained. "I tried, but I can't reach it."

"No, don't do that." Lea was on her feet, tucking things in as she spoke. "We'll be right up."

Ben was already at the bottom of the stairs. The sooner he fixed the cable, the sooner he could take Lea to his extra room at the lodge where they could continue like adults, and uninterrupted. "Lead the way."

A few minutes later, he was kneeling behind the TV stand, fastening the cable to the jack in the wall when his gaze fell to the newspaper on the coffee table.

The New York Times.

Classifieds.

With several ads circled in red.

The tightening in his chest returned again, and he was grateful he'd been on the floor, because he felt as if he'd been run over by a tank. Twice. Which was damn stupid.

He knew Lea was going to New York in a few weeks. It was no secret. She hid nothing from him. So the shock rumbling through his body was unacceptable.

But it was real, and he needed to suck it up. And fast.

"That's it," her dad said as the game must have came back into focus on the TV. "Thanks, Ben."

He backed out of his tight spot and slowly rose to his feet. If only he could do something about the tight spot in his chest. It hurt, bad. Like he was having a heart attack, but he knew differently. It was anxiety. He had to have a heart to have a heart attack.

"You're welcome, sir." He nodded at the man, keeping his gaze from the woman who hovered in the doorway. "I'd better get going. Thanks for having me over."

"Any time, son. But, don't leave on my account."

"I'm not," he reassured, holding her father's gaze until the man relaxed and nodded. "I have to head down the Gap before first light."

"Yeah, morning comes early on days like that."

"Sure does." He made small talk, still not glancing at the woman.

"I'll walk you out," she said, apparently tired of being silent…or ignored.

And now he had no choice but to leave the house with her or he'd seem way too rude. But he did owe her an explanation. He chanced a glance at her face. Yeah. His stomach clenched. Confusion clouded her vibrant gaze as she hooked her arm through his then led them outside.

"Okay, what gives?" she asked as they walked from her front porch to the sidewalk.

Ben glanced around, relieved to note none of the neighbors were sitting on their porches at the moment. He and Lea didn't need to become the talk of the town.

Been there done that with another Gablonski.

If only he didn't have an aversion to liars, he'd try to come up with one that would let her off easy. But, she deserved the truth.

When he reached the truck, he removed her hand and leaned back against his door. "I saw the newspaper."

Her forehead wrinkled into a frown. "I don't follow."

"The New York Times. The classifieds."

"Okay." She blinked. "Still not following."

He shrugged. "It was just a reminder that you're leaving."

Why wasn't the conversation easing some of the damn pain in his chest?

"Yes. Something you already know. I've never kept that from you. So, how is that a problem?"

God, he wished he knew. But he didn't have a clue. He felt like he was standing in quicksand. Something in his expression must've given her an answer because she shook her head and sighed.

"You're still trying to protect this," she said, patting his chest. "But I'm not trying to stake a claim there, Ben. I've tried to make it clear. You're safe with me. I'm leaving. It's a perfect set up. I'm attracted to you. You're attracted to me. I don't know why it's so hard for you to understand. I'm not looking for a ring you don't want to give. I just want some fun. Some sex. Some crazy, *fun* sex where I don't have to hold back or pretend or live up to anything…"

She removed her touch, and his body suddenly felt cold.

"You don't need to live up to anything, Lea. You're perfect," he finally said, unable to allow her to think otherwise. "You're the best damn person I've ever met."

Determination and affection and exasperation all crowded her gaze. "Then why are you stopping this?"

He opened his mouth to answer, but he had nothing.

She sighed again and slowly shook her head. "If you come up with an answer before I leave, look me up." She lifted on tiptoe, kissed the corner of his mouth and his cheek, then drew back and walked away.

Didn't look back. Just walked up the sidewalk, onto her porch, then went inside.

He envied her. She knew what she wanted. Wasn't afraid to take risks.

Normally, he wasn't either. He had no issues with risking life and limb for family and country. Had done it on numerous occasions. But to risk his heart for a few nights in her bed? Okay, glorious, hotter-than-hell nights in her bed. Even so, he simply wasn't that brave.

Lea spent the next few days staying busy. Between taking her father to and from therapy, working at the restaurant, cooking and cleaning her father's house, and double-checking on tomorrow's trip to New York City, she was exhausted. And frustrated.

In attitude. *And* sexually.

Dammit.

And it didn't help whenever Ben waltzed into the Eatery, looking all hot and hard and gorgeous. At least he wasn't avoiding her, her mind insisted. True. But, his presence and that wonderful scent of his, all male and soap and fresh cedar, and the way his eyes held hers with a dark, brooding expression…He was killing her.

Would he ever come around? Reverse his decision?

She hadn't called a halt to things. He had. And they really didn't have a *thing* other than sex. Why did he have to go and stop the sex? She'd only gotten one blissful night. And a few teasers. She wanted a few nights.

But she'd made enough moves. Made things perfectly clear. The ball was in his court now. If they were to fall into bed together, then he was going to have to come to her. She was done making the first move.

"Today's the day, huh?" Mr. Tierney smiled up at her from his perch on the bar stool. "Brandi's coming home for a visit and brining them cowboys with her?"

"Yep." She nodded. "And cowgirls, too."

His smile widened. "Whoop! I heard that. You going to pick them up?"

"Yes. Just waiting for the call. They left Texas..." She glanced at the train on the wall "Three hours ago." She couldn't hold back a wide smile. "They should land any minute now. One of the Wynes are supposed to pick me up on the way to the airstrip."

"Bet it'll be Ben. He can't keep his eyes off ya. Always playing it cool when you're looking, but when you ain't?" The older man slapped the counter and chuckled. "Boy, I'll tell ya, that young man's got it bad and doesn't even know it."

Well, it was news to her, too. Ben stared at her? Damn, stubborn man. Why the heck was he holding back?

Keiffer rushed into the restaurant, bell above the door unnecessarily announcing his arrival. "Hey, Lea. It's time. You ready?"

Mr. Tierney shook his head, muttered something under his breath about being young and stubborn and foolish.

"Yea," she replied, removing her apron as she glanced at the clock. "Did they call? I haven't heard anything yet." She grabbed her purse from under the counter then removed her phone, noting no missed calls or texts.

"No." He ushered her out the door and into his jeep parked at the side of the building. "We just know they should be landing soon, so there's no need to wait for a call. Ben and Mason are already there. Ethan, Tyler and my dad stayed behind to make sure all the rooms are ready at the lodge."

Her stomach squeezed, and it wasn't from the seatbelt she'd just clicked into place. "And you got stuck with *picking up Lea* duty. I could've driven myself. The airport is only twenty minutes away. I'm sorry."

And she was. Sorry it hadn't been Ben. Damn man worked across the street from her. He should've taken her on the principal of convenience alone. And here she'd thought he'd stopped avoiding her.

"It's no trouble." Keiffer smiled as they drove out of town. "Ben was supposed to take you, but Dad called him two hours ago with a busted water heater. He's been helping Ryder install a new one, so he ended up just leaving from there."

"Oh…that's terrible."

Then why did she suddenly feel better?

He nodded. "Yeah, great timing, right?"

Even though she'd been ecstatic over seeing her best friend again, and finally meeting her new ones in person, Lea's mood had lifted considerably, and all because of a busted hot water heater. Silly, but knowing Ben hadn't deliberately pawned her off on his youngest brother made the difference between breathing, and painful breathing.

She was even glad she'd taken a little extra care getting ready that morning. Because of her duties at the restaurant, she couldn't dress chic, but she could wear a sensible dress that still flattered. Gwen had taught her that much. She wore a light gray, cap sleeve dress that hugged her figure without squeezing and fell halfway to her knees, then paired it with gingham print, peep-toe flats with an adorable little bow above the hole. They were cute and comfortable and made her feel flirty. And after the past few days, she needed to feel flirty.

"Looks like we got here before Brandi," Keiffer said, parking his jeep next to Ben's truck before they got out and joined the vigil by the gate.

"Hi, everyone," she said, ordering her pulse to slow down as she stood next to Ben.

He was just a guy. A guy who was holding back. Although, he missed a piece of heat, because a spark had flittered through his gaze for a few beats before his neutral expression arrived to save the day.

She forced herself to ignore the man and stared out over the private airfield used by businessmen and tourists alike. The runway was empty, and the hangar was opened, but also empty. Her friend hadn't landed yet. Other than her and the Wynes, the place was pretty deserted. Just a few workers stood about, glancing up at the sky.

Family owned, the airstrip was convenient for those who wanted quick access to the Poconos, or needed to get to one of the neighboring big cities. The Wynes had some sort of shuttle service deal with the owners, but today, she knew the guys wanted to come get their sister and her new extended family.

"Looks like them there," Mason said, pointing to a small blip in the cloudless blue horizon.

Everyone stood silently, watching, and smiling as the blip grew from a dot to take the shape of a plane that eventually landed without a bump on the airstrip several yards out. As the Gulfstream jet taxied onto a different runway on the way to the hanger, Lea's excitement picked up.

It was going to be great to see Brandi again.

The jet stopped, and the airstrip workers rushed forward to help as the door opened and steps were lowered. Then beauty and testosterone emptied onto the tarmac.

Holy wranglers did the Texans ever know how to fill out a pair of jeans. And cowboy boots. And Stetsons. She'd talked to each of the cowboys on Skype at one point over the past few months, so she immediately recognized them, but wow, the computer failed to convey the punch of their actual presence.

"Hello-o-o," Keiffer said under his breath as a pretty, light-haired woman she recognized as Caitlin, Shayla's younger sister, stepped off the jet.

"Down boy," Ben warned. "These are Brandi's friends. No messing with them."

Mischief danced in the younger brother's eyes as he cracked a smile. "Oh, you mean like you and Lea. Got it, bro."

Ben clenched his jaw, but didn't respond as the new arrivals waved.

Lea rushed forward and met Brandi halfway, hugging her friend close. "You're finally here."

"I know. And I'm finally getting married." Brandi squeezed her tight and cried, which made Lea cry, then she turned and went on to hug each of the girls.

God, it felt good to belong without trying. To be appreciated without having to push herself on someone.

When they broke apart, Jordan McCall smiled at her. "Wow, girl. Is there a reason you're not modeling alongside your sister? Look at you with your long black hair and vivid blue eyes. Can you say Elizabeth Taylor? Oh, wait, no. I've got it. You're the female version of Kevin."

142

Everyone stopped with the handshakes and hugs, and hit her with their gazes. The invisible force nearly knocked her backward, but she managed to remain still. She couldn't stop the damn blush for reaching her face, though. "No. I'm just the bookworm."

"What a coincidence, I love books, too. It's nice to finally meet you in person, darlin'." The blue-eyed cowboy rushed closer to give her a quick hug, while a cute little mini-version of Shayla, she knew to be Amelia, clutched his neck. "Jordan's right. If I didn't know my father better, I might question if we were related."

He did have a point. Now that she could see Kevin Dalton up close, they did share similar features like the same color eyes, dark eyebrows and hair, high cheekbones.

"No, she's not a pain in the rear, like you." The groom-to-be elicited snickers from the crowd while he pulled her into a hug. "How are you, Lea? It's good to see you again."

"You too, handsome." She smiled, drawing back to gaze into Kade Dalton's amazing gray eyes. "Did you have a good flight?"

He released her to drop his arm around Brandi's shoulders. "Yes, we had a great flight. The pilot is flying back tonight so he can bring the rest here tomorrow."

"The rest?" Keiffer frowned as he glanced at the crowd. "You mean there's more?"

Brandi laughed. "Yes. Mr. and Mrs. McCall. Mr. and Mrs. Masters. Jen, Brock and Cody, plus two of Kade's guard buddies, Jace and Tanner."

"The Gulfstream only sits sixteen," Cole McCall explained, nodding to the jet. "So we broke it up between two flights."

"Well, we would've had room had you gone with my suggestion, bossman," Kevin said, slipping his arm around

143

Shayla, who now held a smiling Amelia in her arms. The picture the young couple made of a happy family wasn't lost on Lea. She knew from Brandi that their journey hadn't been an easy one. It was gratifying to see them so happy.

"Yeah." Cole's gaze was warm and tolerant as he drew Jordan's back against his chest and smiled over her head at his friend. "I think there are safety laws against having the women sit on our laps during flight, buddy."

"Too bad," Connor McCall, Cole's brother and the tallest cowboy, spoke up, hugging his wife Kerri at his side. "I thought it was one of Kevin's better ideas."

"Thanks, *McMoose*." The dark-haired cowboy nodded. "I appreciate it."

As Lea watched the interaction, it struck her how well the cowboys and their women fit together. How comfortable they were with each other. How well Brandi fit in with the Texans.

Pain banded around her heart and squeezed. She was beginning to understand how her friend could leave the people she loved and the place she grew up and move so far south. Because she'd found her *happy*. A place where she fit, doing what she loved with the man she loved. Brandi and the other women appeared complete. But not because they had a man in their life's that they loved and who loved them back, no, the women were complete because they found themselves. They were at peace with themselves.

Who wouldn't move to the ends of the earth for that?

She certainly would.

Her gaze was inexplicably pulled to Ben's, and she sucked in a breath when she found him watching her. He'd greeted the Texans, joked with his sister, made the appropriate comment here and there, but she could sense

144

he was off balance. Out of whack, and her heart squeezed because she had no idea how to help him. How to make him happy, other than sexually.

Whatever was eating away at his laid-back nature needed to be stopped.

Now, if she could just figure out what was eating at hers…

Two hours later, the guys were all off on some sort of outdoor adventure with Tyler and Amelia while Lea and the women enjoyed their spa appointments. There had been no need to try on their bridesmaids and maid-of-honor dresses because the others had gotten fitted in Texas. A bridal shop in town had carried the same dress, so Lea had been able to have hers fitting locally. They were all set.

The thirty minute relaxing massage she'd passed on last weekend was pure bliss and had almost put her to sleep. But the eyebrow waxing woke her right up. It was as if they'd yanked two caterpillars off her forehead. She had no idea how a woman endured waxing in other delicate areas. One pull down there and her screams would've been heard clear up into Canada.

"Thanks for setting all this up, and our New York City trip tomorrow," Brandi said as they all sat their newly manicured and pedicured bodies on the private residence deck and enjoyed a class of wine or two in the late afternoon sun.

She reached next to her and squeezed her friend's hand. "You're welcome. I just want you to have the perfect time. You deserve it."

"Okay, you're going to make me cry. Cut it out." Kerri sniffed and the others nodded.

Brandi shook her head and squeezed her hand back. "If anyone deserves it, it's you. Between putting your life on hold and moving back home to take care of your dad, and the restaurant, and your pain-in-the-ass friend's wedding arrangements, you must be exhausted, hun."

"No." She smiled and released her. "I'm good." And she meant it. Mostly. "Your brother has done more setting up than I have."

"He's used to coordinating drills and trainings. He's practically a producer for the Army." Brandi laughed. "Helping me put together a wedding was something he could've done in his sleep."

"Speaking of something he could've done in his sleep," Jordan said, gaze fastened on Lea. "How goes things with you two?"

"Yeah." Shayla leaned forward. "Every time he glanced at you, he had this, I don't know, strange, sad look in his eyes."

Her heart rocked. God, she didn't want him to be sad.

"I noticed it, too," Kerri said.

Even Caitlin nodded. "So did I."

"No more action on the blue negligee front?" The long-haired sheriff sipped her wine and studied her.

Lea laughed, but it sounded sad even to her ears. "Not that I'm aware of."

Her best friend with sun-kissed brown hair and warm brown eyes reeled back and frowned. "What does that mean?"

"I no longer have it."

"You don't? Why?"

"Because, when we were getting ready to leave the colonel's house that first weekend, I kind of stuffed it into Ben's duffle bag."

146

Amongst the coughing and intakes of breath, Jordan's laugh could be heard ringing the loudest. "Oh my God, I love you," the woman gushed.

"So, Ben has your nightie?" Brandi asked, then shoved a hand over her smiling mouth when Lea nodded. "Oh, what I wouldn't have given to have seen his face when he first discovered it."

"Me, too," she mumbled around a gulp of wine.

The dark-eyed chef leaned forward. "He hasn't said anything or returned it?"

"Nope and nope."

Jordan's smile widened. "You have him, honey. All you have to do is reel him in."

"No, I don't." She shook her head as she poured more wine. "No one has Ben. Ever."

"Maybe in the past, but considering the way he looks at you, that is no longer true," the redhead stated.

Maybe she didn't need another glass. All the wine was going to her head. She could've sworn the girls were telling her that Ben was stuck on her. A laugh escaped. "The guy is too afraid to let go long enough to enjoy a few weeks of just sex. He is certainly not going to let himself fall for anyone, especially me."

"Why not you?" Caitlin asked, eyeing her over her barely touched wine.

Lea blinked. "Because I'm not staying. I'm going to be working in New York soon…I hope."

"You will." Brandi patted her leg. "Have you sent out your resumes yet?"

She shook her head.

"Why not?"

"I was waiting to talk to my dad's physical therapist yesterday to see when she felt he'd be able to go back to work."

"And…?"

"She said he was doing well, and she saw no problems with him going back to Gabe's for light duty by the beginning of November."

"That's terrific. So did you send them out?"

"No. Not yet."

"Why not?" her friend repeated.

Truthfully, she had too much on her plate right now, between her dad, the wedding…her sister driving in tomorrow for the wedding. Yeah, too much to deal with, but nothing she could admit to Brandi.

She conjured up a smile and hoped it read true. "Because my best friend is getting married, and I'm too busy enjoying that and everyone's company right now." She shoulder bumped Brandi. "It's on my Monday's to do list."

Yes, she'd definitely start answering ads and sending out resumes next week.

"Okay." Her friend smiled. "Good. I just don't want you to miss out on your dream, hun."

"I know. And I won't. I'll send them out next week. I promise. Now, enough about me and my limbo life. This is your time, your weekend. It's all about you," she said, then raised her glass for a toast. "So, here's to Brandi. May you have the best life. The happiest life."

"I already do." Her friend sniffed as she clinked everyone's glasses then drank.

And Lea was more than happy to return the attention where it belonged. On Brandi. Her friend was the one with her life pulled together and complete. And it had been a long time coming.

That was worth celebrating in Lea's book.

Wyne and Dine

Thursday evening, Ben sat at one of the tables at the bachelor party he helped Kevin set up for Kade in one of the small banquet rooms at the resort. Brandi's bachelorette party was going on down the hall in a similar room. Every once in a while, music and laughter could be heard over their own entertainment, which consisted of poker, chicken wings and pizza, and drinking beer.

Best damn bachelor party he'd ever attended.

Stripers and porn were highly over rated.

"I have to admit, I was a little relieved to hear you'd helped my cousin set up this party," Kade said, sitting next to him.

He waved his beer at the room. "Kevin supplied me with the itinerary, and I supplied the goods."

"And there are no stripers or porn involved?" Connor asked, looking a little green.

Ben nodded. "None."

"I have to admit, Kevin, even I'm surprised." Cole slapped his friend on the shoulder and smiled. "You all belly *dancered* out?"

"As you may recall, I wasn't the one who had danced belly-to-belly with Charity. Isn't that right, cuz?" Kevin stared pointedly at the groom-to-be, then quickly glanced at Ben and his brothers. "This was way before he and Brandi got together."

"Yeah." Connor nodded. "Right after he'd gotten back from deployment. Sort of a relieve the tension kind of thing, if you know what I mean."

Keiffer clinked his glass with Kade. "Heard that."

Then Mason, Jace, Tanner and Ethan all followed suit.

"Relieving tension is good," Ben said, bumping his glass off Kade's.

He was antsy, and tense, and annoyed for no reason, and was finding it difficult to just sit there and shoot the shit about it. The unusual behavior made no sense. He had no idea of the cause, therefore he had no cure. And that only added to his tension. He put out fires. Acted on issues. Came up with solutions to problems.

So, why the hell couldn't he fix himself?

"Maybe you should've gotten that belly dancer for Ben," Keiffer said, raising his beer in a salute.

Ah, hell, when was the idiot going to learn to keep his mouth shut. Now the guys all stared at him.

"Oh boy, who is she?" Kevin asked, leaning back in his chair. "The gorgeous maid-of-honor by chance?"

"That'd be her," Keiffer answered, apparently asking for a punch to the face.

He curled his hand into a fist, but kept it on the table. "Shut it, Keif."

"See? He won't even talk about her." His younger brother shook his head and continued as if he wasn't there. "The idiot has the opportunity to enjoy himself with the best woman he's ever known—beautiful, smart and funny—and he's blown it."

"Really? You and Lea?" Ethan tipped his head to stare at him. "Seems I've missed a lot the past two weeks taking guests up on the mountain."

"Yep. They've had sex, so now he's all freaked out." Keiffer glanced at Ryder and had the decency to look contrite. "Sorry, man. I keep forgetting she's your sister."

"No worries. It's like I told Ben last week, I stay out of my sisters' love lives, and they stay out of mine."

Yeah, Ryder told him that *after* Ben's face met his friend's fist in the back of Gabe's parking lot once Lea had gone back inside. Now, they were good again; at least, they were until Keiffer open his big fat mouth.

"Smart man," Kevin said, then shuttered. "Wish I had known that back when Jen was dating Brock."

Kade chuckled. "You paid for it big time. I thought it was funny."

"You would. You weren't the one pimped out to the nursing home."

"Ah, quit your whining," Connor said with a shake of his head, and Ben was happy to have the heat taken off him for a change. "Those little old ladies were harmless."

"Harmless? They wanted to play strip bingo."

"So?" Cole frowned at his friend. "It's not like you don't know how to strip."

"Not me, you idiot. *Them*. They were taking their clothes off, and growing hands faster than I could run. Damn women pinched hard, too. No mercy, I tell ya. No mercy."

By the time Kevin was done telling his tale, the whole room was laughing, and Ben had to admit, he'd even felt a bit better.

"Speaking of striping…" Kevin held a finger to his mouth to quiet the room, then opened the door to listen to the music down the hall. "Yep, I'd say it was time for *Magic Cowboy*." He set his Stetson on his head and nodded to the door. "Time to crash the party. Who's with me?"

Without waiting for a reply, the crazy man left the room, and everyone glanced at each other.

"Is he really going to do a striptease in there?" Mason asked.

Cole nodded. "Yep."

"I'm in." Keiffer jumped to his feet and disappeared through the door.

Ethan shot to his feet. "Oh, this I've got to see."

"Me, too." Mason surprised him by following.

And before Ben knew it, he was heading down the hall with all the guys about to crash his sister's bachelorette party.

Mason held the door open for him, so he snuck in with the rest of the bachelor party attendees and stood in the back of the darkened room, watching eight very beautiful women laughing and clapping as some guy gyrated on a makeshift stage, in what was left of a police uniform.

It wasn't Kevin. Or Keiffer.

Not yet, at least.

His stomach soured. The only good thing was the classic rock song blaring out of the speakers.

When a Maroon Five song came on, the stripper looked puzzled...until the cowboy came dancing out, along with his idiot of a brother. The *cop* had the good sense to leave the stage to his brother and the cowboy, who was receiving hoots and shouts from the girls jumping to their feet.

Now that the women were standing, he could see they all wore skimpy black dresses, a few of them with a white sash with *Bridesmaid* on them. Lea's had *Maid-of-honor,* and his sister's said *Bride-to-be.* Ah, hell, she had a crown on her head, too, with some sort of frilly pink stuff sticking out. Yet, instead of looking ridiculous, Brandi managed to look cute.

And even though it should've been weird to watch his brother and the cowboy shaking their junk in front of a bunch of screaming women, Ben found it vaguely amusing, as did the rest of the guys who all leaned against the wall and snickered.

On stage, Kevin and Keiffer slowly unbuttoned their shirts then tossed them to Shayla and Caitlin. All the girls whistled and hooted some more.

How the hell did his brother know to dance that like?

Kevin continued to shake it, and when his hands when to his belt buckle, Shayla got up on stage and stopped him.

"Okay, cowboy. Enough," she told him with a grin. "The rest of you is all mine, and you know I don't share very well."

An unfamiliar tug pulled at Ben's gut. He didn't recognize the emotion, but he did recognize the shaft of envy that followed. In all his years, no woman had ever treated him like he mattered more than what he could provide—whether it was sex or help or safety.

The shared respect and affection he saw pass between Kevin and Shayla was something Ben hadn't ever realized existed anymore. The one and only time he'd seen it was with his dad and Brandi's mom, who was an exception. He suspected all four cowboys had found exceptional women, and wondered if they knew how damn lucky they had it.

Hopefully, for their sakes, it would last more than a few years, because it would inevitably end.

It always did.

"Well now, darlin'." Kevin grinned, pulling Shayla close. "You know you're the only one for me."

The beautiful redhead stood on tiptoe and kissed the cowboy.

"Smooth." Ryder grinned, shaking his head.

Cole nodded. "He wasn't dubbed the Casanova cowboy for nothing."

"I'd say the Japanese triplets helped him gain that fame," Connor added.

Jesus...

"Trip-whats?" Ethan blinked at the tall cowboy.

"Three women at the same time?" Even Mason got in on the conversation.

"Yep, and the same night." Cole nodded. "It was a few years back when we went to Japan for a tradeshow."

153

"Your cousin's crazy," he told Kade, who stood there, shaking his head, a small smile tugging his lips.

"So's your brother," his soon-to-be-brother-in-law replied, nodding toward a shirtless Keiffer before taking a pull of his beer.

Ben laughed. "Yeah, sorry."

The man turned to him and frowned. "Why?"

"Because in two days time, you'll be related to them both."

The Texan threw his head back and laughed, which caught the attention of the bride-to-be...and the rest of the women.

Ah, hell.

Ben would've been happy to remain anonymous in the back, but now he had no choice but to join the others by the make-shift stage. So much for his comfort zone. The cowgirls claimed their men with rather heated kisses, which left the rest of the guys to congregate around Lea, Caitlin, Jill from the chocolate place, and Gwen.

The latter he'd already greeted when he'd bumped into her in the hall before the parties had started. He no longer felt the punch to his gut whenever he was in the presence of the beautiful, long-legged blonde. That sensation had disappeared along with his teenage years. Although they couldn't exactly be classified as friends, they'd both gotten over their past and had no issues tolerating each other.

As he drew closer, he held back, letting the others go ahead of him. He noted interesting shaped chocolate candy and an assortment of suggestive party favors on the table. *Damn*. He'd wager the girls were a bit more rowdy than the guys, which surprised him considering he knew they'd spent the day traipsing around New York City. All that walking and shopping and stuff should've made them tired.

Wishing he could sneak out as quietly as he'd snuck in, Ben swallowed his groan down with the rest of his beer, then quickly glanced around for another. That's when he caught sight of Lea laughing at something one of the cowboys had said. It wasn't a forced laugh, or little giggle. It was a real, honest laugh that only Lea could deliver with a combination of grace and effervescence.

Jace and Tanner sandwiched her, looking like they'd...well, like they'd be happy to sample some of her effervescence. His empty hand curled into a fist. If they tried anything, he'd...

What?

These feelings of possessiveness and protectiveness over her were not new, and he was beginning to realize that maybe there was a reason. But he had no hold on her. No claim. And it was his own damn fault.

Feeling as if he'd gotten run over by that damn tank again, he set his empty bottle on the table and blew out a breath.

She *meant* something to him.

That's what the tight feeling was in his chest, the one that knocked him on his ass.

How had that happened?

Lea glanced to him, smile still lingering on her very kissable lips. And instead of her guard coming up and smile fading, her grin increased and gaze warmed until it was hot, blazing hot, and aimed directly at him.

The tanked reversed and rolled back over him. Twice.

Then she hit him with a look that said, *I've had sex with you, and I'd be happy to have sex with you again.*
Shit.

Chapter Nine

"Hey, Ben." Brandi stopped in front of him and stood on tip-toe to kiss his cheek. "I was coming over here to thank you for keeping Kade out of trouble, but it looks like you've found some of your own." She motioned toward Lea with her head. "Although, I'm not sure exactly what the trouble is, Lea looks quite interested in you."

"That's the trouble," he said, trying not to notice how the cowboys were back to sandwiching the woman again.

By her relaxed posture and genuine smile, she didn't appear to mind at all. He glanced at the half-empty glass in her hand. How much wine did she have?

"You don't want her to be interested in you?"

"No."

"So, it's okay then if Jace asks her to be his date for the wedding?"

That got his attention. "No. Yes. Why? Did he say he was going to ask her?"

Damn Texans worked fast.

Brandi laughed and set her palm on his chest. "Relax, Ben. No, he didn't say a word. I was just curious."

Jesus, she nearly gave him a heart attack. His chest continued to feel the weight of that damn tank.

"Are you still going to help me convince her to come to Harland County with me when I get back from my honeymoon?"

He opened his mouth, ready to say, *Sure, of course*...but the words wouldn't form. There were more cowboys there. What if one...

Brandi smiled, placing her finger under his jaw to close his mouth. "It's okay. You're smart. I know you'll get it sooner or later."

He was glad she was convinced, because he sure as shit was not. All he knew was he didn't want to hurt Lea. He promised himself he'd leave her alone. He'd let her enjoy her stay in the Poconos with her dad without taking advantage of her.

But watching her laugh and joke with Jill, her brother and sister and Brandi's friends from Texas, he realized he enjoyed being around the unpretentious woman. She didn't put on any airs, didn't made demands. She just made him feel good. And when her gaze met his again and turned just a little bit naughty, he was hard in an instant, and he had to fight the urge to go to her, pull her close and extract one of her hot kisses.

"Well, because I love you, and I love her, too, I'm going to do you a favor and help you out," Brandi said, slapping her palm against his chest again.

Ah, hell. "What does that mean?"

"Nothing."

Nothing my ass. That determined gaze glinting in her brown eyes always managed to scare the shit out of him.

Before he knew it, his sister hooked her arm through his, but instead of pulling him toward Lea, she led him out of the room.

"Are you okay?" he asked as she guided him back to the deserted bachelor party.

Once inside, she let him go and headed to the food. "Just a little hungry. It's time for my snack, and, boy, the smell of this food was killing me."

It did smell good.

Brandi cut a slice of pizza in half and placed one part on her plate and handed him the other. Since being

157

diagnosed with Hashimoto thyroiditus a few years ago, Brandi had adjusted her eating habits to several small meals and snacks throughout the day, plus, she didn't go over a certain calorie count since she had absolutely no metabolism left. Before the diagnosis, this had caused her to gain over fifty pounds. He was proud of her and her determination to lose the unwanted weight and drop down to where she didn't have trouble breathing walking up the steps.

Ben was used to being his sister's garbage disposal. A twinge of sadness rocked through his chest. He'd actually missed it the past year and a half. As he ate all the *halves* she placed on his plate, he wondered if Kade was her disposal now.

"Here she is. I found her," Lea called, walking into the room, followed by Kade. "Kind of thought it might be snack time." She walked to the table and grabbed a plate without missing a beat. "The smell of these wings were tempting me all dang night."

"Yeah, me, too." Brandi nodded. "Not that I didn't enjoy my chocolate snack a few hours ago." His sister waggled her brows at her friend. "That was quite a mouthful."

Lea snorted, and had to place a hand over her mouth to keep the chicken from flying the coop.

God, she was adorable.

After a few swallows, she wiped her hand on a napkin then drank the water he handed her. "Thanks," she said, then smacked Brandi. "Next time, wait until I don't have a mouthful."

"Sorry." His sister's eyes sparkled too much for him to believe her words. She finished her food, then tossed her plate and walked over to Lea and hugged her. "Thanks for taking me and the others to the city today, and for the party. It was a ton of fun."

"You're welcome. I'm glad you enjoyed it. The girls asked me to get the dancer, but they should've just told me to ask Kevin instead."

Brandi drew back and laughed. "Yeah, and my brother Keiffer. Who knew? Did you, Ben?"

He shook his head. "Hell no. And I don't think I want to know."

Kade chuckled, then thrust out his hand. "Thanks for keeping my party 'dancer' free."

"My pleasure." Ben shook his soon-to-be-brother-in-law's hand then released him. "But like I said, Kevin really was the one who planned it. I just put in the orders."

"Well, in any case, thanks for helping with this, and the whole wedding. You, too, Lea. Both of you have made things so much easier for Brandi."

Lea smiled. "You're welcome."

"Thanks, Ben." His sister stepped close and hugged him tight.

"Any time," he said, hugging her back.

God, he'd missed her, and until that moment, locked in one of her special Brandi hugs, the kind that was sure, and tight, and warm, Ben hadn't realized how much.

"Well, what do you say, hun?" She released him and turned to Kade. "Ready?"

"Yes." The cowboy nodded, gaze affectionate as he stole a kiss. "Any chance we can call it a night?"

His sister's smile grew. "I'd say there was a great chance of that. Why do you think I snuck out?"

"Beautiful and smart. I knew there was a reason I was marrying you."

"You mean it's not for my endearing, clutzy nature?"

"Well, there's that, too."

159

The happy couple disappeared into the hall, which left him alone with Lea and his attraction for the misty-eyed woman. His gut twisted at the look of deep envy darkening her watery gaze. She brushed at her face. Then sniffed. Then brushed her face again.

"Dammit. There's something wrong with my eyes," she said, groping for a napkin.

Losing the inner battle to keep his distance, Ben grabbed a napkin and proceeded to gently wipe her face. "Better?"

"Yes." She nodded, but more tears spilled over. "Shoot. I'm sorry. It's just so dang good to see Brandi happy and loved by a man who actually appreciates her, faults and all. God, who does that anymore? You know what I mean?"

He nodded, not trusting his mouth to keep things uncomplicated. But he should've been worried about more than speech, because his mouth took over for the napkin and carefully, and with great precision, kissed the wetness from her cheeks.

Nothing complicated about that.

Or the fact he thrust his hands into her hair and held her head while his mouth finally found hers, and he kissed her long and deep. All the tension coiled inside him ready to snap. The anxiety and heaviness in his chest dissipated from his body as they held onto each other, and he reacquainted himself with her taste.

Damn, he loved her taste, was addicted to her taste, couldn't get enough of her taste or the feel of her. He ran his hand over her sexy little black dress that had been driving him nuts since they'd crashed the bachelorette party, cupped her breast and brushed his thumb over her tight peak.

She moaned, and the low, hungry noises she made in the back of her throat had him, hard and hot, and, oh hell yeah, bothered.

Her hands were everywhere, too. In his hair, brushing his collarbone, down his chest, slowly stroking his abs…driving him crazy with need.

She drew back, ragged breaths puffing into his face. "Thanks."

He stared into her hazy gaze, flushed cheeks, puffy lips still wet from his kiss, and he blanked again. *Damn it.*

"For…taking care of me."

He'd like to take care of her. Right into his damn bed. And would've told her…or showed her, but Keiffer choose that moment to call for him from down the hall.

They broke apart, and he twisted around to face the door, using his body as a shield to block her from view while she readjusted her dress.

"Ben? There you are," his brother said, waltzing into the room. "You missed it, bro. Kevin was teaching me and some of the guys how to bust a move. It was classic. We—" Keiffer grabbed a piece of pizza, then stopped dead when he spotted Lea standing behind him. "Oh, hi, Lea. Sorry, my bad. Carry on. I was never here." He set his pizza down and began to back out of the room, his gaze colliding with Ben's. "Maybe you didn't blow it."

Running a smirking gaze over him one last time, his brother disappeared into the hall with a big ass smile on his face. Ben was pretty sure he knew the reason for the grin. Because of the huge boner straining the zipper in his jeans.

"What was that all about?"

He twisted around to face her and shrugged. "Who knows with Kief."

"You do. You know how everyone is."

"He shoots his mouth off without thinking sometimes."

She just stared at him, waiting for him to continue.

"He thinks he knows what's good for everyone but himself."

"Sounds like another Wyne."

"Yeah, Mason should really work on that, too."

"You know that's not who I meant," she said quietly. "You don't want to talk about *you*. I'm getting too close again. You need your distance."

When he didn't confirm or deny, *couldn't* confirm or deny because he had no damn idea, she sighed softly, sadly, and walk out of the room.

Lea spent the day working at the restaurant, happy for the steady flow of customers to keep her too busy to think about Ben or her lack of restraint when he was around. Darn man had made it clear, numerous times, he didn't want anything more from her. But whenever she got too close to the man, all her brain cells took flight, and she made the mistake of giving into her attraction.

Well, no more. Nope. She wasn't going to let herself fall into that trap of desire again. It wasn't his fault, either. She knew this. The guy did try to keep his distance, but something would happen to throw them together then…*Bam*. They were lip-locked and ready to explode.

"Heard Gwen was in town," Mr. Tierney said, buttering his bread. "That true?"

"Yep." Lea nodded, grabbing the pot of coffee. "She came back with us yesterday when the girls and I went into the city."

"Must've been awkward for Ben to be at the same party with the two of you."

How in the world had Mr. Tierney heard about the guys crashing the bachelorette party?

"He managed." She refilled his coffee before escaping into the kitchen only to stop dead when Gwen entered through the back door.

"I figured you were here," her sister said, reaching for an apron hooked on the wall.

Lea frowned. "What are you doing?"

"I'm relieving you. It's already going for three. You should be at the lodge getting ready for the rehearsal and dinner."

She blinked. "Who are you, and what have you done with my sister?"

Gwen laughed. "I know, I'm usually the last person to be considerate or responsible, but I'm trying to change that."

Lea nodded. "Okay, but are you sure? It's been a few years since you've worked here, and it can get nuts on a Friday."

"No worries. I remember. Now, go and have a good time, and don't worry about coming home tonight after the dinner. You should stay at the lodge like the others so you're there bright and early for Brandi in the morning."

Lea's heart rocked in her chest. She grabbed her sister's hands and peered into her eyes. "What's wrong? Are you sure you're okay? You can tell me anything. You know that."

Gwen's gaze grew watery, but she blinked the tears away and squeezed Lea's hands. "I'm fine, and so sorry that my trying to help is so out of character that you think I'm sick or in trouble. I promise you, I'm neither." Her sister pulled her into a hug and some kind of emotion akin to guilt fluttered in Lea's stomach.

She should probably tell Gwen about Ben before she heard it from someone else, if she hadn't already. Clearing her throat, she drew back and blurted it out. "I slept with Ben."

The clattering of pots reminded her they weren't alone. She glanced at the cook who tried to look busy, even thought he'd heard all this last week when Ryder was here with the Wynes.

"I know," her sister said, regaining Lea's attention.

"You do?"

"Yeah, at least, I suspected. Man, the way he looked at you last night, devouring you with his gaze, he never did that with me."

She didn't even know how to respond to that.

"Maybe it's because we never had sex."

The sound of a ladle hitting the floor echoed through the kitchen, but Lea was too busy reeling to care. She ushered her sister into the storage room, flicked on the light and closed the door.

"You and Ben never had sex? I find that really hard to believe, Gwen. I walked in on you two making out downstairs, remember?"

"Of course I remember, but that's all you walked in on. Me and Ben making out. We never took it any further." Her sister began to pace. "In hindsight, I wish we had, I'm sure it would've been a hell of a lot better to lose my virginity to him than that bastard photographer."

Lea just stared, trying to take in what her sister was saying.

"Anyway." Her gorgeous sibling stopped and blew out a breath. "I just wanted you to know I was happy for you. Ben's a good guy, and he deserves someone good like you."

That scared Lea. God, did her sister not think she was a good person? "You deserve to be happy, too."

Gwen laughed. "Maybe. I need to work on myself first, then worry about finding a man, besides, they all only want to be with Gwen Gabel, not Gwen Gablonski. Never Gwen Gablonski," she muttered under her breath.

Lea set a hand on her sister's shoulder and squeezed. "Then you just haven't met the right one, yet."

Color entered her sister's cheeks.

Or maybe she had met him…

"No, don't. This isn't about me. It's about you and Ben."

Now it was her turn to laugh. "There is no me and Ben."

"What do you mean? I thought you said you slept together."

"I did…we did. But he doesn't want more."

"Honey, that's not what his gaze was saying last night."

What the hell was everyone seeing that she wasn't? "Well, then you're wrong, or he's too stubborn. It doesn't matter anyway. Next week, I'm going to start sending out resumes."

"For museums in the city?" Gwen's gaze sparkled with excitement.

"Yes." She nodded, unable to stop the answering smile. "Dad's therapist said if he stays on target, he'll be able to come back to work sometime in November."

"Oh, Lea, that's terrific." Gwen pulled her close. "I'm glad for him, and for you. I know you've waited for so long and had to work at that museum in Philadelphia for two years to fulfill part of your scholarship. And now you're schlepping at the train museum until Dad is better. But here's the thing, I'll stay with him."

Something was definitely wrong. "You want to leave New York?"

"Yes. I know that sounds crazy after all these years. I mean, I do love the city, but I don't know. I need a change. I'm tired of modeling. I'm actually starting to get too old for it, but I'm not interested in moving on to acting or anything like that." Her sigh filled the air between them. "I'm not sure what I want. Just something not industry related."

"I'm sorry, hun. Sounds like you've had something happen."

Tears filled her sister's eyes again, but she blinked them back, again. "Yeah, but I don't want to talk about it right now. Okay? I'm good. And in a few weeks my contract runs out and I've already told my manager I'm not renewing."

Lea pulled her sister in for another hug and held onto her for a few minutes. "Okay, I won't pry, but you know you can tell me anything, right?"

"I know. And thanks. Same goes for you," Gwen stated, then drew back and sniffed. "Now, go on with you. Have fun with Brandi and her Texas friends. They seemed really nice."

"They are." Lea nodded. "Are you sure about tonight? Brandi does have a room reserved for me, but I told her I wasn't sure if I was going to use it. I'm okay with driving back in the morning."

Although, staying there tonight would be so much easier to be at her friend's beck and call for last minute details and mishaps.

"I'm sure. Now go. And I'll see you all tomorrow at the wedding. Dad is excited about going. He hasn't stopped talking about it. Poor guy is going stir crazy I think."

A shaft of guilt shot through Lea's gut. She should probably start taking him out to more than just doctor's appointments now that he was somewhat mobile.

"If you have any trouble—"

"I'll call Ryder."

She laughed. "Okay. I'll see you all tomorrow." Lea opened the door then turned around to face her sister. "Thanks."

A genuine smile lit Gwen from the inside out, and she radiated beauty. The effect stole Lea's breath. Her sister's beauty had always stolen her breath.

"You're welcome."

On the short drive home, she called Brandi to let her know she'd be staying the night, then she called Ryder to see if he knew what had happened to their sister to make her want to give up a career she used to eat, drink and breath. He had no clue.

Whatever it was, Lea would figure it out.

It would take something pretty traumatic or powerful to cause her to give up on her dream. She couldn't imagine giving up the life she loved.

Ben was running late. He hated being late. The only times he was ever behind were because he had to wait around for someone…and they were late. Or his reports were not on time because he had to wait for others to finish theirs first, and they were late. He didn't mind helping people out, he really didn't, but when they didn't do their job and others suffered? That didn't cut it with him. Like today. He'd taken five days leave and wasn't supposed to work today, but someone had dropped the ball and forgot to order rations for a Gap drill next month, and it was past the required sixty day window to get food ordered. So, he had to step in, call in some favors, smooth over a few feathers, and make sure the soldiers were taken care of for October's drill.

Now, he was running late for his sister's wedding rehearsal.

At three-thirty-six, he was out the door and halfway to his truck when he changed course and headed to Gabe's. Something was drawing him there, pulling him, and he'd learned long ago to never ignore those feelings when they hit.

Maybe Lea was there and just happened to need a ride.

As he entered the restaurant, he half-expected—no, he was hoping—to see her smiling face. He was pathetic. But it was the truth. He hadn't slept much last night. Hell, he hadn't been sleeping good for the past few weeks, ever since Lea had…

He stopped dead just as he reached the counter, and Gwen came out of the kitchen, hair in a ponytail, blue apron over her designer dress, carrying a tray of food. She halted and nearly lost the entrées, but he darted forward and helped her to right the tray.

"Thanks," she said, face red, but she moved past him and delivered the food to an elderly couple sitting in a corner booth and a party of three sitting near the window.

"You just missed her."

He twisted around to see Mr. Tierney sitting at his usual perch at the counter.

"Missed who?"

"The other sister." The older man smiled.

Damn, then that meant he was drawn here to see Gwen. He couldn't imagine why. They had nothing to say to each other. None that he could think of, anyway. Not in the mood, he headed for the door, but his ex-girlfriend moved pretty quick in heels and blocked his escape.

"Don't leave. We need to talk."

He leveled her with a stare.

Her face turned pink, but she didn't move. "Please."

It wasn't the word, or her beauty or their past that had him relent and nod. No. It was the sincerity he'd seen in her pleading gaze that had him following the model-dressed-as-a-waitress into the kitchen, past a startled cook, then into a storage room where she shut the door.

Ah hell. "Look, Gwen, I don't know what this is about, but I really don't have the time."

"It's about Lea."

He had the time.

"Is she okay?" His heart rocked in his chest. He hadn't felt anything to the contrary, but his radar was all out of whack lately.

"She's fine, although she could certainly be better."

He blew out a breath. "You need to get to the point."

"Okay. I wanted to say I was sorry."

The one thing he'd longed to hear in his teens, but had never expected to hear from her just left her lips. A decade too late. He stared.

"I should've said that many years ago, I know. And for that I'm sorry, too."

Wow, two apologies.

"Are you okay?" This was not at all like Gwen. He had to admit, he was starting to worry about her.

"Lea asked me the same thing a half-hour ago when I came in here and made her leave."

She smiled, a genuine smile that lit the room. The kind that used to light his world, but now left him feeling nothing.

"I'm fine, or at least, I will be after I try to make amends for what I did to you," she said, with that earnestness still in her gaze. "It was wrong, and I'm sorry, and I should've told you sooner. But I was stupid and young. I know that's no excuse, but it is the truth. I got caught up in the ambience of France, and dealing with the new world of modeling, and being the center of attention. It went to my head, and I let it shove you out. I screwed you over, Ben, and I'm so very sorry. That's no way for a human being to treat another." Tears filled her eyes and ran down her face.

And even though she didn't deserve it, he felt sorry for her.

She brushed her tears away and lifted her chin. "I just wanted you to know you deserved better than the way I treated you. And I'm so happy you've let Lea into your life. She'd never let you take a backseat. You deserve someone good and kindhearted like my sister."

Those invisible bands returned to squeeze the hell out of his chest. "No. I don't. I'm not the relationship type."

"Because of me." More tears ran unchecked. "Oh, Ben, don't do that. Don't shut out all that is good in you, all that deserves to be shared."

"You're giving yourself more credit than you deserve, Gwen. Yeah, you didn't help revise my opinion of women and relationships, but I'd already had a crash course in that before and after you."

"Then you apparently need a different one, because there are relationships out there that do work, and Ben, they can be wonderful. So wonderful it makes all the hurts go away."

Her gaze became dreamy and warm and something in her sincere tone told him she was talking from experience.

"You have to be willing to work at it, but first of all, you have to be willing to give the relationship a try."

This was the first time since they were in high school that Gwen had ever talked to him from the heart. Because of that, he respected what she was trying to say and do, and didn't remind her he wasn't looking for a relationship.

"It doesn't have to be a marriage kind of thing," she continued, stepping close. "All I'm saying is open up, Ben, and let—"

"Lea in." He blew out a breath. "I get it, Gwen, but I told you, I'm not interested. And she could do better."

"That's just it, you're wrong on both accounts."

He frowned, and she laughed.

"I was going to say you need to open up and give yourself permission to feel. Let someone get to know the *real* you, because you're pretty terrific… And Lea does. You're also wrong about my sister when you said she could do better than you, because she can't."

If Gwen was trying to help, it wasn't working. The tightness in his chest increased, and his need to escape propelled him to the door. "I've got to go."

Yeah, he was wuss, but didn't care, and wasn't lying. Rehearsal was at four thirty, and it was already almost four.

"Okay, but are we good?" she asked, grabbing his arm.

He stared down at the woman who had broken his teenage heart all those years ago, finding her just as beautiful, if not more, but he didn't feel any attraction, or anger, or pain. Just a little bit of sadness that she'd blown a good thing for nothing.

It wasn't for nothing, his mind insisted. They'd been wrong for each other, and she'd done him a favor; although, she could've handled it better. This realization eased something inside him. A smile tugged at his lips, and he nodded at her.

"Yeah, we're good."

Tears filled her eyes again. *Ah, hell.*

"Thank you." She released him to swipe her face. "And remember what I said about Lea. The two of you are good for each other. Take a chance, Ben. Let her in. Life's too short. Have some fun. It'll do you good." With that, she released him and opened the door. "Now, you'd better hurry or Brandi will be stressing."

If there was one thing he took away from Gwen's unexpected open talk, it was that women were damn confusing.

And now he was really running late.

Making up for lost time on the back roads, Ben arrived at the lodge with seven minutes to spare. Enough time to take the tux he'd picked up that morning from the rental shop, and his duffle bag, up to his room, then change into black dress pants and gray dress shirt.

He was tucking in his shirt as he rushed to the outdoor gazebo and pavilion area Brandi had them add for weddings. Brilliant idea. The place was practically booked solid all spring, summer and fall. He and his brothers had been surprised by how many couples wanted outdoor weddings. But with the mountains and lake as a backdrop, he had to admit, it was actually a decent setting.

"There he is," someone shouted.

"Now, we just need the reverend," Keiffer said.

Good. At least he wasn't the only one late. He nodded to his brother, smiled at his beautiful sister, all glowing and happy, then he spotted Lea, and his heart caught. All the tension and anxiety and frustration of the day did its magic disappearing act, again.

She was hugging Kade, smiling her usual smile, the one with her heart in her gaze, the one he felt clear to his bones and knocked him on his ass. And today, God, today she was absolutely gorgeous in a royal blue dress with a little hint at cleavage, and a lacey, cutout type thing making an upside down V above her left knee. Then there were her shoes. *Damn.* It didn't take much for him to imagine her in nothing but those black do-me heels.

He couldn't take his gaze off her.

That continued through most of the evening. Try as he might, Ben's gaze kept returning to Lea, all through the rehearsal and dinner, and even now, as the wedding party sat in the corner at the Knotty Pine, enjoying a final round before calling it a night. Nursing his beer, he vaguely listened to the conversation, watching Lea's animated expressions, captivated by the life in her face as she recanted a story about the girls and their outing yesterday in New York City.

"I bet that caused a stir." Connor chuckled.

"Seven women with hot dogs in their hands running after the guy in Grand Central Station? Yeah, you could say that."

Wait...what? His stomach suddenly knotted. Who were they running after? Were they trying to get hurt? He'd been too distracted by Lea's beauty to let her words sink in.

"Dude picked the wrong place to snatch-n-grab." Brandi laughed.

Chapter Ten

"Right in front of a Texas sheriff," his sister continued.

Jordan nodded. "Lights were on, but nobody was home."

Cole hugged his wife's shoulder and kissed the top of her head.

How could he be okay with that? Jesus, they could've been hurt. They had no business running after a thief. The knot in Ben's stomach twisted.

He hated that goddamn city.

"Well…" Kevin rose to his feet. "My cousin's getting married in the morning, so I'd better get my beauty sleep so as not to embarrass the kin."

Kade rose, too, slapping his cousin on the back. "Not enough sleep in the world for that, Kev."

A collective laugh went around the group, all rising to their feet. Good. He could call it a night, too. The newly disclosed information about the girls doing a rundown in the city had ratcheted up his tension, and caused a dull throbbing behind his eyes.

But he wouldn't sleep. He was too keyed up to sleep. He'd probably exchange his beer for a scotch and sit outside for a bit.

"Goodnight," Brandi said, hugging and kissing everyone.

He was hanging back, talking to the McCalls as the room cleared.

"You've got a great spread here," Connor said, dropping his arm around his wife as Cole and Jordan nodded in agreement.

"Thanks," he said. "Brandi was key in getting the place up and running." Something he and his brother never took for granted.

"Well, I'm warning you now, we'll be back up here again next year, but we won't be alone."

Ben had been surprised to discover at dinner both Kerri and Shayla were in a first trimester or something of pregnancy. Other than their pallor, the two hadn't shown any signs.

He smiled, and held out his hand. "Congratulations. I heard."

The big guy's grin couldn't have grown wider or his chest broader. "Thanks," Connor said, shaking his hand. "But I had help."

Ben laughed with the others. "Well then, congratulations to you, too, Kerri."

"Thanks." She smacked her husband's chest, then yawned. "Sorry, I never realized how tiring it could be. I'm exhausted, but haven't done much all day."

In a swift move, the cowboy scooped up his wife, and her startled cry echoed around them.

"Put me down, you big goof. I can walk."

"I know, darlin'." Connor winked at his wife. "But I like you right where you are."

And with a nod to him, Cole and Jordan, the cowboy ambled out of the bar and disappeared.

Jordan glanced up at Cole and smiled. "Did you ever, in million years, think that would happen?"

"No," her husband immediately answered, gaze full of affection and warmth. "I just thank my lucky stars every day that our parents had 40th wedding anniversaries that brought you and your sister back into our lives three years ago."

Ben stilled for a minute. Their parents were both married *over forty years*? Well hell, he'd never known anyone married that long. And still happy, by the looks of it, too. He'd met the older McCalls and Masters yesterday when they'd arrived with Kade's cousin Jen, her husband Brock and their five-year-old son Cody, whom Tyler had been ecstatic to see again. The two couples still held hands. He had to admit, it had been nice to see.

"Uh oh. Lea forgot her bag," Jordan said, holding up a small, light green gift bag Brandi had given to each of her attendants. "She's staying in the guest room in the residence area by you. Can you give it to her?"

Shit. No. "Sure."

She handed him the bag and smiled. "Thanks." Then she turned to her husband who had a small smile twitching his lips as he shook his head for some reason.

"Come on, Mrs. McCall, before you get into more trouble," Cole said, then glanced at him, his gaze appearing almost apologetic. "Good night, Ben."

"Yeah, have a good night, Ben." Jordan's grin grew wicked before she turned around and walked out of the room with her arm around her husband.

Having no idea what any of that was about, Ben eyed the scotch behind the bar, longingly, but left with the damn bag clutched in his hand instead. Picking up his pace, he headed for the residence area, hoping to catch Lea before she made it to her room. The last thing he need was to be alone with the woman in a room with a bed. Ah hell, what was he saying, they didn't need a bed.

The sexy woman's sweet scent drove him crazy all night. She smelled like cotton candy, and he wanted to eat her up, and go back for seconds. And thirds.

Shit.

Now he was hard. Again. His zipper dug into the erection he'd sported most of the night thanks to her sexy, damn dress with peek-a-boo lace and her mile-long legs.

By the time he passed through the common area, it was quiet. Too quiet. *Damn.* Everyone was in their rooms. Including Lea.

Making his way to her door, he set a time limit in his head. One minute…two minutes tops, that was how long he gave himself to hand over the bag and get out of her room.

No. Hell no. He wasn't even going to *step foot* in her room. Just hand over the bag from the hall. *Yes*, he nodded to himself as he stopped outside her door, staying in the hall was the smart thing to do.

Shoulders back, resolve set, he checked the time on his phone, then knocked on her door.

One minute. Two tops.

"Ben?" Lea frowned as she opened the door, still wearing that sexy, damn dress. "Is everything okay?"

"Yes…no." *Damn it.* He cleared his throat and shoved the bag at her. "Jordan said you forgot this, and asked me to bring it to you."

Mission accomplished in less than a minute, and he was still in the hall.

"But it's not mine."

Shit.

He pushed the bag back at her, this time *into* her, his knuckles brushing fabric and skin…soft skin.

She took the bag, small smile tugging her lips as she stared at him. "I'm almost afraid to look inside."

Not my problem. Turn around. Walk away. "Why?" *Damn.* He was pathetic.

"That's why," she answered, pointing to something just inside the door.

Careful to keep his feet in the hall, Ben leaned in a little and glanced at…an identical bag sitting on the credenza.

"So, if Jordan said this is mine, then…"

He watched, pulse beginning to pound loudly in his head, as she stuck her hand inside the bag and pulled out…another sexy, damn negligee. His heart rocked in chest as she sucked in a breath and choked out a laugh. He was going to kill Jordan…right after Lea finished killing him, with the flush that swept into her face and heat seeping into her gaze.

"She is so wicked."

So were his thoughts.

And the woman didn't help when she dropped the bag and held the light green lacy number against her lush body.

"She sure knows my size."

So did he.

And oh, look it was all ready for her. Standing at attention. Behind his zipper. Wrinkle free.

The same couldn't be said for his mind; it was rutted with restrictions and caution as it battled with his body's need to step over the threshold and take her up on the silent invitation blazing in her eyes.

"What do you think?" she asked, molding the silky material to her curves.

He wanted her, there was no denying the fact, but Ben knew by giving into need this time, if he *let go*, he was agreeing to have sex as friends for the next few weeks until she left.

Sex with the sexy-as-sin woman.

Often…

What the hell was wrong with him? Of course he wanted that.

Leaving the hall and his restrictions behind, he stepped inside her room and closed the door. "Any chance of you slipping into that?"

The thought made him throb. A sinful gleam entered her eyes and stopped his heart.

"Yes, but I'm pretty sure you'll like the one I'm already wearing."

Ah, hell. His stopped heart dropped to his throbbing groin. "You're wearing sexy lingerie under *that* right now?"

Her lips curved into a secret smile. "Yep. I've been wearing it *all* night."

Everything inside him stirred. Hard.

"But before I show you, I think we need to be clear on what we're doing. Agreed?"

"Agreed."

"So…what *are* we doing, Ben?"

Damn, he hoped this wasn't a trick question, because he wasn't firing on all cylinders. A serious blue gaze stared at him…waiting.

He sucked in a breath and latched onto the first thing that came to his mind. "Having fun?"

Apparently, it was the right answer, because her smile returned; the one that always reached in and chased away the chill around his heart.

"For a few weeks?" she asked, gaze hopeful and wide. "Until I leave?"

He nodded, not trusting his voice, because when he stared into her eyes, he wanted to touch her, hold her, be with her. Those thoughts, those needs petrified him. But not enough to make him leave.

"Good," she said, reaching behind her to unzip the dress and send his pulse into the outer hemisphere. "Because I'm a friend, and you're a-Ben-that-fits."

179

He choked out a laugh, then swallowed his tongue as her dress fell to the floor revealing a one-piece, black satin number that hugged her hourglass curves to perfection. Still wearing her sexy black heels, she stepped out of the dress then turned around so he could have a heart attack.

There wasn't one inch of her he didn't want to kiss or lick or touch.

She sucked in a breath. "W-what are you thinking right now? Your eyes are like emeralds…"

"That you're sexy as hell, and I want to take you with your shoes on."

She trembled in front of him, but held his gaze, hers darkening to a delicious navy. "Then take me."

Damn. She was bold, and it turned him on. Big time.

Years of practice at following orders, Ben knew the drill and was more than happy to comply. He stepped to her and lightly trailed his fingers up her arms, holding back a smile as she trembled under his touch. "Yes, ma'am," he said, wrapping his fingers in her hair as he tipped her head to the side and leaned in to inhale her scent.

She smelled great, like woman and candy and heat. He brushed her throat with his lips then sunk his teeth in the curve where her neck met her shoulder. She gasped and clutched at his arms, breathing his name.

"Yes, ma'am," he repeated before he covered her mouth with his, kissing her a little desperate, a lot hot, and very deep.

Pressing his tongue to hers in the same glide and pull his body ached to achieve, he ran his hands down her curves, stroking and caressing with equal fervor. She was soft, so damn soft and hot. He drew back, untied her satin straps and watched, his body tightening, as he tugged the black satin down her mouthwatering breasts, until her nipples were freed. "Perfect," he muttered before dipping to suck one peak in his mouth and cup the other with his hand.

"Mmm…" Her grip on his arms tightened, and she leaned into him, filling his mouth with more of her delectable curves.

When he switched his attention to the other nipple, he trailed his hand between her quivering thighs, finding her wet.

Her breath shuddered out in a sexy, low purr, and his need to taste the woman increased to an unreasonable, insatiable ache. He released her, tugged the silky garment down her body until it hit the floor and she stood before him completely, gloriously naked—except for her black do-me heels.

Finally.

"All damn night, I wanted you in nothing but those heels," he murmured, running his lips and hands up her naked body, lingering on some of his favorite parts, until he had her panting and sweating.

"I-I don't think I…c-can stand," she said, voice shaky with need.

"No problem." Kissing her neck, he guided her backward to the cushioned bench in front of the bed and helped her sit down. "I've got you." He dropped to his knees, spread her legs with his shoulders and kissed one inner thigh, then the other. Then in between.

Her breath caught as she grabbed his head, and her fevered responses fueled his desire to give her more. Running his tongue over her in feather-light strokes, he increased the pressure when she wiggled against him.

The mewling sound she made nearly ripped him in two.

He lengthened his stroke, and she cried out and arched up into his mouth.

"You taste so damn sweet." *So damn sweet.* He licked her again.

"Ben—" She thrust into him and clutched his head.

He upped the pace and pressure of the stroke. With a long, low moan, she bucked up off the cushions, but he held her, and stayed with her, watching her as she exploded, nearly taking him with her. Eyes glazed over, head thrown back, she had her bottom lip pulled between her teeth as she rocked against him.

So damned hot.

Letting her down gently, he moved his mouth to inner thigh, then slowly drew back before he stood and stared down at her. "I needed that."

He also needed to be inside the sensual woman eying him with a lazy, sinful smile.

"Me, too."

Her satisfied sigh shook through him.

"You have on too many clothes."

What he wanted to have on was *her*, so he stripped in several, swift, economical movements. "Better?"

She smiled a wicked ass smile. "Almost…"

Before he knew it, her hands were on his hips and she twisted them around so he was seated and she was kneeling.

"Better," she murmured, surging up to put her mouth on his chest while her hands pressed into his thighs to keep him there. "Much better." Her lips moved lower.

"Wait. Don't…" He grabbed her shoulders to hoist her up, but he was too late.

Her fingers wrapped around his erection, and she licked him.

He muttered a curse. He wasn't going to last. "Lea...don't. I want to come inside you."

She glanced up, heat smoldering in her eyes, steeling his strength. Shit. He nearly lost it right then.

"You will." She licked him up one side then down the other. "I promise."

A light sheen of sweat broke out over his shoulders and chest. "This isn't how—damn—"

Her tongue swirled over the tip of him and he groaned, the deep rumbling sound filled the air between them. Then she slowly took him into her mouth.

Ah, hell. She was so warm and wet and moving in a rhythm he loved. "Lea..." The exquisite feeling became too much. His hands moved to her hair, and he closed his eyes as his hips arched up to meet her. He'd been sporting a hard on all day, dreaming of her all damn week. Heat skittered down his spine, and the tell-tale tightening in is groin signaled he was about to lose control.

He forced his eyes open to stare at the vision of the sexiest-damn woman he'd ever met, kneeling between his legs, naked except for her heels, dark hair falling to form a silk curtain around them, as she worked him in her mouth.

She slayed him. Her inhibition. Her acceptance. Her need for him, which matched his need for her.

She picked up the pace.

"Ah...yeah...hell, yeah..." His eyes rolled back in his head.

It was all too much. The pent-up frustration he'd endured all week. The wicked things she was doing with her mouth. The feel of her soft breasts bouncing off his thighs.

She brushed her thumbs over his sac and hot pleasure like he'd never known rushed through him. He was done.

Cupping her head, Ben thrust up into her mouth and came so hard he saw stars.

When his vision finally cleared, he focused on the woman smiling up at him.

"How's that for fun?"

Ben laughed and hauled her up on his lap, feeling lighter, better. He always felt better with her around. "It's a start," he said, kissing her lips, plans for round two already forming in his brain.

Lea awoke to the feel of a soft caress down her back. She opened her eyes and found a sexy man in her bed. "Good morning."

"Yes it is," Ben said, running his hand down her body and back up. "But it's getting late, and we need to get ready for the wedding."

He still didn't stop his caresses, trailing a finger down her breast to touch her nipple. Heat pooled low in her belly, and she squirmed.

"Then you have to stop that."

A wicked grin claimed his lips. "Make me."

Now all her good parts were tingling. So she reached out and did some stroking of her own.

"Hey, none of that," he warned, making to grab her hand.

Laughing, she pushed him onto his back and sat on him. "I prefer all of *that*." And to prove it, she wiggled her butt right over him.

He let out a curse. "You're killing me."

"No." She shook her head, and bent down to nip at his chin, her body on that delicious slow burn he was so good at achieving. "Just starting the morning with a bang."

Which, surprisingly, he was up for, considering they were up most of the night having *fun*.

Twenty-seven minutes later, she was dried off from their shower and slipping into a robe, her gaze never tiring of watching the play of muscles across his back and arms as he began to get dressed.

She sighed. "Seems a shame to cover up all that goodness."

His hands stopped buttoning his shirt as he lifted his gaze to her. "No worries. If you play your cards right, you can have more goodness tonight."

"Is that right?" She smiled, walking over to the credenza to pick up the green negligee he'd unknowingly delivered last night and dangled the delicate material from her finger. "And if you play yours right, you can unwrap yours."

He stilled, the amusement gone, replaced by unmitigated heat. "You're really going to wear that today?"

"Yep. All. Day." She dropped it back into the bag. "But you don't get to see me in it, unless you play your cards right."

Emerald eyes stared a moment before he growled and reached for her. But the knock on the door stopped whatever he was about to do.

"Lea, it's Brandi. Are you awake?"

At the look of panic that crossed Ben's face, her frustration turned to compassion. But then his moment of crisis was gone, and he was the one who opened the door.

"Hey, sis. Yes, she's awake, but I can't say for how long. The woman had me up most of the night." Then he surprised her again by pulling her in close and kissing her right in front of his sister. As her body took over and she began to melt into him, he drew back and grinned. "I'll leave you with that thought."

She grabbed his arm to stop him, and lifted the nightie still clutched in her other hand. "And I'll leave you with this one."

He let out another of those sexy growls and mumbled something about her killing him before he turned to hug his sister. "Morning, you. I'll talk to you later. Before you become Mrs. Kade Dalton."

"Okay." Brandi smiled up at her brother and tapped his chest. "You don't have to leave on my account. I can come back. There's still time—"

"No." He shook his head. "You two have things to do, and I have a wedding to get ready for." His gaze found her, and she was happy to see it was warm and open. "Lea and I are good."

She responded with a smile and a nod, then watched him kiss the top of Brandi's head before he left the room.

Brandi turned to face her and blinked. "Wow. What did you do to my brother?"

She laughed, unable to stop the blush from finding her face. "We had wild, monkey sex."

"Well, you two need to do that more often," her friend said, walking farther into the room. "I don't think I've ever seen him smile with his whole face before. It was in his eyes and everything."

"I know." She nodded, feeling all kinds of warm and, yeah, smug, because she put it there.

Brandi narrowed her eyes and studied her. "Same goes for you."

"That's because we had fun."

"How did you get him to agree to that?"

She smirked. "Jordan had a hand in it." She lifted the negligee and bag. "Seems she told Ben I'd left this downstairs last night, and he thought it was the gift you gave me. But when I pulled this out, whatever reservations he'd had, they flew the coop, and he told me he was on board with having fun until I leave for the city."

Brandi shook her head and laughed. "That woman is too much."

"I know. And I'm glad."

"Me, too." Her friend admired the garment. "I can't believe it's the same color as your maid-of-honor dress."

"I know," she repeated, and grinning, dropped her robe to put the negligee on. "Now I can wear it underneath today without it showing…and I told him that, too."

"Oh my God." Brandi's hand flew to her face as she smiled. "You're as bad as Jordan. That's going to drive him insane."

"I hope."

"Yep, as bad as Jordan."

Slipping the robe back on, she glanced at the clock on the nightstand. "Enough about me and Jordan. Today is your day. Time to focus on you. Since Kade stayed in a guest room last night, I have the hair stylists meeting us all in your room in an hour. So, what do you say we start getting ready for this wedding?"

"Sounds good." Brandi pushed the hair back from her face, and that's when Lea noticed the necklace glinting on her neck.

"Oh, how beautiful," she gushed, stepping close to admire the vaguely familiar square-cut diamond pendant. "From Kade?"

Her friend shook her head, tears filling her eyes. "No. My dad. He gave it to me a little while ago. He had my mother's engagement ring made into a pendant for me."

Now that her friend mentioned it, Lea remembered how she'd once admired the stone on Mrs. Wyne's finger way back when childhood had been perfect. Before car accident and cancer had robbed her and Brandi of their mothers.

"It's beautiful. Come here." Throat hot and tight with emotion, she pulled her friend into a hug, and together, they held onto each other in solidarity of another milestone they'd never get to share with their mothers.

After a few minutes, they pulled themselves together and wiped away their tears. It wasn't right. It wasn't fair. Her friend's mother should be in the room with them, celebrating this wonderful occasion. But, she wasn't, and they would cope. They always did.

Her stomach was knotted, but it was time to push the sadness aside and focused on all the good the day had to bring. "All right," she said, conjuring a smile as she hooked an arm through Brandi's while she held her garment bag with the other. "Let's go get you ready to marry that handsome Texan."

Chapter Eleven

Ben wasn't an overly emotional guy. Hell, he buried them deep, under years of layering he'd built around his heart as a shield. Between women and New York and deployments, he had a veritable fortress in his chest. But Brandi had always had a secret passage, and today was no exception. And probably Lea had something to do with it, but he preferred to blame the feelings on the day.

He knew his dad had given his sister the necklace he'd asked Ben to help him have made from the engagement ring his father had given to Brandi's mother. The sentiment was huge. Not only for obvious reasons, but from the not so obvious. The one where his no-nonsense, hard-driven, emotions-are-for-wusses father actually came up with the idea.

Yeah, that was huge.

And it had meant the world to Brandi, as Ben knew it would. He saw it shining in her eyes when he'd shared a quiet moment with her before the wedding. Sure, they were filled with tears, but there was also a deep love and a deep affection for their father, and no one would ever guess, if they hadn't already known, that the two weren't blood related.

Just as, later on, when the older Wyne had walked down the aisle, head held high, chest out with a radiant Brandi on his arm, Ben had felt the honor and pride rolling off his father in waves. His sister had been stunning in her white satin gown, reminencent of old Hollywood, with only a few white satin roses sewn at the hip. She was a lot like Lea, not pretentious, so he wasn't surprised to see she'd picked out a gown that was simple, elegant and graceful with a little playful air, just like the woman.

Despite his dire outlook on relationships, he stood watching, with the Pocono mountains a breathtaking backdrop, as his radiant sister professed her love and devotion to a good man, whose humbled gray gaze held the same deep love and affection glowing in his sister's open gaze, and he couldn't help but be happy for them. Kade had gone through hell, and Ben was glad Brandi would bring joy and peace into the man's life as she had to him and his brothers and father.

With the ceremony now over, and tears and hugs and handshakes had passed, Ben was more than ready to clip his emotions and return back to normal. Too much emotional overload. His chest was tight with it. But now, it was over. His sister was married; it was time to eat, drink and be merry.

And turned on. Again. *Damn it.*

Try as he might, all damn day, Ben couldn't help see past Lea's elegant green dress and picture her walking down the damn aisle—or on a gorgeous rescued horse as the wedding party rode around the resort—mingling at the reception—or standing in the damn food line—in the negligee of the same damn color. She was very distracting, but he welcomed the distraction; it helped him to get through whenever the day got too emotional.

Yes, he much preferred the emotion she tugged from him.

Lust.

Lea's pretty hairdo all piled high and sexy on her head with little pieces hanging down, made him want to twirl them around his finger and pull her luscious mouth to his, and as he stood in line behind her at the buffet, he gave into the need to lean closer and inhale her scent. A wuss move, he knew, but didn't care. She smelled as sweet as she tasted, and he was looking forward to easing away the tension of the day as he lost himself inside her sweetness.

"Hello, handsome," she said, sending him a sideways glance full of the heat rushing through his body. "How are you doing?"

Behind the heat, there was more, there was a knowing in her gaze. His heart cracked open a little. She always could see past his pretense, his tough exterior and knew, just knew he was dealing with shit.

"I'm good, but I'll be better later when we're alone."

She smiled on that one, then nodded. "Me, too."

He spent the next hour reliving that conversation, using it to get him through. Everything had been going fine. He was standing in the corner having a drink with the guys, watching Lea swaying to some Latin type pop song, imagining her in that damn nightie, when Kevin ambled over with Shayla's cute little baby girl, Amelia, in his arms.

"Ah, what's the pout for, pumpkin?" Cole asked, smoothing the little girl's brow.

"She's not too keen on going home tomorrow without Tyler," Kevin answered, blowing raspberries on the flower girl's arm, eliciting a sweet giggle.

He knew Tyler had been thrilled to have Cody and Amelia around the past few days.

"And I suspect she'll be asking for him for a week or two once we get back to Texas." The cowboy's tone, usually light with mischief and amusement, held an undercurrent of concern and deep affection.

For some reason, the tension ratcheted up in Ben. The invisible bands returned to squeeze his chest tight. He had no idea why, and refused to dwell on it. So, when the music turned slow, he was happy to escape with an excuse to go ask Lea to dance. And within two point one seconds of her wrapping her arms around him and holding him tight, that unreasonable tension dissipated in her warm embrace.

"You're awfully tense," she said, brushing her nose into his neck as she snuggled close. "We should do something about that."

He smiled and gathered her close, already feeling so much lighter. "What did you have in mind?"

Her chuckle rumbled through him. "You'll have to wait and see."

Forty minutes later, his sister and her new husband said their goodbyes and left for their island honeymoon. Which meant he no longer had to party. At least, not with all the guests. No, he just wanted to party, privately, with only one.

But she was walking her father out to her brother's car. Mr. Gablonski was getting tired. He'd done really well, Ben thought, for his first all day outing.

"You two staying out of trouble?"

Jordan appeared at the bar where he was nursing his seven and seven next to her husband as he watched a few couples dancing. Keiffer was out there with Caitlin again. Gwen was dancing with one of the Texas guardsman, and Mason was dancing with Jill, the woman responsible for the reception's delicious desserts, looking more at ease than he'd been in years.

"Of course," her husband replied.

"What about you, Ben? You having a good time?" Her gaze held just a hint of mischief.

He snorted. "Not sure if I should strangle you or thank you," he said.

Cole lifted his drink. "Heard that."

She ignored her husband and focused on him.

Shit.

"You trying to tell me you didn't like what was in Lea's bag last night?"

"Ah, hell, Jordan, what did you do?" Cole's gaze bounced from him to his wife then back again, "Sorry, Ben."

"No reason to be sorry," she said. "Not if you like negligees."

"She's wearing the damn thing now," he said, then tossed back the rest of his drink, and motioned to the bartender for another. "Underneath her dress. All damn day."

Cole's mouth twitched. "Sorry, man. That has to be tough."

Jordan smiled at her husband. "I have one on, too." She pulled at her dress where only he could see, then patted his cheek before she turned around and walked away.

The bartender handed Ben another seven and seven. He handed it to a wide-eyed Cole. "Here, I think you could use it more than me. She must be a handful."

Although, that probably made the man a lucky bastard.

"No thanks," Cole refused the drink. "Yeah…she is."

Warmth and satisfaction and something he didn't quite recognize flittered through the man's gaze. He winked, then walked straight to his wife, and Ben watched as Cole pressed her against one of the posts and whispered something in Jordan's ear that had the tough as nails woman melting into the cowboy.

He turned away and downed half the drink in one gulp, his gaze searching the crowd, wishing Lea would appear so they could call it a night. And he could make her melt into him…and then he in turn could melt inside her.

"Did you miss me?"

He twisted to the right, and his shoulders relaxed as he gazed into Lea's smiling face. "Yes. You ready to call it a night?"

Her smile faded. "I…actually, I won't be able to stay the whole night again, Ben. Sorry. My sister's catching the bus back to the city tonight, and I don't want my dad to be alone."

"Can't you ask your sister to stay?"

Lea stared at him as if the idea was new. Because it was. She never asked for help. Always did things herself. The woman needed to give up control and let others help, too.

"It's not as if Gwen has a photo shoot tomorrow, right?"

She shrugged. "I don't know. I don't think so."

He ran his hand down her arm and softened his tone. "Then ask her to stay one more night. Why does it always have to be you who takes care of your dad?"

She pulled away from his touch, her normal, open and friendly expression closed and tight. "Excuse me for being concerned about my dad," she huffed then marched out of the pavilion.

Ben muttered a curse and strode after her. "Lea, wait up."

She stopped near one of the big oaks, still close enough to catch the light from the party, but out of earshot, then turned to face him. "Look, I'm not going to apologize for caring about my dad."

"It's not about that and you know it. It's about giving up control. Letting your brother or sister help out. Have you even asked them?"

"They're busy. They have careers. I'm here—"

"Stalling your own. Putting your life on hold," he cut her off, tired of hearing excuses. "You need to start living it, Lea."

Her chin rose. "I thought that was what I was doing."

"To a point. But now that your dad is near the end of his recovery, you should start getting your life back on track."

"I thought that was what I was doing," she repeated.

"Was it? Have you sent out your resumes? Or do you need to talk to your father's doctors again?"

Anger flashed through her eyes. "What's that supposed to mean?"

"It means you have to stop using your father as a crutch. Start living your life. Let your brother and sister help with your dad. Share the responsibility." He held his breath, hoping she'd see the merit in his suggestions. He liked control, but he'd also learned, long ago, to delegate authority because one person could not do it all.

She blew out a breath and nodded. "You're right," she said, surprising the hell out of him. "Since I've been back, I haven't really asked them to do anything. I've just kind of jumped in and did it myself."

"I know. I tend to do that myself, too. But it's okay to let others help." He chanced touching her arm again. "He's their father too. Let them help."

"Ben's right," Gwen said, appearing out of nowhere. "I can help. Just didn't think you wanted it."

Lea frowned at her sister. "Sure I do, but you have a career to worry about—"

"As do you," Gwen pointed out. "So, how about we work that into all our schedules and between you, me and Ryder, we can all make sure Dad gets back to work, without putting any of our lives on hold. Okay?"

"Okay."

"Good. It's settled then," Gwen touched Lea's arm. "You enjoy yourself tonight. Let me worry about Dad. I'll go back to the city tomorrow night. I'll give the bus station a call right now and switch my reservation." The woman already had her phone out as she turned and walked back toward the party.

He grabbed Lea's hand and squeezed. "Are you okay with that?"

God, he hoped she was okay with that.

"Yes. I'm a bit surprised, but definitely okay with that." She squeezed his hand back. "Thanks for pointing out I wasn't asking my siblings for help. I thought I was trying to make their lives easier, but I can see where you were right. I need to let them help, too."

He nodded. "It doesn't mean you don't care. It's all right to give up control once in a while."

A playful gleam entered her eyes. "I like when you give up control. Or take it."

And just like that, he got hard.

"Speaking of taking…It looks like you get to take me out of that nightie after all." She smiled and reached up to touch his face, and he had all he could do not to give voice to the *whoot* rolling around in his head.

"What a coincidence. I happen to be great at removing nighties," he said, hooking her arm with his as he led them to the lodge.

Out of respect for his father, and Brandi and her guests, Ben resisted the urge—barely—to toss Lea over his shoulder and put boot to heel and rush to his room.

It was the following weekend when Lea received a quick call from Brandi letting her know the newlyweds had arrived back in Harland County safe and sound from their honeymoon.

"How was the beach?" she asked, envious of the week her friend had had of uninterrupted sex in a secluded hut on Bora Bora.

"Heaven. Nothing but sun, sand and sex."

Lea's insides tightened at the thought of enjoying a week like that with Ben. It didn't compute. Between his work and his family, her work and her family, not to mention seeing all the Texans off last Sunday, they hadn't had much more than a few stolen caresses in the supply room, or her basement this week. "I'm so envious."

Brandi laughed. "I take that to mean things are still *fun* with you and Ben?"

"Yeah, when we can fit some time into our schedules."

"Speaking of schedules. Did you send out your resumes?" her friend asked.

What was with everyone pushing her about her resumes? They should know she didn't need pushing. Much. She had to admit, her finger had hovered over the button a few extra seconds, but she did hit Send.

"Yes. I sent a few out on Monday." After her sister had reassured her she'd be home by November should the doctors not give their father permission to go back to work. "There hasn't been anything in the classifieds this week."

"You can always apply in Houston..." Her friend's voice was hopeful as it trailed off.

"True." She smiled. "But I'd like to give the Big Apple a try first."

"Okay. Just keep it in mind," Brandi said before she hung up.

It was tough to keep anything in mind but Ben these days. Darn man occupied way too many of the brain cells he so easily destroyed when given the chance.

After three incredible nights at the lodge last weekend, she'd been forced back to reality by work. His. Hers. Gwen's. Her sister had left Sunday evening, but not before *she* also reminded Lea to send out her resumes.

Applying for a job had been more of an issue than she had imagined, and Lea knew, deep down, it wasn't solely due to her concern over her dad. It was Ben. The reality of her feelings for Ben hit her the moment she'd hit the Send button.

Finally, after all these years, she was having a...*something* with the man, something wonderful, and she didn't want it to end. Each time she saw him, it was becoming increasingly clear to her. Whatever was going on between them was much more to her than having fun, and now she wasn't sure what to do. She couldn't tell him. He'd freak out and end their *fun* before she could blink. No. Those thoughts were better kept to herself, so she could enjoy him right up until she left...and beyond.

If he'd been lenient with his dating routine with Charisse and the woman's out-of-town work schedule when he had been seeing the blonde, surely he'd consider still seeing Lea when she moved to New York. Their *fun* shouldn't have to end just because she wouldn't live in the Poconos seven days a week. There were daily buses to and from the city, eliminating the aggravation of driving, and then there were the weekends he didn't have drill.

Maybe they could still see each other occasionally.

But even as her mind came up with these more than reasonable ideas, she knew they wouldn't cut it with Ben. He hated New York City. Plain and simple. Hated it. He understood her desire to work there, but would never visit. He hadn't stepped foot in the city since a few months after the towers fell.

He'd lost a good friend that day.

She could still remember waiting with Ben at the bus station. Waiting for his friend to return. After a few days, there were two cars. Two that sat unclaimed. Because their owners hadn't made it.

Ben had been one of the volunteers to help out afterwards. He'd been gone only one week, but he'd come back a changed man. He'd already been somewhat closed off, but after volunteering, it was as if a switch had been flipped or a wire had been cut that accessed emotions.

That was over a decade ago, and Ben was just now starting to show signs of life.

He was also starting to show signs of being late. He was due to pick her up ten minutes ago to spend the day on the lake. When the phone rang, she knew it was him without even looking. It wasn't like Ben to be late. She just hoped he was okay.

"Hi, Lea," he said, that low, sexy voice of his never failed to receive a tremor of applause from her body. "As you already know, I'm running late. Sorry. I was helping Ethan inventory the supplies at the lodge when one of the guests went into labor while on the lake."

From anyone else, she would've considered his explanation as an excuse. But this was Ben. He didn't lie. And she'd been around the lodge and seen firsthand how some off the wall things could happen.

"No problem. Is the guest okay?"

"Yes. Scott arrived, and she's now on the way to the hospital." The relief in his voice was audible. "Anyhow, just wanted to let you know why I wasn't there yet."

"Thanks. That's sweet," she said. "Do you want me to drive out? This way you could finish your inventory?"

"You wouldn't mind?"

"Of course not. I know how hard it is to keep up with two jobs. How about if I leave here in an hour?"

"Okay. Thanks." His voice sounded a little strange as he hung up.

Could she dare to hope that mentioning two jobs had made him think about her leaving? Could he actually be a little upset at the thought?

It was the third week in October, and Ben was out behind his cabin, stacking the wood he'd cut earlier that day, getting it ready for the wood burning season that was upon them. He wasn't sure what had happened to September. That month had flown by, and now, three quarters of October was already gone.

Time flies when you're having fun...

The old adage shot through his mind, and a small smile tugged his lips. He'd certainly been having that. Lots of fun, although, he did limit himself to only seeing Lea once or twice a week, and since Brandi's wedding, he hadn't spent the full night with her again. Always keeping it to a few fun hours at his section at the lodge, or in her basement...or her office at the restaurant.

His smile broadened on that one. That lunch had been unexpected, and the sex hadn't been planned, either, but as always the case whenever he was around the woman, he couldn't help himself. He had to kiss her, which always led to more.

But he was working on that, by keeping away from her whenever possible. Limiting himself to those one or two rendezvous a week. Of course, his body wanted to rendezvous daily, more than once a day. That was why he disciplined himself to stay away. Keep occupied.

Like cutting and stacking wood.

His gaze shot to the hundreds of spliced pine lined up and stacked in a neat pile, waiting for his brothers to come and take over to the lodge. Yep. Lots of discipline. Hence his stacking today. It was a Saturday, and he and Lea both had the day off. He also knew for a fact she didn't have work at the museum tomorrow, since last Sunday had been her once a month day. And that's why he was avoiding her today. Because he'd give into his desire to stay the whole night with her again, like he'd done last month, during the weekend Brandi had gotten married.

Ben never fell asleep with the women he had sex with, but he'd done it continually with Lea. Not good. She was leaving as soon as she landed a job, and he knew she had several resumes out there. Resume he'd pushed her to send. He didn't want her to get too attached, because he had no intentions of continuing their *fun* once she started working in the city.

What would be the point? They didn't have a relationship. Just sex, and okay, *friend*ship, but not a relationship. Her life would be centered in the city. And that was a good thing for her, but he wanted no part of the city, so once she started working there, he could no longer have any part of her. And since that was in her very near future, it was best to keep things as they were. Sex, but no falling to sleep together. No spending the whole night.

Best thing for him to do when he felt the need to see Lea, outside of their appointed time, was to get physical— by introducing an ax to firewood.

Grabbing the next piece to be split, he pushed Lea out of his mind and swung the ax, sending the blade into the wood. He lifted the ax with the wood attached and slammed the log into the stump, splitting the wood in two.

Keiffer walked into the back yard with Mason. "Hey, bro."

"Of course you'd show up now that I'm almost done."

His youngest brother stopped dead and whistled at the large pile. "Paul Bunyon called. He wants his ax back.

And Babe. You been messing with Babe? Oh, no. That's right. The only babe you're messing with is Lea."

Ben straightened and glared. "You really think it's wise to be an ass while I have an ax in my hand?"

"He's got a point," Mason said with a smirk. "I'd listen, Keif."

"Fine. We just came for the wood you told us to take for the lodge."

"There it is. Have at it."

"All of that?"

"Of course all of it." Mason shook his head. "He's sexually frustrated and needs to make room so he can cut more wood."

"Now who's the idiot egging on the man with the ax?" Keiffer asked before Ben could respond. "At least all I was doing was pointing out he has feelings for Lea that go beyond the bedroom."

Ben reeled back. "Bullshit. I do not." He swung the ax, driving the blade into the stump to leave it there until later when he needed to take out his frustration…*shit*. No. Not his frustration; he wasn't frustrated, except maybe with his siblings.

"That was a pretty quick denial," Keiffer pointed out.

"True, Ben, it was," Mason agreed. "And you know what that means."

That they wanted their heads knocked together.

Keiffer nodded. "He definitely has feelings for Lea."

Ah, hell.

"Exactly."

"You two need to can it." He glared again.

"So, you really don't care for her?"

"No," he replied, scooping up the wood he'd just split.

It was one word. A little word, and it was out of his mouth without much work. But it felt wrong. And Ben knew why.

Because he didn't lie.

And that word felt like the biggest damn lie he could ever tell.

But it was said, and he wasn't going to retract it, he decided as he stacked the wood at the end of the pile.

"Then you won't be upset to hear she landed a job from one of those interviews last week, and left for New York this morning?" Keiffer asked.

"What?" *Shit.* "She left already?" He whirled around to face his brother in time to see a sly smile on the guy's soon to be bloodied face. "Very funny."

"It was, actually. You should've seen your face when you thought she'd left without saying good-bye."

"It was kind of comical. And telling," Mason added, wise enough to back up and keep plenty of space between them.

"Speaking of telling," Keiffer continued, apparently happy to live on the edge. "You should think about telling her how you feel, Ben. Ask her to stay. Or make plans to commute. Whatever floats your boat."

"There's no need to ask because I don't *feel* anything."

"Except sexually frustrated," Mason supplied.

"Yeah, there's that." Keif nodded toward the split wood. "And there's the proof, so don't even try to deny it, Ben."

His jaw cracked from his clenched teeth that were having a contest with his fists to see which could clench the tightest.

"I don't see what the big deal is anyway. So you have feelings for Lea. That's a good thing. She's a good person. You know she wouldn't screw you over."

His jaw was winning.

"He's right, Ben."

Ah hell, not Mason, too. If any of his brothers would've been on his side, the one where you boycott relationships, he would've thought it was the brother who'd been dump on his wedding day. Yes, that's the person Ben would've expected in his corner.

But no. Mason was staring all serious, singing Lea's praises.

The thing was, he knew she was a good person. That wasn't the issue. The issue was the relationship.

He didn't want one.

With anyone.

"You're both missing the point. I'm not interested. So can it."

"The point is New York City. You hate it. And because she loves the city and wants to work there, you're going to hold it against her. And dump her."

"Yeah, you're willing to let her go live there when you know damn well you're going to be miserable here."

"Yep, that's it exactly. You have me pegged." He decided to appease them so they'd let him alone. "Now, can we please get to loading up this wood?"

Ben knew his brothers meant well, but they were way off. He didn't have feelings for Lea. Other than sexually.

"No." Keiffer shook his head. "It's not healthy. You need to admit your feelings, bro."

"For the last time, I do not have feelings for Lea!"

An audible gasp had the three of them turning to see Lea standing behind them, mouth open, face pale, arms full of white take-out bags, and from the aroma, his nose detected bacon.

Chapter Twelve

Ah, hell. Ben's stomach clenched tight, then twisted at the pain he saw her trying to blink from her over-bright gaze.

"Sorry." She set the bags on his picnic table then cleared her throat. "There were some specials left over from breakfast. I just thought I'd bring them here so they didn't go to waste." Then she turned and walked back around the house.

Shit.

He glared at his brothers before rushing after the woman. "Lea. Lea, wait up. Would you wait?" he asked, cutting in front of her to lean against her car so she couldn't leave. "I'm sorry. I didn't—"

"Don't," she said, placing a finger to his mouth, cutting off his words. "Just don't. If you try to explain, you'll lie to me, and you don't like to lie, Ben."

Christ. He was the one who hurt her, and here she was worried about him.

"And I don't want to be lied to, either." She removed her hand and smiled. "It's okay. It's my fault. I forgot. Got mixed up. The lines got blurred a little in my head. We're friends, and we have sex. That's all."

He blew out a breath and ran a hand over his head. "Look, I'm sorry, Lea. I didn't mean to hurt you."

"I know." She squeezed his arm. "You've always been upfront. You told me from the start, it's just sex. An added bonus to our friendship. I remember now. We're good."

He stared at her. Her face was no longer pale, but her gaze wasn't quite full of life. It was more guarded, not open, just…friendly.

Something rippled through his gut.

She was just giving him friendly.

"You should eat that breakfast while it's still warm," she told him.

Now that she was here, he didn't want her to go. "Why don't you stay and eat it with me."

She smiled, but it didn't fully reach her eyes, and he was staggered to discover how much he missed the warmth.

"Sorry. I can't. I have to get back to the restaurant. Mary called off sick. I just stopped by on break."

The woman was always thinking of others.

"I-I was also stopping by to tell you I got a job."

His chest tightened. *Damn.* He thought Keiffer had been kidding. "In a museum?"

"Yes." She nodded. "In New York City."

"That's terrific. Congratulations. Just what you wanted." He pulled her in for a hug, and hoped he sounded sincere, because for some reason, he didn't feel too good.

"Thanks." She hugged him back. "I start next Monday. I can hardly believe it."

That was what had been missing, that life, that light, it was back in her voice, and he drew back in hopes he'd catch a glimpse of it in her eyes. "I'm happy for you," he said, and meant it.

If working in that damn city could put the sparkle back in her eyes, then he was glad she'd gotten the job, because she should always have that sparkle. And looking into her eyes, he was drawn in, again, and filled with that strong need to touch her and be with her.

And that shook him.

Now, more than ever, he needed to distance himself. She was leaving next Monday. In nine days. *Shit.* Probably sooner. His chest was tight again, so tight it hurt to breathe. He cleared his throat. "When do you leave?"

She released him to lean back against her car. "Not until next Saturday. I don't need to look for a place to stay. Gwen said I could stay in her penthouse." Lea laughed. "It's ironic. I'm moving to New York, and my sister is moving back to the Poconos."

Yeah. Ironic.

The ball of anxiety increased in his chest. He didn't want her to go to the city. She might get hurt there. Who would protect her?

Who had protected Gwen? *No one, and she was just fine*, the voice in his head reminded. But there were others who used to work in the city, and they weren't fine.

The increasing pressure in his chest was causing a dull ache behind his eyes. He knew he should say something to Lea, but he couldn't figure out what.

"Well, I'd better get back to the restaurant." She straightened from the car and stared at him.

When he realized he was still blocking her door, he moved, but not before he placed a hand on her arm. "Are we good?"

She smiled, and all was right with the world because it reached her eyes. The warmth surrounded him and chased away the invading chill.

"Yes, we're good."

"Can you come back here later tonight? Maybe get your brother or sister to stay with your dad?"

She blinked, eyes wide. Yeah, he couldn't blame her. He'd never asked her to spend time at his cabin. Just the resort. But, he couldn't explain it. He needed her here. Needed to have a memory or two of her here, before they were done making memories...

"Ah, yeah. Gwen's on her way in now. She's been coming in almost every weekend." Her gaze was still disbelieving, and it gave her an impish quality. "I'll bring us leftovers from the restaurant to eat, if that's okay."

Without giving it much thought, he pulled her close and kissed the tip of her nose. "Perfect. Does six work for you?"

Her hands crept up around his shoulders as she tipped her head back and smiled. "Trust me, Ben, you're packing more than six inches."

He barked out a laugh that relieved some of his mounting pressure, then he cupped her ass and ground against her. "How does six o'clock sound for my more than six inches?"

"Perfect," she repeated his earlier reply.

Her breath was hitched as he captured her lips for a hot kiss he hoped would hold them both over until later. She tasted of coffee and pumpkin spice, and hot. Her fingers brushed the back of his neck, and his body tingled to life. And wanted more. Now. So he broke the kiss and set his forehead to hers. "You're damned addicting." His breathing was ragged as he tried to rein in his rampant desire.

"Ditto."

By the time she backed out of his driveway, he was already counting down the hours until she returned.

A few hours later, Lea refilled the napkins in the holders on the tables at restaurant. There was a lull in the rush. Mr. Tierney and old man Simpson sat at the counter discussing the recent World Series. More like arguing, but that was how they discussed. Three other tables were occupied, but they were all served and almost finished eating. Her gaze kept drifting to the clock on the wall. Three forty-seven.

Was it broke? Darn hour hand didn't seem to be moving. She wanted it to be five o'clock so she could leave to get ready to head to Ben's.

A smile tugged her lips as she carried the extra napkins back into the supply room. She still couldn't believe he'd asked her to come to his house. His *home*. This was huge, but she knew not to make a big deal out of it or it would be a short visit.

She also knew it wasn't nice to eavesdrop, although, technically that wasn't what had happened this morning. Her presence had gone undetected by the three brothers as she'd rounded the corner of Ben's cabin. Lea had been about to greet them when Keiffer told Ben to tell her how he felt. Her heart had shot to her throat at the thought of him actually feeling more for her than lust. And if he was talking to his brothers about her, then he must care.

But, then he'd opened his mouth and stopped her in her tracks.

For the last time, I do not have feelings for Lea!

The unexpected remark, coupled with the unexpected vehemence in his tone had crushed her heart, which then dropped to sink in her stomach. That's when she knew. That was when Lea realized and acknowledged what she always knew…she was in love with Benjamin Wyne. The debilitating pain of feeling as if someone had reached in and ripped out her heart was the confirmation. For a second, she had been incapacitated. To hear the man she loved loudly state he had no feelings for her had sucked.

Even now, her stomach turned just thinking about it.

But her saving grace from being completely and totally devastated had been the look of deep remorse that had darkened his eyes when he'd seen her standing there. If the man didn't have feelings for her, he would not have given a rat's ass about her overhearing his remark, therefore, he would not have any need for remorse.

Those thoughts had given her the strength to walk to her car, then to hold her head high when Ben had followed and tried to explain. *Again*, not the actions of a man who had no feelings for her.

Still, the sting did remain. She knew he didn't *want* to feel anything for her, but he was fooling himself if he didn't realize he already had them. Those unrealized feelings were the reason she'd agreed to see him tonight. They had one week left. Correction. *She* had one week left. One week to help the emotionally challenged man realize she meant more to him than just good sex.

She was back at the counter, checking out the last customer when two very good-looking Wyne brothers entered the restaurant, dark gazes full of regret.

"Lea, can we talk?"

"Sure." Her heart suddenly rocked. "Is something wrong? Is Ben okay?" Did he change his mind about tonight and send his brothers to call it off?

"Ben's fine," Keiffer rushed to reassure, and she felt lightheaded with relief. "But we aren't."

Mason nodded, coming closer. "We feel really bad about this morning."

"Yeah." The younger Wyne eyed her anxiously. "We wanted to make sure you were okay."

"And to tell you not to pay any mind to what Ben said. The idiot actually cares about you. He's just too stupid to realize it."

God, she hoped so. She was counting on that.

"Yes, our dimwitted brother is too busy controlling his feelings and bottling them up to even know he has them."

"I know."

"Then you know he cares about you?"

She sighed. "Yeah, just probably not as much as I care for him."

There, she said it out loud. Funny, it didn't make her feel any better.

"I wouldn't be too sure." Mason grinned. "Ben is happier when he's with you."

"Hell ya," Keiffer exclaimed. "You're the only one who can make him smile, a genuine smile that reaches his eyes. And he's less sharp when you're around, too. Not so grumpy."

They were sweet, trying to make her feel better, trying to point out her affect on Ben. But in truth, it was probably the age old feel good antidote.

Sex.

Yep, sex could also be the reason the man was happier with her, the reason he smiled a genuine smile, and wasn't so grumpy. Yeah, because she helped him relieve stress. With sex.

"And then there's the fact he's asked you to go to his cabin. He never has women at his cabin, Lea," Keiffer pointed out.

"I know." She had to admit, she was a little surprised Ben even told his brothers about her upcoming visit.

"Then you also know it's a big deal," Mason said.

She nodded, trying not to get those hopes up again.

"Just don't say anything," Keiffer advised. "Or my dumb brother will clam up tight."

She smiled. "I know that, too."

The younger brother laughed. "I keep forgetting you grew up with him. You know him as well as we do, well, okay, maybe more now, which is cool for you but—"

"Keiffer, shut up," Mason said, shaking his head.

"Shutting up now."

"Thanks, guys." She smiled at them both. "I appreciate your concern. I'm okay. Just taking it one day at a time. Not poking the bear too much at once."

Mason nodded. "Smart."

"And patient. I sure as hell couldn't put up with the lot of us," Keiffer said, then cocked his head as if he'd just remembered something. "Hey, I almost forgot. Congratulations on the job." He pulled her in for a hug. "I'm going to miss you around here."

"Yeah, congratulations, Lea." Mason gave her a hug when his brother released her. "Gabe's won't be the same without you."

"Thanks, guys." She fought back tears, having always known leaving her friends and family would be hard. "I'll be back on the weekends and stuff, so I'm sure we'll bump into each other."

The guys stayed for pie and coffee, and when they were gone, Lea had less than thirty-two minutes to kill before she would leave to get ready to meet Ben.

Ben got out of the shower and dried off, his thoughts on nothing but Lea since she'd backed out of his driveway that morning.

She was leaving.

Moving to New York City.

No more rendezvous after this week.

You could go see her...

No, he couldn't, and wouldn't. September 2001 he vowed never to set foot in that damn city ever again, and he wasn't about to break that vow. Not even for Lea.

He rubbed at his chest, still unbearably tight. Their time was coming to an end. He had to face it, and admit he was going to miss the incredible woman. Miss that cute little laugh that fluttered its way through him, making him smile. And her smile, he was going to definitely miss the way she smiled with her whole heart in her eyes, and the way it always made him feel alive. *Damn, yeah*, he was going to miss that, and her laugh and her sighs, the hitched ones, her breathy-little pants that turned into long, drawn out moans as she came.

A knock sounded on the door.

Ah hell.

He was too hard to wear jeans, and too hard to wear sweatpants. He either painfully covered his condition or prominently showed off his condition.

Dropping the towel, he glanced at his alarm clock. Quarter to six. Since he wasn't sure if it was Lea, he carefully slipped into his wranglers, leaving his top button undone, and rushed to answer the door.

It was Lea, holding another white bag with more delicious smelling food, and staring slack-jawed at him, heat and need suddenly smoldering in a gaze that slowly swept him from head to toe and back. "Hi."

"Come in." He took the bag from her and used all the restraint he had not to act on the desire blazing in her eyes, or they'd never make it out of the foyer.

Opting not to speak, he backed up to let her in and motioned for her to walk before him until he got a handle on his control. Which needed work because he couldn't stop himself from leaning in to inhale her sweet, sexy scent as she led the way to the open kitchen. He set the food on the counter then turned to face the silent woman, standing only a few feet away, devouring him with her gaze.

"Is there a reason you're only half-dressed? Not that I'm complaining."

Her voice was so deliciously low and hungry he felt it to his very tip. He pulsed.

214

Damn, she was potent.

"You were early. I just got out of the shower when you knocked." He swallowed. "Maybe I'd better put on a shirt, so we can eat."

"No. Don't," she stepped forward, blocking his escape. "I love what you're wearing. You're so hot I can barely breathe."

He clenched his jaw against the heat skittering down his spine. "Lea, if you don't stop looking at me like that, we—"

"God, I hope so."

His zipper was cutting off his blood supply. "But the food…"

"Can wait. I can't."

He sucked in air. "Are you sure, Lea? I don't want you to think that's all we have to do."

What the hell was he saying? Of course that was all they did. They didn't have a relationship. They had fun.

"I'm sure."

Cocking his head, he gave into the mischief whispering inside. "One of us has on too many clothes."

An answering grin pulled at her lips. "True," she said, then shocked the shit out of him when she lifted her blue sweater over her head, unhooked her bra and dropped them on the floor at his feet.

Oh, hell yeah! He was definitely on board with this. She was right. She looked hot. Smoking hot with her hair hanging down, gorgeous breasts hanging out, tempting peaks tightening right in front of his eyes.

Jesus, he was about ready to burst.

"Well?" She held her arms out and did that turn around thing of hers, making him smile. "Better?"

"Hell, yeah, you look hot."

She smiled back. Then blinked at his feet. "Oh, wait."

Backing up, she leaned against the wall and yanked off her boots and then her owl socks, her breasts jiggling lusciously with each move. His mouth was watering by the time she stood back up and smiled again.

"There. Now we're even," she proclaimed, wiggling her burgundy tipped toes.

Fire flittered through his veins at the sight of her. "No. Actually, we're not." He stepped to her, unable to remain at arm's length any longer.

"We're not?"

"Nope." Using one finger, he traced a circle around her belly button before drawing a line down to her jeans, where he popped her top button. "Not unless you're commando under these."

Her intake of breath cooled the air between them, and he watched her nipples pucker.

"Y-you don't have…"

"Nope. I just got out of the shower, remember?" He smiled, tracing a circle around her breast before he skimmed her gorgeous peaks. Both of them. He just had to touch them.

She trembled, but instead of moving forward into his touch, she stepped back and grabbed his hands. "Ben, look, I know this is just for fun, that we've been having a lot of fun for weeks now, but, I need to know that when I'm gone you won't think of me as one of your regulars. Someone who is here today, gone tomorrow. I really couldn't bear it if you thought of me like all the other women you've had in your life."

How could she even think such a thing? She was head and shoulders above those women.

"I don't." He'd never lump her into that category. "You're not." She stepped to him then, sweet scent calming his senses. "It has been fun. Hasn't it?"

216

"Yes," he replied, then let out a long, shaky breath when she slid her hands up his chest, over his shoulders to lock behind his neck, and pressed her glorious curves against him. The feel of her breasts brushing his chest was too amazing for words, but he knew she needed them right now for some reason, so he used that one. "It's been amazing."

She nodded, nuzzling his neck; she breathed him in and sighed.

The woman was so enchanting and hot and soft. He ran his hands down her back and turned his head into her hair and inhaled, took her in, imprinted everything about the moment in his mind for later, when she was gone.

"Ben?"

She drew back enough to catch his gaze and peer deep inside, seeing things only she could see, things he couldn't hide from her, things he never showed anyone else.

Her mouth was so close to his he could feel her talk when she whispered, "It's been real, too. Thank you."

"You're welcome. Thank you," he said, mouth tingling by the almost brush of lips. She was incredible and exciting and fresh. So damn fresh and wild he was always just a little bit out of control with her.

She was also steady and reliable, a true constant for him, something no other woman had ever been for him.

"Sorry, I'm not commando."

He chuckled and tightened his hold on her. God, she was adorable. He was going to miss the hell out of her. And because of that, he closed his eyes and breathed her in again. Sweetness, fruity shampoo and warm woman. He was not likely to ever forget her. Then he kissed her, slow, tentative kisses, tasting first one corner of her mouth, then the other, then everything in between.

Her hitched breathes took away his and he rode the anticipation of all he knew was to come. Their amazing connection. Being with her was a crazy, incredible ride.

Crazy, because for years, he'd created a wall around his heart and emotions, keeping them guarded and untouched, then Lea came along and inched her way past his defenses, past layers of barricades and resistance and stripped away every last one of his barriers, leaving him vulnerable, exposed, and bare. And yet, the incredible woman treated that find as if it was as precious as air.

If he was in his right mind, he'd no doubt run. These were very serious alerts. Threat level red. Yet, he was still with her, holding her, savoring her kisses. Wanting her. Wanting to be with her.

"I hope you don't have to go home tonight," he said against her jaw.

"No. I'm all yours."

An unnamed thrill raced through him as he twisted them around and pressed her back against the wall. "Good."

Grabbing both wrists, he set her hands above her head and held them loosely with one of his while he kissed her deeper, longer and trailed his other hand down the curve of her throat, over her collarbone, to lightly trace her breast.

She moaned; her body trembled, and she arched into him, driving him out of his mind, but he would not be rushed.

Not tonight.

No. He was going to savor this night.

Chapter Thirteen

Lea's heart rocked in her chest, and she could hardly catch her breath. The man was incredible, and driving her mad with his feather light, barely there touches and kisses. She was going to be certifiable in seconds.

He drew back and released her hands. "Keep 'em there," he ordered, eyes so deliciously dark and heated, her core contracted.

His mouth was on her neck, nuzzling that spot behind her ear, and she couldn't stay still. She gasped and squirmed, and silently pleaded for him to touch her. But still, his hand brushed around all the good parts, skimming down her belly and hip to her thigh where he lingered, inching ever so close she could feel the heat of his hand through her jeans. Then it was traveling back up, while his other one traveled down, creating circles of sensations, and she was having a hard time concentrating on just one.

He was a force of nature; the reactions he drew from her were fierce and untamed, and she loved ever blessed minute. His touch grew firmer and bolder until finally, *finally* he brushed her nipples.

She cried out, and he drew back to cup both breasts and tweak her nipples. Lea arched into him, always remembering to keep her hands up. But she wanted to touch him. Oh, God, how she wanted to touch him and taste him.

"Not yet," he said, as if reading her mind, dipping down to kiss her breast and elicit a moan from deep in her throat.

And when he started to pull her zipper down, she felt the rumble of every single tooth as he neared the bottom.

Then a hand was inside, and she shameless sucked in her gut so he would have more room to get to her tingling center. And then he did, and she could feel his ragged breath against her skin.

"So wet…"

He slid his thick finger inside her, and she was so close already, so darn close he ripped a needy sound from her, but she didn't care. She rocked into him, and he upped the pace of his strokes, captured a nipple in his mouth, and when he pinched the other with his fingers, she exploded with a shameless, low, needy cry filling his kitchen.

Catching her before her knees completely buckled, Ben helped her put her arms down and held her close while she found her way back to the world and regained feeling in her fingers.

"That was…incredible," she gushed, and his dark, smoldering gaze had her belly heating again.

"Just the prelude," he said, then tossed her over his shoulder and carried her down the hall to his room, where he dropped her on the mattress. "We have the whole night."

With a thrill shivering through her at the heat in his words, she propped up on her elbows and watched as he stripped off his jeans.

Yep, commando.

His erection stood thick and long and proud, and her body ached to have him inside. She was such a Ben groupie. His six-pack abs and defined chest were on her list of *must tastes* for the night. He fished a condom from his jeans, and she loved the way his muscles rippled.

"You want help?"

"No," he said, voice low and gravely. "If you touch me now, I'll burst."

Her mouth watered, and body quivered as she watched him roll on the condom. She was *such* a Ben groupie.

Then his hands were on her jeans, and in one swift move, he yanked them and her panties right off. "Oh!" she gasped. His take charge, determined movements had her heart racing and body heating in anticipation.

Ben crawled up her body, kissing and licking on his way to her mouth where he plundered with a groan. His hands were gliding everywhere, spreading the heat that was simmering inside. She traced his abs and would've gone lower, but he drew back, nudged her legs apart then entered in one thrust.

Lea's cry of pleasure mixed with his, and they were both damp with need.

"You feel so good," he said, his voice a throaty whisper.

Then he began to move, and she closed her eyes, riding the sensations. And when he spread her thighs and thrust in farther, she gasped and clutched his arms.

His mouth was on her throat as he pulled nearly all the way out, then drove back in, over and over again. "So damn good."

Heat flooded through her belly and settled between her legs. *Oh, yeah... He* felt so damn good, all big, and thick and thrusting. "Ben…"

He drew back and stared down, his gaze incredibly open and trusting, sharing emotions with her he wouldn't normally reveal. Her throat tightened, incredibly humbled by the trust.

She arched up, pressing her chest to his, needing to connect as much of her body to his as possible as she neared that blissful edge.

The angle afforded him to push even deeper inside. He made a raw, rough, rumbling sound deep in his chest as he captured her mouth, and their tongues matched the push and pull of their bodies. Then he upped the pace, and it was all too much, and just right, and perfect. So perfect, she came with him buried deep inside, with barely any room for air between them. Irrevocably connected, she trembled around him, calling his name, and as he thrust deep and hard one last time, he followed her over the edge with her name falling from his lips.

Ben woke the next morning to find himself wrapped in a *Lea blanket* of warm, soft, naked woman. He decided then and there that was the only way to wake up in the morning.

Too bad she's leaving...

The truth in that statement slammed into him, and he stilled, willing the tightness in his chest to ease. He was confused; the woman put the tightness in his chest, but she was also responsible for taking it away. *What the hell?*

She wiggled closer, and the feel of her soft curves brushing his skin pushed the confusion away.

Last night had been another incredible night with the giving woman. It had also been more, but he refused to dissect what had set last night apart. Her cries, and touches, and responses, and the way she panted his name as she clutched tight...they were always good. He could still hear the soft, throaty little mewling sounds she made as he stroked her just the right way.

And now he was hard.

Which was actually pretty amazing considering the marathon they'd had. In the bedroom, on the kitchen island, outside on the back porch swing. That one had been tricky, but with a little ingenuity, they'd found their groove, and lost the last of their strength in the process.

They had been too exhausted to go back inside. Okay, he couldn't feel his legs, that's why they stayed put. They'd been relaxed, warm and satisfied. Yeah, they weren't going anywhere.

Surrounded by woods, the fifty-two acres he owned were private, so he hadn't been concerned with exposure to either the public or the elements.

After Lea's sexy, low cries scared the night creatures while they were in the throes, he hadn't been too worried about falling asleep outside. The heavy blanket that was now thrown over their snuggling bodies had kept them warm. There had been no need to go back inside. And despite the cold temperature, the two of them had generated enough heat to keep them toasty.

He was acutely aware of the fact he was ready to generate more.

She snuggled close again, this time running a very wicked hand down his chest to splay over his abs, just inches from where he needed her touch.

"Mornin," she said, voice muffled against his chest. "You feel good."

He ran his hand down the curve of her ass and gripped her tight. "So do you, but I know how to make you feel better."

"Mmm...not sure that's possible, because I feel pretty damn good." She lifted up on her elbow to stare down at him, the slight movement sending the swing into motion.

That wasn't the only thing moving. His heart rocked hard then started to race, and chest squeezed tight, real tight, and he tried but couldn't drag in any air. What the hell happened to all the air? They were outside, for Christ's sake.

He didn't know. Couldn't think past the need to get away from the soft, sweet, emotional look in her eyes, directed at him.

Shit.

No, he didn't do emotions. He didn't want them. *Ah, hell*, why did she have to bring emotions into this?

He didn't mind some of them. Desire. Passion. Lust. Lust was a great one. One of his favorites. But those weren't the ones shining in Lea's eyes this morning, softening her face, making her all doey eyed, and him feel all warm inside.

Shit. Shit. Shit.

This was bad because right now, he was responding to the look of fondness, affection and…love.

Christ, his chest hurt.

The feelings she generated reached in and touched something deep inside, cracking something open.

Damn it. She broke him. That's why his chest hurt so bad.

What the hell did he do now?

Call Scott?

No. He needed to go outside for air.

He was outside.

"Ben, what's wrong?" She touched his face, concern mixing with the emotions still warming her gaze.

He opened his mouth, but the only thing that came out was a squeak. So he lifted the blanket, rolled off the swing and tripped his way back inside his cabin where, apparently, all the air was being held captive because he sucked in several good mouthfuls.

Until Lea followed him in.

"Ben?"

He couldn't look at her, not yet. "Yeah?" he asked, taking the wuss' way out by walking to the laundry room in the hopes of finding some clothes, any clothes to throw on so he could get out. Go for a drive, hike, unicycle ride. He didn't care. He just needed to think, and he couldn't do that around Lea. That wasn't an excuse. It was fact.

"You okay?"

Jackpot. He found clean clothes stacked on his dryer.

"Yeah. Just need to be somewhere." Anywhere she wasn't so he could find his brain.

He pulled on clean clothes, slipped into the cowboy boots he'd left by the wall, and nearly jumped three feet when he felt her hand touch his shoulder.

Ben twisted around and lost his air again.

Ah hell, she was naked. Gloriously naked, and he was hit with a foreign urge to reach for her and cradle her close, hold on tight and never, ever let her go.

Damn. Oxygen deprivation was setting in. He was worse than he thought.

"Where are you going? Panicville?" she asked, her voice soft.

He didn't deserve soft because he was an ass.

She stood in front of him, unconcerned by her lack of attire. How did she do that? He was piled under clothes and had never felt more naked in his life.

"Nope. Just need to be somewhere." He brushed past her out of the laundry, grabbed his keys off the rack and headed for the front door.

"Ben."

"Just need to be somewhere," he repeated, as if saying it three times made it not a lie.

Ah hell. He was telling her lies. She so didn't deserve it, but damn, he just needed to think. Needed space, and if he'd been smart, that is what he would've told her.

"Fine."

The softness had disappeared from her voice, and he knew, with an inexplicable certainty and chest-tightening dread, if he had the balls to turn around and face her, the warm light, the soft look, the happiness would no longer be in her eyes.

"Have a good life."

He was a jerk. Who needed to run.

"I'm sorry," he said, glancing over his shoulder, but not meeting her gaze. He couldn't bear to see the pain he'd caused in her eyes.

She didn't answer.

He didn't blame her. This stupid panic attack and the horrible way he'd handled it proved Lea Gablonski was better off without him.

And as he closed the door, he already hated himself.

Chapter Fourteen

Wednesday evening, Lea parked her car at the lodge and got out to head to the residence wing for a good-bye dinner the Wynes insisted on throwing for her. She loved them dearly, and wanted to say her good-byes to them, but Ben would be there, and she hadn't talked to him since he walked—no ran—out of his own cabin Sunday morning, after giving her the most incredible night of her life.

He'd been sexy, and charming, and he'd shown her his heart. Several times that night. In several ways. She'd seen it in his eyes. Felt it in his touch. Heard it in his voice. The night had been magic. But apparently, he'd missed all of it because he sure as hell hadn't expected to see her heart.

She was in idiot.

Why couldn't she have remembered to not show her feelings?

Oh, right, that would be because she'd been overloaded with mindboggling orgasm after orgasm the night before and had no damn brain cells left. That's why.

Idiot.

She was definitely angrier with herself than him. The guy was emotionally dysfunctional going into the *liaison* thing they had. She'd known that about him, right from the start. He'd reminded her, too.

On Monday, he'd shown up at the restaurant, his gaze all haunted and remorseful. But there had been a bus rush at the time, and he'd left before business had calmed down.

Lea blew out a breath as she walked through the lobby. This was on her…this mess. She'd fallen in love

227

with a man, a good man, but a man who didn't know how to love back. His heart and emotions were wrapped tight under so many layers of lock and keys, it'd never see the light of day. At least, not for her.

She wasn't the right fit.

God, she wished she was.

But her key didn't work.

Since she considered the Wynes family, and had no intention of avoiding them when she returned to the area for visits, Lea was determined to salvage whatever she could with Ben. She set her shoulders, walked straight to the residence wing door and typed the code for admittance.

"Hello," she called out, surprised to find the area quiet as she walked down the hall toward the kitchen and family room.

Had she gotten the day and time wrong?

As she rounded the corner, her breath caught. "Ben."

"Hey," he said, leaning his long frame up against the counter, arms crossed over his chest as if he'd been waiting for someone.

"Am I here on the wrong day?"

He shook his head. "No. I asked everyone if I could have some time alone with you. They're all at Timbers waiting in the back room for us."

Her heart slammed into her throat. Time alone with Ben…why? Hope wanted to take flight, but Lea had learned years ago never to give it premature wings.

"Okay," she said cautiously as she chose a spot across the room from him and adopted his stance against the cabinet. "What did you want?"

"To apologize for being the biggest ass in town."

Her lips quivered, wanting desperately to smile, but this was serious, and he had stuff to get off his chest.

"I'm really sorry for running out on you. I don't have an excuse other than I panicked. It felt like something was choking me. I had to get out. That's all I knew."

God, she made him feel that awful? "I'm sorry my feelings for you have caused you distress, Ben."

He blew out a breath. "Lea...don't."

"Don't what, Ben? Feel? I told you." Several times now. "Too late. You knew I had feelings for you way before we started having sex."

"I never wanted you to get hurt."

She sighed. "You were upfront with me. Always. I know that as well."

"I'm sorry."

"I know that, too. And I understand you panicked, but at least know why you panicked."

"I was there, remember? I think I know why."

"But you don't, Ben." She shook her head. "You think it's because of my emotions for you. But you're wrong. It was because of *your* emotional response to me."

He opened his mouth, and she could almost hear the denial on his lips, but he hesitated, just a little, and she knew she had been right. He hadn't considered that possibility. But now he could.

"So, if you're ever naked, laying out on your back swing wrapped in a blanket with a naked girl, at least know why you're about to panic," she said.

His lips twitched into a smile. "Yes, ma'am. So, what do we do now?"

"That depends," she said, eyeing him close.

"On what?"

"On whether or not you want to continue to have sex."

He swallowed, clearly not expecting that.

"I'm moving to the city in two days, but I'll be coming in on weekends, every once in awhile, and I would like to continue to see you."

He clenched his jaw and inhaled, heat and regret and need all mixing to darken his gaze before he blew out a breath and shook his head. "I don't think it's a good idea."

"Can I ask why?" Yea, why was he breaking her heart?

"Because I'd end up hurting you, and I don't want to do that, Lea. You deserve someone who can give you what I can't."

She wanted to grab him by the shoulders and shout, *you* are what I deserve. *You* are what I want. *You* are already hurting me. But, she knew he was still a far way from facing his emotions. Hell, he hadn't even acknowledged them yet.

"Okay, so, what do we do now?" she asked, throwing his earlier question out there again.

"How about we go to your going away party as friends?" he asked, holding out his hand.

Reaching for his hand, she brought a smile to her lips. "Deal."

Definitely not how she wanted to go to the party, but she had vowed to patch things up with Ben, and if this was all he was capable of giving, then she would just have to accept things, even though her chest felt like it had caved in.

All day Saturday, Ben had kept busy, thankful it was drill weekend. He didn't need to think of Lea. But her smiles and laughter and sighs constantly flittered through his head. If he could just figure out how to stop them, then maybe life could get back to normal. Back to the way it was before…sex with Lea.

That was how he labeled things in his head, now. Before sex with Lea, and after sex with Lea. The latter made him sweat just thinking about the things they'd do after sex.

Swallowing a curse, he yanked the door closed on the equipment cage on the drill floor when he turned around and nearly ran into both of his brothers. With their military haircuts, uniforms and dark eyes, they could've passed for twins, except Mason had a good inch on Keiffer's six foot frame.

"What's up, girls?" Ben asked, already finding the conversation old.

"You tell us."

Grumbling, he pivoted around and marched across the drill floor. The soldiers had been dismissed twenty minutes ago, and the armory had pretty much cleared out. He removed his hat and ran a hand over his head. It had been a long day, and tomorrow they would all be back to do it again. The last thing he needed was prying from the peanut gallery following close behind him.

"We're just wondering how long you're going to go around with your head up your ass."

"Nice," he muttered. Keiffer sure had a way with words. "As long as it takes." He shoved the hat back on and shook his head as he bounded up the stairs, taking them two at a time. The sound of boots clapping off the steps behind him echoed in the stairway as he headed to his third floor office.

Damn, they still followed.

"As long as it takes for what?" Mason asked.

He yanked the door open and glanced over his shoulder. "For both of you to get off my damn case."

Keiffer nudged Mason. "Yep, he's got it bad."

"And still doesn't know it."

"What are you talking about?" he asked, opening his office door.

"Your feelings for Lea."

Ah hell. "Are you back to that again?"

"Yes," Keiffer replied, dropping down in a chair in front of Ben's desk. "Until you admit it, until you look deep down inside that buried heart of yours and realize you're in love with the woman, then we're going to keep going back to that again."

In love?

Hell no.

He wouldn't be stupid enough to do that. The burning pain in his chest was just anxiety from everyone wanting him to feel. He twisted around and stared both his brothers down. "What kind of bullshit are you spouting now?"

"It's not bullshit," Mason said quietly as he shut the door and leaned against it, as if to make sure he didn't bolt from the office. "It's the truth. For someone who hates liars, you're becoming very good at it."

"Yea." Keiffer nodded. "Can you honestly look back on all the time you spent with Lea and say with utter certainty that you have no feelings for her?"

As much as Ben wanted to say *yes* so damn bad, he couldn't. It would've been a lie. He'd had feelings for her since he was a teenager. She'd been a good friend, not only to Brandi, but to him, too.

She'd been there when he'd had issues with his mother leaving for New York. There when Brandi's mother had died. When Gwen had left him. Standing vigil with him that terrible September, while he waited all day, all night and all day at the bus station parking lot for his friend to return. There when he didn't.

There when he'd returned from Ground Zero two weeks later, numb. Broken. Hardened.

232

Lea was a rock. His support.

She was his anchor.

He walked over to the window and stretched an arm out to lean against the frame as he stared down across the street at Gabe's. Customers came and went. A waitress in a blue apron weaved around the tables, but it wasn't Lea.

His heart sank. Would never be her again.

She was gone.

If he thought the pain in his chest had been bad before, this was worse. This was much worse. Tight, unrelenting. Suffocating. He sank down into the nearest chair and blew out a breath.

Lea had always been there with a ready smile. She was always first to volunteer when someone needed help. Working side by side, filling sand bags during the flood of '06. If it wasn't sand bags, she was feeding the troops. Lea was everywhere in his life.

She was his life.

Ben began to shake. He didn't want to feel. He wanted to run, to turn it off, but it was too damn late. The floodgates had opened and all the emotion he'd buried behind the dam burst free and washed through his system unchecked.

"Here." Mason shoved a cold drink in his hand. "You look like you could use it."

Keiffer cupped his shoulder and held tight. "Yeah. You look like you just got a clue."

He nodded, cracked open the soda and tossed back half the can. Yeah, he got a clue. Several days too late, but he finally got a clue. He set the cola on his desk and slumped back in the chair.

Son-of-a-bitch. His brothers were right.

He *was* in love with Lea Gablonski. And he let her leave without telling her.

"So, what are you going to do about it?" Mason asked.

He shrugged. "Nothing."

"What do you mean, nothing?" Keiffer frowned next to him.

He stared hard at his brother. "She lives in New York now."

"So? You love her, you go after her," Keiffer said, incredulous look on his face.

Ben shot from his chair and began to pace. "It's not that simple."

"Sure it is."

"No, it's not." He twisted around to stare down at his brother. "Didn't you hear me, she's in the city. I don't go there, remember?"

His youngest brother rose to his feet and leveled a serious gaze on him. "Maybe you should. It's been a long damn time, Ben. You used to love the city."

Yeah, before all hell broke loose. Before good people died. Before lives were torn apart. Before the carnage…

He needed air. He strode to the window, grasped the pane and yanked it open. That didn't help. He pulled at his collar. His chest was so goddamn tight.

Two strong hands clamped around his shoulders and held him still. "It's okay, Ben. You're okay. Breathe. Look at me."

He blinked, and Mason's concerned brown gaze came into focus.

Yeah, there was no way he'd be visiting the city anytime soon.

Chapter Fifteen

By three o'clock Saturday afternoon, Lea was already settled into Gwen's place. She hadn't packed too much, so there wasn't much to unpack. Just some clothes, her laptop and of course, some books.

And three photos. One of her and Brandi at the wedding. One of her and her brother, sister and father at the wedding. And one of her and Ben her sneaky sister had taken of the two of them dancing to a slow song. She remembered the exact moment. Could hear the Joe Nichols song. Feel Ben's strong arms around her. Feel his heart beating strong and steady under her palm. See the affection in his gaze, the affection the poor guy never knew he'd revealed. It warmed her, even now, with them in different states. Living different lives.

She swallowed past her tight throat, and swiped away the tears. Dammit. She said she wasn't going to cry anymore.

Her phone buzzed with a text message from Brandi.

Skype?

Okay, she texted back, then wiped her face again before walking over to open her laptop. She inhaled then blew out the breath as she sat down and answered the call.

"Surprise!"

"Congratulations!"

Horns blew, confetti fell into view as her five friends from Harland County filled her screen.

Lea laughed, her heart warmed by their thoughtfulness. "Thank you."

"You're welcome. Of course we weren't going to miss congratulating you on this momentous occasion. I'm

235

sorry I'm not there, hun," Brandi said, gaze filled with emotion. "You've wanted this forever. I'm so proud of you. You went out and got it. You *got* it."

Now her eyes were filling with emotions. "Yes, I did."

She swiped at the tears. But they weren't happy tears. They were miss him tears. *Dammit*. She'd wanted Ben forever, and she tried to get him. She really did, and at one point, God, she almost had him. She knew it. She'd felt it, but…his walls were too strong. Impenetrable. And she'd failed.

She had her dream job, but not her dream man. Ecstatic over one, and devastated over the other. It left her a mixed up mess.

She sniffed.

"Oh boy. I know that sniff," Jordan said.

Kerri nodded. "Me, too."

"I know that look," Shayla exclaimed.

"Yeah, been there." Even Caitlin chimed in.

Brandi moved closer to the screen. "What has my brother done now?"

"Nothing. It's all me. I was the dumb one. I fell in love when I knew it was a bad idea. But I couldn't help it. I did it anyway."

"You're human."

She nodded.

"Does he know how you feel?" Brandi asked.

A small snort escaped her. "Yeah, I'm pretty sure he'd seen it in my eyes the morning he panicked and left me naked."

Kerri shook her head. "Men."

"Yeah, typical," Jordan said, as the girls all murmured their agreement.

"So, what now?"

"Nothing." She shrugged. "I start work on Monday. My life is here now. I'll stay here and love my job and be miserable without him. It wouldn't be so bad if he didn't care about me. If it had just been sex for him. But it wasn't. I saw actual emotion in his eyes, Brandi. He does care about me."

"Of course he does, hun. I saw the way he looked at you, too. When he thought no one was looking and his guard was down. My idiot brother is in love with you. Maybe this absence will force him to admit it."

God, she hoped so.

"It will. It worked for Cole, although, I have to warn you, Lea, men can be stubborn," the somber sheriff said. "It took my husband several months, so don't give up on Ben. Just because he doesn't come around the first few weeks, doesn't mean he won't."

Hope did that little flicker flutter thing, and she found she could breathe again.

"Okay. Thanks." She sniffed and wiped her face. "Now, how 'bout we get to celebrating?"

The girls cheered, blew horns and tossed more confetti, and Lea did her best to push her sadness aside and focus on the positive. On her achieved goal. After all these years, she was finally working in a museum in New York City.

Yes, that was definitely something to celebrate.

She just wished her mother was there to help celebrate.

That Ben was there for her to share her achievement.

Neither were possible.

By the middle of November, Ben was miserable. He was going through Lea withdrawals. His body even shook at times. It was pathetic. So was the fact he was sitting on his back porch swing, just to be close to the memories. Just to be close to her.

Yeah, pathetic.

Two weeks had gone by and still no Lea. She hadn't come home on the weekends. And he needed her to come home because he couldn't go *there,* damn it. And he couldn't breathe or get warm. Something was missing inside him. So much was missing.

He hated being weak. But he broke out in a cold sweat every time he considered getting on a bus to go to her in the city. And he didn't even know if she wanted to see him. He'd been an ass. Didn't really deserve any kind of a second chance with her.

But, hell…he wanted one.

Of course, he had no idea what he could possibly offer her. It was all new to him. He had no damn clue how to be in a relationship, then he realized, they'd been in one all along. It had never, ever really been just sex with them, no matter how much he'd try to sell that to himself. His heart had been involved from the get go.

Then it hit him. The familiar warning of an impending feeling. It started at the back of his head and tingle down his neck to spread out in his shoulder blades and chest. Then the heaviness appeared. He didn't breath. Didn't move. He let the feeling wash over him to get a sense of who was in trouble.

He got flashes of the city. Museum. Buses. Kids...

Lea.

Ben was on his feet, phone in hand as he made his way inside the cabin and dialed her number.

Straight to voicemail.

"Damn it."

He began to pace, his chest tightening to unbearable whenever he glanced at his keys on the hook. His head was pounding, ears ringing, and he broke out in a cold sweat.

"Get-it-the-fuck-together," he said between clenched teeth.

Then another feeling hit him.

The museum. Kids. Buses. Lea.

Goddammit, that told him nothing.

He sucked in a deep breath and glanced around his kitchen. The memory of Lea still haunted him. Her smile, the heat in her gaze when she'd told him he was hot. The way her breasts bounced when she'd ripped off her shirt and bra and stood in just her jeans. The light and affection warming her eyes as she gazed at him on the swing.

He glanced around the empty cabin, feeling just as empty. Nothing new. In fact, most of his life had been empty. His doing. He'd held people at bay. Sought out a warm body when the emptiness became too much. Then he'd retreat back to his solitary existence...and existed.

Until Lea.

She'd always sneak in past his defenses with a smile, or laugh, or touch, never asking or demanding. Just giving.

And now she was in trouble. He had to go.

Lea needs me.

Those three words cut through the haze fogging his mind and the ringing subsided in his head. His vision cleared.

He could breath.

Swiping his keys of the rack, Ben said a silent pray he wasn't too late and rushed out the door.

This time, he was going to be there for her.

Chapter Sixteen

Friday of Lea's second week of work was coming to a close. She usually walked through the lobby of the museum with a light step, but something was dragging her today. She couldn't place it. Had she forgotten to do something? Her mind raced through her to-do list, appointments, research notes, visit to the archives. Nope. All done.

So what was eating at her gut?

Ben?

Ben was always eating at her gut. She missed him. Ached for him. Needed him. Picked up her phone every day to call him, and always put it back down. Nothing worse than a pest. Besides, he needed to call her. Not just for her sake, but his. He had to take that step.

As she left the museum, she had the overwhelming urge to call him, but she'd rushed out of the penthouse without her cell phone this morning. It was probably dead by now, too, since she'd also forgotten to charge it last night. *Idiot.*

The mid November air was chilly but not cold, and she lifted her face to the sky and let the breeze refresh her. She already felt better. Smiling, she skipped down the cement steps in the pair of Gwen's black, knee-high leather boots she wore with a navy sweater dress, topped with a black wool overcoat and followed the daily path she took to the subway two blocks away.

She loved her job. It was everything she'd always hoped it would be and more. She couldn't imagine her life without it.

She also loved Ben. Why couldn't she have him, too? *Dammit*. She was trying to give him space, to not go to the Poconos until Thanksgiving next weekend, but God, she missed him. And she just couldn't wait anymore. She was going to get on a bus and go to the Poconos tonight.

With her mind made up, she upped her pace, excitement rushing through her veins. And then a thought occurred. What if this was drill weekend? Not being at Gabe's, she wasn't privy to the scuttlebutt of drill dates, so she had no idea if this was drill weekend or not.

She'd call Ryder when she got back to the penthouse.

As Lea crossed to the second block, her gaze was drawn to a crowd and commotion on the street. An accident. She hadn't seen or heard it. Must've happened while she was still at work. There were ambulances, and police cars, and she sent up a silent prayer that whoever was involved would be okay. Her gut tightened. No one needed to go through what her family had years ago.

Slowing her steps as she neared to accommodate the crowd, she tried not to look at the street. She didn't want to see, but a movement caught her eye. A familiar stride and set of shoulders. Her heart rocked hard in her chest.

"Ben?"

He twisted around from where he stood talking to a policeman and paramedic. Her gaze ran down him then back up, reassuring herself he was real. Reassuring herself he was unharmed.

"Lea."

A smile spread across his face and lit his eyes, and she suddenly felt warm. Blessedly warm.

"Give me a minute, okay?" he asked, and when she nodded he turned back around to talk to the men.

What was he doing here? He hated the city. Couldn't step foot in it. She remembered how he'd tried to get on a bus one year, to see Brandi play at Carnegie hall, but he'd turned ashen and shook so bad, he couldn't step on the platform.

She studied him now, looking for signs of distress. His stance was sure, authoritative. His color was good. She could still see a line of tension in his shoulders and jaw, but no panic. The anxiety that usually overwhelmed him seemed to have taken a back seat at the moment.

Her heart leapt. He did it. He overcame his debilitating fear. She was so damn proud of him she wanted to barrel into his chest and hold on tight, forever.

Instead, she watched as he signed something, shook a few hands, then twisted around and headed straight for her. His emerald gaze glinted with a determination that hiccupped her pulse.

She couldn't believe he was here. Again, she wanted to go to him, but her legs were shaking too much. And as she listened to the murmurs of the crowd, she'd pieced together a little of what had happened.

Ten minutes ago, as she was inexplicably dragging her feet, a car had swerved to miss a bus and jumped the curb, hitting two pedestrians. Where she normally walked. A chill raced down her spine. If she hadn't been dragging her feet…

And if Ben hadn't been there, walking down the block, he wouldn't have been able to grab the two little boys and pull them out of harm's way.

Ben saved them.

Without a word, he pulled her close and held her tight. God, she missed this. He felt so damn good. His warmth and strength surrounded her, and she soaked him all in and eventually stopped shaking. When she finally drew back to ask if he was okay, and why he was here, he placed a finger on her mouth and graced her with a smile, as a grin tilted his lips.

"Wait. Not here," he said, then took her hand and led her back down the street to the museum, and she wondered briefly how he knew where it was. She'd never told him. He'd never asked.

By the time they went inside, her pulse was pounding, palms sweating, and she had to keep talking her knees out of buckling, again.

He led them to a quiet corner, then turned to face her. She opened her mouth, but his finger returned to her lips, and he looked down at her with so much emotion in his eyes, her heart rocked hard in her chest. Then it was pounding so loud she was surprised he didn't hear it.

"I have a few things I'd like to say first, if you don't mind." When she nodded, he grabbed both of her hands and stared at their fingers for a few seconds. "I'm sorry, Lea. Sorry that I let you go. I should never, *ever* have done that. It's not a mistake I'll ever make again."

She squeezed his hands to convey she heard him. She always heard him. And she didn't need his words now. Just him. But she knew he needed to get this out.

He squeezed back. "I've been a fool. Didn't recognize the signs because I'd cut myself off from emotions so long ago. Off from everyone but you. I don't need anyone but you, Lea. You've always been there for me. Letting me teach you how to swing a bat. Having my back when Gwen left. The towers fell. With Mrs. Dankirk. You always helped without question. You have always been there for me. You're my history, Lea." He smiled at her. The perfect smile. The one with his whole heart in his gaze, reaching, connecting with hers, warming her from the inside out. "And I love you."

Overwhelmed with happiness, she finally barreled into the man and held him tight. "I love you too, Ben. I've always loved you."

He hugged her hard and just stood there holding her for a few minutes. His heat and acceptance and love all seeped into her and made her whole.

When he drew back enough to stare down into her eyes, his gaze held nothing back, so full of emotions her breath caught again.

"Right here and now, in this museum, Lea, I want you to know you've got your job *and* me. I'll do whatever you want, commute to the Poconos, I don't care as long as you let me in your life."

Tears fell down her face as she nodded. "Thank you. Because I want both, Ben. Very much. And you don't need to commute. I will." Her sister had a killer penthouse, but the thought of staying with Ben in his cabin sent a thrill through her. "I love your cabin. Especially that swing…"

He growled as he brushed the tears from her face. "Me, too."

"I was trying to wait until Thanksgiving to see you, but I couldn't do it. I had to see you and was coming home tonight." She drew in a breath then released it. "About what happened out there…I normally only work until four, Ben. But today, I'd stayed behind. I was dragging my feet for some reason. If I hadn't, that car…"

He pulled her in tight, buried his face in her neck where he breathed in deep. "All the way here I was willing you to be safe, Lea. I tried your phone, but it went to voicemail." His whole body shook.

"It's at home. I forgot it. I'm so sorry." She hugged him tighter.

"I'm just glad you listened to your intuition. So damn glad."

244

"And I'm glad you were okay, and so proud of you." She drew back to cup his face. "God, Ben, they said you'd saved those little boys."

He nodded, but surprised her when he didn't use the incident to complain about the dangers of the city. This was great progress.

She smiled. "I still can't believe you're here. You came to see me. How did you know where I worked? I don't think I'd ever mentioned the name."

"Gwen. I stopped by Gabe's on the way out of town, and she gave me her address and this one," he said, running his finger down her cheek as he held her gaze. "I had this feeling about you and a bus and kids and the museum." He shuddered. "I had to come. Nothing was going to stop me. Not even my phobia. For once, I listened to my gut where you were concerned. I didn't ignore my feelings. They were full of you, Lea. Full of you."

Then he was kissing her, so slow and tender Lea had never felt more cherished in her life. Ben was real. This was real. Everything was right. And perfect. And she was so happy she thought she might burst.

Never in all of history could that eleven year old girl have imagined, all those years ago, she would actually have her dream job *and* her dream man.

♥

Jill is a chocoholic with a big heart, a flair for baking and confection, and a knack for getting into predicaments, including the one where she was almost financially ruined by her ex. Now she's in a new town with a new business and is determined to stay away from trouble. Especially, the gorgeous guardsman with the haunted gaze, brooding expression and miserable attitude. Her days of helping people were over.
Too bad her new business venture puts her in daily contact with the man who melts her heart.

♥

Please turn the page for a sneak peek at:

Wyne and Chocolate
Citizen Soldier Series: Book Two/Mason
Available February 19, 2015
Pre-Order **HERE**

♥

Chapter One - Wyne and Chocolate

If the road to riches was paved with potholes, then judging by the size of the one that just sent Jill Bailey into a ditch, she was going to be a freakin' billionaire.

If she didn't freeze to death first.

Camouflaged under nine inches of still-falling snow, the crater big enough to swallow a man whole hadn't been visible until she was upon it. Even though the rapidly falling white stuff filled the hole, and she'd deployed her quick-swerve maneuver, neither had saved her from wrecking her car against a tree.

Idjit.

Only a moron would ignore warnings and travel on a closed interstate during a blizzard. Especially if that moron was desperate. She was both. A moron and desperate. Which made her dangerous. Yeah, to herself.

"Ouch," she muttered into the silent car as she pushed at the deployed airbag to tentatively touch her throbbing nose, then pulled her hand away to stare at her wet fingers. "Oh, goodie. Blood."

Her stomach churned. Nope. She was not going to be sick. If there was one thing Jill hated more than the sight of blood, it was being physically sick.

And spiders. She really, really hated spiders.

Ignoring the pain throbbing her face, she tried starting the stalled car, but it was no use. Nothing happened. She was stuck. Turning off the ignition, she kept the lights on in hopes someone would happen by and see her in the ditch. Maybe if she tapped the brakes once in awhile too, it could catch attention. Jill glanced to her left, trying to eye the dark, deserted interstate up the small hill. Maybe she could flag someone down for help. Yeah, not going to happen. She was the only one foolish enough to venture out on a night like tonight, completely blowing the New Year's resolutions she'd made last week vowing to be smart and fierce in business and not to let her heart rule her head.

Yeah, blew that one eight days in.

She hissed out a sigh, the rapidly cooling temperature lending visibility to her disgusted breath. Shivering, she turned the key and pushed the button to roll up the window. No sense in filling the car with snow, and cold air. Judging by the smoke emanating from the hood of her car, the radiator was now shot. Or was that just snow? She flicked on the heater. Nothing. Great. It could be a long night. She fished out her phone, but wasn't surprised to see there weren't enough bars to make a call. Not in the boonies.

Running her gaze ran down the dress coat covering her wrap-around-dress and the high heeled boots she'd worn to pitch a new candy line to a major New York confection conglomerate, she sighed again. Perfect for the meeting. Horrible for being stranded in her car. In the middle of a blizzard. Apparently, not only was she going to have to wait for an answer about the candy, she was going to have to wait for help, too. Even though the last sign she'd passed said she was only five miles from her exit, there was no way she could walk safely in her outfit.

Fudge.

Okay, her mind reasoned, if she remained calm, and kept those New Year's resolutions, she would survive this mess and live to pay her uncle back. Keeping those resolutions were key. She couldn't afford to blow even one if she was to get her life back in order. Especially that last one. *Don't let her heart rule her head.* That's what had sent her into the downhill spiral that was her life over the past three years.

But things were finally looking up. Desperate for finances, she'd added chocolate shaped penises to the lollipop menu of Confection Connection, her bakery/candy shop, when her friend Lea Gablonski had asked if she'd create penis pops for a bachelorette party last September. The lollipops had been so successful, Jill hadn't been able to keep up with the demand.

Finally, after accepting a large order last week, she'd commissioned a new mold from a company in NYC, with more penises per mold. It had been ready today. With the costumer scheduled to pick up the pops in two days, Jill had no time to wait for the mold to arrive in the mail. She needed it today, so she could start creating tonight. The new pattern would shave a ton of time off her schedule. She was very pleased with them and the fact she'd had the company increase the size of the pop because…well, size did matter.

Her bark of laughter quickly turned into a wince as pain radiated to her temple. Yeah, even the silent winter night didn't appreciate her ill humor.

But, if she didn't laugh, she'd surely cry. Thanks to her *dratsab* ex-husband. Okay, he was a bastard, but she hated the word and preferred to say it backward. He was a jerk and a gambler who mooched off her until he got her fired from the major New York bakery she loved when he waltzed into her boss's office and demanded they give her a raise.

Even now, color flooded her cheeks at the memory. She welcomed the warmth, but not the accompanying embarrassment from that mortifying day. That had been her last straw. Jill had packed up what little she had left, which wasn't much because most of her things had been sold so she could eat, pay rent, pay his never-ending gambling debts.

She straightened in her seat. That was in the past. She was moving forward. Rebuilding her reputation and her life. She left her old one behind to start anew where she'd been the happiest. In the Poconos. She had many wonderful childhood memories of visiting her cousins Evie and Nico Martelli, and helping her uncle out over the summers at his pizza shop in Pennsylvania.

God bless her uncle. He'd loaned her the money to hire a good lawyer and get a divorce. Thanks to her ex running their joint credit cards to the hilt and not paying them, her credit had tanked. Again, her uncle stepped in and loaned her the money to open Confection Connection. He said he believed in her and was happy to invest in her future.

Tears blurred her vision, but she blinked them away. She had vowed to pay her uncle back, and was finally in a position to start making payments to him. Well, she would be once she fulfilled this latest order.

Who would've guessed chocolate penises would lead her on a path to financial freedom?

A loud knock reverberated through the silent car and sent Jill straight up until her head hit the roof.

Pain radiated across her face, again. "Ouch."

Unable to make out more than shadows, she twisted the key and rolled down her window, her heart hammering in her throat, praying an axe murderer wasn't on the other side.

"Are you okay?" a familiar voice asked, and it took her a second to focus on the handsome man in fatigues.

Her mind registered the National Guard uniform with the name WYNE on his chest, while her body registered just which of the four gorgeous Wyne brother was outside her door.

Mason. The grumpy one. Serious one. The one whose mere presence always interrupted her pulse and sent a tingle to all her neglected good part.

But he was a man, and she was off men for a bit. For over a year-and-a-half now. So, her body was just going to have to starve because she was still fasting.

"Jill?" Another face appeared. Another Wyne brother. The youngest. Keiffer. "Is that you? Are you okay?"

"Yeah," she finally answered, and pushed at the air bag. "I got in a fight with this and lost."

"What the hell are you doing out here?" Mr. Grumpypuss asked, withdrawing a huge knife from his ACUs-Army Camouflage Uniform. "Turn your head and close your eyes," he ordered before she even had a chance to answer his question.

A second later she heard a huge pop, and felt a burst of air. When she opened her eyes and turned back around, the airbag was deflated and she could breathe a little easier.

"Well?" Gaze dark and narrowed, Mason stared down at her in a handsome face creased with aggravation as snow blew all around him.

"Thank you," she replied.

Muttering under his breath, he shoved the knife back into his pocket. "No, I mean why the hell are you out here? The interstates are closed."

She glanced at Keiffer who was wearing a strange expression on his face as he stared at his grouchy brother. Then he transferred his gaze to her and a slow smile slid across his lips.

Whatever the younger Wyne was thinking, she knew she didn't like it. Nor did she appreciate his brother's tone.

Lifting her chin she stared right at the irritated man. "What does it look like? I drove out here so I could hit a pothole, lose control of my car and ram a tree because I had nothing better to do than aggravate you." Her chin lifted higher. "So, are you going to rescue me, or should I wait for another patrol to go by?"

If they were out on the roads in uniform, then the National Guard had definitely been activated and she was more than happy to wait for the next team, even if her chattering teeth balked at the idea.

And to show she didn't care for him or his attitude, Jill pushed the button and rolled the window back up. There. Let Mr. Grumpypuss deal with that.

A second later, she heard Keiffer's laughter disappearing in the distance and she blew out a breath that frosted in front of her. Okay, so she put one Wyne in his place and made the other laugh...but she was still stranded. And cold.

...And stuck in the snow with a broken car, and probably a broken nose. Thank goodness she had been going slow. Hitting a tree at a high rate of speed usually ended much worse.

The passenger door suddenly swung open and a very handsome, very pissed off Guardsman folded his large frame into her car and slammed the door.

"W-what are you doing?" she stammered like the *idjit* she was.

"I'm waiting with you."

"Why?" She blinked, and sucked in more air from a car that suddenly felt very cramped. Damn, the man took up the front seat while his presence filled the back.

"Because our humvee broke down up there and we were waiting for another when we spotted your lights," he replied, his voice aggravated and gaze cold and intense as he leaned closer. "So, you're stuck with me until they arrive. You got a problem with that, sweetheart?"

🕸

Supernatural huntress Pilar relies on her empathic gift to help track down her missing cousin last seen on an island country off the Romanian coast rich with werewolves, vampires and a deadly black dog. Determined to find Lilly before the young woman comes into her powers others would seek to use for evil, Pilar must enlist the help of three princes topping her suspect list and fight her attraction to the oldest one. What dark secret rules his soul? Does it involve Lilly? Will her desire for the dangerous man jeopardize her investigation, or will he prove invaluable when unleashed.

♥

Please look for the upcoming release of
Royally Unleashed
Royally Unleashed Series: Book One/Duncan
Coming October 13, 2014

♥

♥

Ever wonder how Kevin's sister Jen got together with her husband Brock before Cody was born? Before all the Harland County cowboys were tamed?

Join me this holiday season for the tale of Jennifer Dalton and Brock Kincade, and how the couple got together amidst the unsettled cowboys of Harland County.

♥

Please visit the cowboys of Harland County
And see how it all started…

Harland County Christmas
Harland County Series: Book .05/Jen and Brock's story
Pre-Harland County
Coming December 1,2014
Pre-Order **HERE**

♥

♥

Holly's stay in Harland County, Texas is limited. She's only there to help run her uncle's ice cream business while he recuperates from an operation. Her home is in Colorado. Her life is in Denver. Her dream job is in Denver but won't be if she doesn't get back before her leave of absence runs out. Everybody knows this, but apparently her heart and body didn't get the memo because they spark to life whenever her uncle's smoking, hot doctor is around.

The cowboy isn't looking for a relationship. She isn't staying. Perfect set up for a fling. What harm could there be?

♥

Please visit the cowboys of Harland County
Her Healing Cowboy
Harland County Series: Book Five/Jace
Coming May 2015

♥

***

For announcements about upcoming releases and exclusive contests:
Join Donna's Newsletter
Visit me at: www.donnamichaelsauthor.com
***
Harland County Series

Visit my **Harland County Series Page** at my website www.donnamichaelsauthor.com for release information and updates!

Book One: Her Fated Cowboy
Book Two: Her Unbridled Cowboy
Book Three: Her Uniform Cowboy
Book Four: Her Forever Cowboy

Coming soon:
Prequel Book .05: Harland County Christmas-Novella
Book Five: Her Healing Cowboy

Become a *Cowboy Tamer!*

Drop me a line at donna_michaels@msn.com and request some Cowboy-Tamer swag!

***

Harland County Series
Book One: *Her Fated Cowboy*

L.A. cop Jordan Masters Ryan has a problem. Her normal method of meeting a crisis head-on and taking it down won't work. Not this time. Not when fate is her adversary. Having kept her from the man she thought she'd always marry, the same fickle fate took away the man she eventually did. Thrown back into the path of her first love, she finds hers is not the only heart fate has damaged.

Widower and software CEO, Cole McCall fills his days with computer codes and his free time working the family's cattle ranch. Blaming himself for his wife's death, he's become hard and bitter. When his visiting former neighbor sets out to delete the firewall around his heart, he discovers there's no protection against the Jordan virus. Though she understands his pain and reawakens his soul, will it be enough for Cole to overcome his past and embrace their fated hearts?

***

Harland County Series
<u>Book Two: *Her Unbridled Cowboy*</u>

Homeless and unemployed thanks to an earthquake, divorced California chef Kerri Masters agrees to head back to her hometown to help plan her sister's Texas wedding. It must be her weakened state that has her eyeing the neighbor she used to follow around as a child. Her tastes tend towards gentlemen in suits, cultured, and neatly groomed— not a dimple-glaring, giant of a cowboy. He's big and virile, and makes her want things the inadequacies brought out during her divorce keep her from carrying out.

Connor McCall's brotherly feelings for the pesky former neighbor disappear when the grown up version steps on his ranch in her fancy clothes and shiny heels. Too bad she's a city girl, because he has no use for them. Three times he tried to marry one, and three times the engagements failed. He's not looking for number four no matter how much his body is all for jumping back in the saddle and showing the sexy chef just how it feels to be loved by a cowboy.

Turns out the earthquake was nothing compared to the passionate, force of nature of an unbridled cowboy, and Kerri learns far more about herself, and Connor, than she ever expected. But when events put his trust in her on the line, will he choose his heart or his pride?

***

Harland County Series
Book Three: *Her Uniform Cowboy*
Crowned Heart of Excellence – InD'tale Magazine
Voted BEST COWBOY in a Book/Readers' Choice-LRC
NOR Reviewer Top Pick – Night Owl Reviews

Desperate for change after a verbally abusive relationship, Brandi Wyne leaves a symphony career, her family, and the Poconos to fall back on a designing degree and a chance to renovate a restaurant/pub in Texas. Even though part of a National Guard family, she'd sworn off military men when the last one proved less than supportive of her thyroid condition and subsequent weight gain. Too bad her body seems to forget that fact whenever she's near the very hot, very military local sheriff.

Texas Army National Guard First Sergeant Kade Dalton never planned on becoming Harland County Sheriff or the attraction to a curvy, military-hating designer from Pennsylvania. Heavy with guilt from the death of a soldier under his command during a recent deployment, and dealing with his co-owned horse ranch and a bungling young deputy, it's hard most days just to keep his sanity. But it's the Yankee bombshell who threatens not only his sanity, but tempts his body...and his heart.

Fighting their attraction becomes a losing battle, and Kade soon finds sanctuary in the arms of the beautiful designer. Does he really have the right to saddle Brandi with his stress issues? And if so, can he take a chance on the town's newest resident not abandoning him like others in his past?

***

Harland County Series
Book Four: *Her Forever Cowboy*
NOR Reviewer Top Pick – Night Owl Reviews
Voted July's Read of the Month/Readers' Choice-SSLY Blog

Single mother, Shayla Ryan, longs to put down roots to create a stable environment for her baby girl and her younger sister, but the threat of her abusive, ex-con father finding them has made that almost impossible. Her newest residence in Harland County, however, holds a lot of appeal, especially in the form of a Casanova cowboy with eye-catching good looks and easy charm. Those two qualities took her down the wrong road before, and though the sexy cowboy interferes with her pulse, she can't let her heart get in the way of the safety of her family, or give it to someone who doesn't believe in forever.

If there's one thing software company vice president, Kevin Dalton, loves more than puzzles, it's women. Size, shape, race doesn't matter as long as they don't want a relationship—he's not looking to repeat the past, and more than happy to remain single. Until two beautiful redheads drop him to his knees—one with her cutie-pie smile, the other with her elbow. Too bad the elbow-toting beauty is both hot and puzzling. A killer combination too strong to resist. And without realizing it, the redheads slowly rewrite the code around his heart.

But when the danger from Shayla's past shows up, can he rise to the challenge to keep them safe...and really be what they need? A *forever* cowboy?

***

Time-shift Heroes Series
Book One: Captive Hero
2012 RONE Awards Nominee Best Time Travel

When Marine Corps test pilot, Captain Samantha Sheppard accidentally flies back in time and inadvertently saves the life of a WWII VMF Black Sheep pilot, she changes history and makes a crack decision to abduct him back to the present. With the timeline in jeopardy, she hides the handsome pilot at her secluded cabin in the Colorado wilderness.

But convincing her sexy, stubborn captive that he is now in another century proves harder than she anticipated— and soon it becomes difficult to tell who is captor and who is captive when the more he learns about the future, the more Sam discovers about the past, and the soul-deep connection between them.

As their flames of desire burn into overdrive, her flying Ace makes a historical discovery that threatens her family's very existence. Sam's fears are taken to new heights when she realizes the only way to fix the time-line is to sacrifice her captive hero...or is it?

Can love truly survive the test of time?

Time-shift Heroes Series
Visit my **Time-shift Heroes Series Page** for release information and updates!
Book One: Captive Hero
Book Two: Future Hero
Book Three: Unintended Hero

**

Cowboy-Sexy

Honky Tonk Hearts Series with
The Wild Rose Press
by <u>Donna Michaels</u>

4 Star RT Magazine Review*&*NOR Reviewer Top Pick

Finn Brennan was used to his brother playing practical jokes, but this time he'd gone too far--sending him a *woman* as a ranch hand, and not just a woman, but a Marine.

When Lt. Camilla Walker's CO asks her to help out at his family's dude ranch until he returns from deployment, she never expected to be thrust into a mistaken engagement to his sexy, cowboy twin--a former Navy SEAL who *hates* the Corps.

The Corps took Finn's father, his girlfriend and threatened his naval career. He's worked hard for another shot at getting back to active duty and won't let his brother's prank interfere. The last thing he needs is the temptation of a headstrong, unyielding, hot Marine getting in the way.

***

She Does Know Jack
A Romantic Comedy Suspense
by <u>Donna Michaels</u>

NOR Reviewer Top Pick

Former Army Ranger Capt. Jack 'Dodger' Anderson would rather run naked through a minefield in the Afghan desert than participate in a reality television show, but when his brother Matthew begins to receive threats, Jack quickly becomes Matthew's shadow. As if the investigation isn't baffling enough, he has to contend with the addition of a beautiful and vaguely familiar new contestant.

Security specialist, Brielle Chapman reluctantly agrees to help her uncle by going undercover as a contestant on the *Meet Your Mate* reality show. Having nearly failed on a similar assignment, she wants to prove she still has a future in this business. But when the brother of the *groom* turns out to be Dodger, the only one-nighter she ever had—while in disguise from a prior undercover case—her job becomes harder. Does he recognize her? And how can she investigate with their sizzling attraction fogging her brain? Determined to finish the job, she brings the case to a surprising climax, uncovers the culprit and *meets* her own *mate*.

***

Thanks for reading!

Made in the USA
Charleston, SC
08 March 2015